The Colours

The Colours

By T.M. Parris

A Clarke and Fairchild Thriller

ISBN-13: 9798736519309

The Clarke and Fairchild series of novels

is written in British English.

Within this novel, a billion is a thousand million.

Chapter 1

John Fairchild lay on the baked earth of the Baja California desert keeping his binoculars trained on the mansion in the distance. Heat radiated through his clothes and dust caught in his throat. He'd been lying there without moving since dawn, but he wouldn't be there much longer. As soon as he was sure this was the place, he'd sent the exact co-ordinates to his client Zack, who then sent them via some back channel to the Mexican authorities. It was purely a matter of what kind of priority they would give it now.

"Anything?" said a voice in his ear.

Zack, on the other end of a satellite phone connection, was frustrated. A US agent, working for the Drug Enforcement Agency, had infiltrated a huge drugs cartel and passed on the location of a secret pot plantation somewhere in this desert, prompting the fury of the man behind the cartel, notorious Colombian drug boss Chico Quesada. That down there was Quesada's house. And inside that house was the unfortunate US agent, who was snatched off the street in Guadalajara several days ago. Fairchild had traced him here, where they were holding him captive.

In other situations Zack would be sending in Marines right now, dropping them loaded with weaponry from helicopters. But this was politically sensitive and proper procedure had to be followed, which meant waiting on others. Not something that came easily to Zack. Fairchild, a paid hire in all of this, could stand it, but he didn't want to think too much about what was being done right now to the guy in that house. So he understood his friend's impatience.

"Anything?" repeated the voice. Fairchild was Zack's eyes and ears right now. Officially Fairchild wasn't here at all, of course.

"No, nothing. Hang on. Wait!"

Fairchild saw movement below, a door opening, figures appearing.

"Two people coming out. No, three. One of them is Quesada. It's him and a couple of minders."

They moved fast and made sharp, impatient gestures. One of them had a phone to his ear. They headed for one of the jeeps at the front of the mansion.

"They're leaving, Zack. In a hurry. They must have been tipped off."

"Any sign of law enforcement?"

"Nope."

"Shit! We needed to get him right here to make this stick. Any sign of our guy?"

"No, he must still be inside."

"Crap."

"They're on the move."

The three men were now in the jeep, whose tyres spun into life, raising a cloud of dust.

"Can you get after them?"

Fairchild was already on his feet, head low, trying to keep some kind of cover while making for his four-wheel drive.

"Sure." He kept speaking to Zack through his clip-on mic. "But they'll make me if I follow them. We're in the desert, Zack!"

"Never mind that, just keep them here! Don't let them go anywhere until the goddam police arrive! You got a tracer on that jeep, right?"

"We'll see."

"What do you mean, we'll see?"

Fairchild said no more until he was back at the vehicle. He started the engine and the screen showing the locations of his tracking devices flickered into life. All of them were operational, and all but one still clustered around the front of the mansion. That one was moving away fast, taking a route that wasn't an official road. As Fairchild reversed and manoeuvred after it, he heard the faintest sound of a siren on the wind.

"Sounds like the police are here," he said, pulling the steering wheel hard to coax the SUV the shortest route after Quesada.

"Great. Just as the guy leaves. How convenient."

"I'm after them. They're off road. They're going to know I'm here, Zack."

"Good! Give them some trouble. Take out their tyres!"

It was easy for Zack to say, sitting in a base somewhere north of the border. The land rose up in front of Fairchild and the engine moaned as he accelerated upwards, his wheels spraying dirt. Then it levelled off and Quesada's jeep came into view. That meant they could see him. Almost immediately a side window lowered and a head and shoulders emerged along with an assault rifle. The shooter opened fire. Bullets punctured Fairchild's bonnet.

He braked. The dust rising from their jeep helped; Fairchild steered left and right, a crazy path. But the shooting continued. A bullet hit the windscreen and cracked it. The jeep sped up. Fairchild was losing ground. With one hand he pulled out a gun, lowered the side window and fired off a round. But from a distance with his left hand it wasn't going to achieve much.

"You still there?" Zack crackled in his ear.

"Yeah, but they're getting away."

"Well catch up!"

Fairchild put his foot down, reminding himself to increase his fee next time he worked for Zack. Whenever he drew closer the shooting started again and he had to drop back. As the land rose and dipped, the jeep would disappear from view but its dot remained on the screen.

"Where are they heading?" asked Zack.

"No idea. There's nothing out here. They're going straight for the middle of nowhere."

But just then Fairchild topped another rise and in front of him all became clear. Low-level sheds nestled between small natural hillocks, and stretching alongside all of them a long flat area made the perfect landing strip. A flimsy turboprop taxied at one end.

"Shit, Zack! There's a whole runway here! I see hangars, storage sheds, a light plane on the move. They must be using it to transport the drugs."

"Holy fuck! How did we not know about this?"

It was a good question, but now wasn't the time to try and answer it. The jeep had pulled in next to a hangar, and the plane was lining up on the runway. Fairchild, on higher ground, was an easy target for the bodyguards, who jumped out of their jeep and started firing on him straight away. Fairchild climbed out and crouched behind the vehicle listening to its windows crunching from the bullets. He could smell diesel mixed with dust. He peered round just enough to see Quesada, covered by his minders, running for the plane.

"Zack, he's getting into the plane. It's about to take off."

"Well, stop him!"

"How? You think I've got anti-aircraft guns here? No one said anything about planes. Can't you find them with satellites?"

"You mean like we found the airfield?"

Zack had a point. Fairchild risked another peep round the wing of the SUV. A bullet dinked the metalwork, far too close for comfort. The plane was powering down the runway. The minders were heading back to their jeep. It was not a good time to hang around.

"I'm out of here, Zack. There's nothing more I can do and these goons are going to come after me now."

Fairchild jumped back into the SUV and spun the wheels as he steered sharply away. In his mirrors he saw Quesada's men in the jeep coming straight for him. As he drove off, the plane rose into the sky.

"He's in the air, Zack. He's gone."

"Shit."

"And so am I. Got to make myself scarce."

Fairchild tuned out the string of expletives in his ear and focused on trying to stay ahead of the approaching jeep.

Chapter 2

Vauxhall Cross wasn't Rose's favourite place in the world. She'd prefer to be out in the field. Admittedly, the MI6 riverside headquarters looked the best it could possibly look today, and the view from Marcus Salisbury's office was probably the best in the place, as befit the top dog, the person who used to only be known as "C". Behind the man's head, the Thames glittered in the sun and looked vaguely blue. Along Millbank, north of the river, the landmarks of London lined up, grey, solid and respectable, familiar as the face of an old friend. Yes, Rose loved her country. Of course she did. That was what it was all about, protecting this nation and her fellow Brits. But she'd still prefer to be out there getting on with the job, chasing down the threats wherever they surfaced. Her six-month stay in London hadn't been unpleasant as such, but she was desperate for it to be over. Which was why she was sitting here today making a special effort to impress the boss.

Salisbury didn't look too impressed.

"Don't get me wrong, Clarke," he said. "I'm sure plenty of people in this building would love to spend a month or so in the south of France. But as you know, we're supposed to be engaging the limited public resources at our disposal to address clear and current threats to our nation."

"That's exactly what this is," said Rose.

She already knew Salisbury wasn't favourably inclined towards her current mission. It was Walter, her line manager of indeterminate but considerable seniority, who had taken on that argument and won. The result was Rose's appointment as the head of a small team whose imprecisely specified remit focused entirely on one person. Some day,

Rose hoped, Walter would tell her what kind of hold he had over Salisbury that enabled him to secure the Chief's support, however reluctant. So far, Walter wasn't talking.

"Gregory Sutherland," she said, "is a real and present threat to this country. He was a traitor when he worked for MI6 back in the sixties, and his opinion of us hasn't improved since then. When he crossed over into the USSR, he established himself within the KGB and used their vast resources to pursue his own aims. He built contacts within criminal circles using the street name Grom, and carried on in similar vein within the FSB after the break-up of the Soviet Union. He has vast amounts of money squirrelled away, which he's desperate to get his hands on now he's been kicked out of Russia. He's still a manipulative, effective operator, despite his age. He has ample means and motive to mobilise all kinds of causes against us. That's what he does. We need to neutralise him, take away everything he could use as a power base."

Salisbury had already heard all of this, of course. From the expression on his face, the man was unmoved.

"Gregory Sutherland died in 1969. The idea that this man you're chasing, this disgraced Russian spymaster now in exile, is in fact British, is ludicrous. Do you have a shred of evidence that proves they're one and the same person?"

"You mean like a DNA test? That would be very difficult to achieve. But people have met him. Spoken to him."

"People other than John Fairchild?"

Salisbury's contempt was obvious. MI6 seemed to divide itself into two parts, those who liked the rootless mercenary John Fairchild, and those who didn't. One of Salisbury's first actions in the top job was to order an investigation into John Fairchild, specifically into whether he was acquiring information from trusted officers and selling it on. The investigation went nowhere, though Rose wasn't sorry it happened, as her role in it enabled her to get back into the Service after she'd been dismissed for an intelligence failure when working in Croatia. And after her experiences with Fairchild, she had some sympathy with Salisbury's view of the man.

"Have you met him, then? Gregory Sutherland?" asked Salisbury.

"I've seen him. From a distance."

He picked up a pen and repositioned it without looking up at her. That was the kind of thing he did when hearing something he didn't like. Deliberately undermining, of course. When in PR or political mode, it was all different: warm smiles, reassurances, firm handshakes. Salisbury was the archetypal "safe pair of hands" favoured by risk-averse politicians and bureaucrats. Someone you could trust to deal with things in a sensible and responsible way. But he didn't necessarily show that side to his own staff, particularly when they were giving him bad news.

Finally he sighed and gave her a quizzical look.

"It doesn't sound very definitive, does it?"

Patience, Rose. "The Russians aren't struggling to believe it. As soon as we fed it through our FSB sources that Grom was actually British, they turned on him. They must have done their own checks and realised his identity was false. So there has to be something in it. Enough to dirty our reputation, at least."

This was one of Walter's winning arguments, Rose was sure. Even the possibility that a corrupt senior FSB officer could turn out to be a UK citizen, trained and previously employed as a British intelligence officer, was enough to damage the reputation of the Service. Which already had a somewhat mixed reputation when it came to Soviet double agents.

Salisbury leaned back in his chair. In a light grey suit but no tie, his dress was formal enough while nodding towards the trend to informal. There was nothing eye-catching or remarkable about Marcus Salisbury. In a spy, that could be a good thing. In the head of a spying service like this one, Rose wasn't so sure.

"He'd been using a false identity for more than forty years," he said. "Clever guy."

"Yes," said Rose seriously. "Very. And he hasn't lost his touch. Somehow he got out of Russia six months ago despite his own team turning on him without warning. An unarmed septuagenarian vanishes into thin air while topping the most wanted list of one of the world's most oppressive states? We've been looking for him ever since. So have they."

"And now you think he's sunning himself on the French Riviera?"

"No. We think that's where his money is."

This was the real purpose of the team that Rose had been appointed to lead six months ago. Through the hands of corrupt bureaucrats and their business and mafia associates, Russian money was exported from Russia in large quantities, to end up stashed in offshore accounts or invested in property and other assets across the globe. With the new security focus on Russia as a threat, teams of analysts already monitored these flows as best they could. Rose's team was doing exactly the same thing, only focused on a particular individual. They made use of financial intelligence expertise known as FININT, but with a specific Russian in their sights. At least, that was what everyone thought. Because the idea, the mere possibility, that this Russian was in fact British, was, to put it mildly, sensitive. That was why Rose enjoyed a certain amount of autonomy. A privileged position, which she felt she'd earned, having suffered at the hands of Sutherland's manipulative cruelty herself.

"You know that tracing Sutherland's wealth has taken us right across the globe," she continued. "Of course none of it is in that name. As you said, officially Sutherland died over forty years ago. Mikhail Khovansky is how the Russians know him. But most of it isn't held in that name either. We've managed to link a whole web of trusts, shell companies and nominee accounts back to him. Cyprus, Panama, the Seychelles, the British Virgin Islands – it's pretty complicated. He wants to keep it hidden, but the Russians are trying to find it. As far as they're concerned, it's stolen money and they want it back. Never mind that most of them are also on the take. They see it as a particular insult, a corrupt thieving Russian official who isn't even Russian."

"And this is helping us how?" asked Salisbury languidly. "We're already watching expropriated Russian funds across the world. Extra resources for a bespoke team just for one person is – well—"

Wasteful? Unjustifiable? Rose barged back in before Salisbury could hit upon his preferred offending adjective.

"We're working closely with FININT. Sharing everything we can. We're adding to their pool of intelligence. We can identify his associates and flag them up. The people who helped him set all this up, the bankers, the accountants, the lawyers. Many of them won't have a clue who he really is or what he's done, but some might be more deeply involved than that, and if they are, they're not friends of ours. We're learning a lot about Russian capabilities as well, now that we're going after the same target."

"Such as?" He sounded bored.

"That their hackers are better than ours."

That woke him up.

"And that they're not afraid of using other powers of coercion," she said. "Any interests they find that are held by Sutherland's former associates within Russia – accounts set up in the names of friends and supposed relatives – that's gone. Those people are under the power of the state. He'll have lost all of that now he's in exile. The Kremlin is quite happy to apply the same techniques internationally. Sutherland's resources are thinning down to a smaller and smaller pool that matters more and more to him. But this is only taking us so far. We need to be ahead of the Russians, not behind them. We need to get there first. That's why we have to change direction. Encryption and firewalls can't all be hacked. You can't do everything from behind a desk. The big leaks, Panama Papers and so on, came from people working inside."

Salisbury paused long enough for the silence to turn awkward, then idly opened a file in front of him and lifted some papers out. He'd already read the proposal, but seemed to want to spin this out for as long as possible.

"And why the French Riviera?" he asked.

"We think Sutherland has holdings in Monaco. Some correspondence we've seen relating to a Swiss account mentions another account at a Monaco bank offering private banking services. To be a customer there, you need Monaco residency. But we can't find an identity that matches any of our aliases. He must be using a different name, a completely separate identity. He could have had that put together in Russia using the FSB. But we don't think the FSB knows what it is either. If we go in on the ground, we have an opportunity to get ahead of the Russians. We can gain some kind of insight into his operations before the Kremlin sends in their bad boys and scares everyone away. They're not after insights. They just want the money back."

"I see."

Rose hoped the idea of getting ahead of the Russians appealed. It might be something he could use to bolster the reputation of the Service – if it worked, of course.

Salisbury was thumbing through the papers again. "You've also requested an art specialist," he said, with a hint of incredulity.

"We think some of his money is in art. As you know, it's an attractive route for money laundering. One of the pieces we're watching may be in Monaco. We picked up a rumour that it was in storage there." She cleared her throat. "I'd like to request Alastair Greenwood from Hong Kong Station. We trained together. He's always had a strong interest in art. There isn't much he doesn't know about it, especially Van Gogh and his contemporaries. As you'll have seen, that might be particularly—"

"Yes, I see you've asked for your friend," said Salisbury. "I'm not sure how Hong Kong is supposed to manage without him."

"We lend and borrow people on secondment all the time. It's only for a few weeks, if that. He could really help."

She hoped it didn't show how keen she was personally to work with Alastair. He'd been her friend since university, before they both independently joined MI6 and found themselves on the same graduate programme. At times in this job, she'd have given a lot to be able to discuss things with Alastair over a glass of wine, like they used to. In a profession of secrecy, friends you could really talk to were valuable.

"We'll see." Salisbury closed the file. Clearly she couldn't rely on him to be persuasive with Hong Kong on her behalf. But there was always Walter.

Salisbury gave her a bland look. "I don't think I'm making a secret of the fact that I have some doubts about the importance of this operation." He held up his hand to stop her coming in. "With respect, Clarke, you don't know what else comes across this desk, and juggling priorities isn't your job. It's mine. I've heard your arguments, I've heard Walter's and I've taken into account the work you've done over the past six months, which the FININT analysts seem to think has been of some use."

Rose retained a neutral expression, though his mealy-mouthed admission was gratifying.

"So I'm going to approve this," said Salisbury. "But reluctantly. I will be watching. I need regular reports and concrete progress, and if I don't see it, I pull the plug. I won't pay for a jaunt, Clarke."

"It's not a jaunt." Rose tried, and almost succeeded, to keep the vigour out of her voice. Christ, was Salisbury a difficult Chief to please. "We need someone on the inside, who can get behind the firewall and give us the name. Someone who has access and can be discreet. Who may be motivated by what we can offer. And we've already identified a target."

A silence. "You already have someone in mind?"

"Yes," said Rose. "We do."

Chapter 3

Zoe Tapoko stood in her brother Noah's bedroom staring out at the huge white blocks of flats that were everywhere you looked in these *quartiers nords* of Marseille. Ten floors below, people crossing the open square walked fast, heads down, from the Metro to the shops, to their homes or back again. A group of young men leaned against a concrete bench, arms folded, legs wide, like they owned the place. In a way maybe they did.

Outside was bright, a clear September sky and sunlight making the distant windows glitter, but inside was gloomy, stuffy with the smell of deodorant and clothes that needed a wash. Noah lay on the single bed, his feet sticking off the end, only seventeen years old, ten years younger than Zoe and half a metre taller at least. On the wall above his head a giant poster of Marseille's most famous footballer Zinedine Zidane stared down. Zoe watched the guys on the bench.

"Is that them?" she asked, breaking a long silence.

"Who?" Noah was gazing at the ceiling.

"Down there. Look out of the window, bro!"

Her bossy tone got him moving like it usually did, but it was like wading through treacle sometimes. He sat up and peered out.

"No, that's not them. Epée and his crowd hang out in that park place." He pointed vaguely. "The school kids go past there."

"They sell drugs to school children?"

He looked at her as if she'd just arrived from a different planet.

"So how exactly did you get involved with this Epée and his crowd?" she asked.

"I didn't get involved. Not exactly."

"Really?"

"Yeah, really." He was only being defensive, but sometimes Zoe could slap the boy. "They asked me to do a favour, help someone out. I didn't realise it would end up…"

Zoe bit her tongue. He could be so naïve. But that was what those gang leaders did, preyed on people's natural niceness and goodwill. Sucked it all away so there was nothing left. It explained a lot about how things were on the estates these days, the suspicion in people's eyes.

"So this favour involved carrying money around?" she asked.

"Yeah, but I didn't know how much. I just thought it was a few Euros. Someone needed cash to get home or something. I didn't think—"

"You didn't think it was drug money? Noah!"

"All right, so I'm a fool, okay? Next time someone asks a favour I'll tell them to shove off. That's how you want it, Zo?"

"If it keeps you out of those people's hair, then sure! So who was it who mugged you, then?"

"How should I know? They just jumped me. They didn't introduce themselves first. One of them had a knife. I just handed everything over. What else was I supposed to do?"

"Yeah, okay, fair enough. It seems a hell of a coincidence that it happens when you're carrying a couple of thousand Euros on you."

"That's what I said to Epée. He said yeah, it's really unlucky."

"He didn't believe you, basically. He accused you of stealing it."

"Well, yeah."

"And now he's saying he wants it back."

And this was the problem. Somehow, her trusting fool of a little brother was in hock to a local gangster for two thousand Euros. Two thousand Euros none of them had, not Noah, not Zoe, and certainly not their aunt Lilian whose flat Noah was living in. It was a problem. A problem? No – a disaster.

"And Lily knows nothing about this, right?"

Noah nodded.

"Well, let's keep it that way. We'll sort it out between us, somehow."

When their parents died within months of each other four years ago, the two of them became even closer than they were before. But Zoe had to move away from Marseille to find work, and Noah was desperate to stay, to keep his place at the Olympique Marseille youth academy. Football was his life, kept him keen and eager even when their parents' passing devastated them both. Noah missed his dad, Zoe saw it in him every time they met. But the discipline of the youth squad kept him going, and their aunt Lily took him in, even though her shifts as a hospital cleaner barely covered the rent. She was at work or asleep most of the time, and didn't need the hassle. Zoe had to wait for weekends to come over. And here she was now, promising to sort things out somehow.

"So, who are these people?" she asked. "This Epée?"

Noah shrugged. "What do you mean, who? It's a gang, the *Pirats*."

"Well, are they black, white, Arab?"

"All of them, Zo. The big guys are on Corsica. Epée's white but all the guys are just local. Marseillais. It's not about that."

Yeah, well maybe she was too taken up with race sometimes. Their parents were of Cameroon descent though she and Noah were born in France. From early on, she'd always felt the colour of her skin held her back, made it even more difficult to break out of the mould. But often the people around her seemed to want to deny that. She didn't know why. What are you complaining about? she sometimes thought people were thinking. You're doing okay, aren't you? You've got a job in a bank! In Monaco! You should be grateful. You got out, didn't you? But she hadn't got out, not really. They were both here now, for sure.

She looked up at the sky, deep blue above all the concrete roofs and the household clutter of hundreds of balconies. She used to love life in Marseille when she was growing up, when everything was okay, when Mum and Dad were still around. They lived in the Centre-Ville, near the Old Port. Out here you couldn't even see the sea. Back then Zoe used to crew on the yachts that went out. Day sails, sometimes longer if school and college allowed. No chance of that now with a full time job. It seemed cruel to be so close to the ocean and have nothing to do with it. But she had to commute to work from her place in Nice – who could afford to live in Monaco? – and that sucked away all her time, and all her money too, it felt. And rents in Nice weren't cheap, either. At lunchtime she'd walk down by Port Hercule and check out the sailboats there. At times she thought of packing it in and going for a crewing career, but the money just wasn't good enough, the work not steady enough. Yachts were getting more automated all the time and crews were getting smaller, proper sailing crews anyway. Zoe contributed to Noah's upkeep – Lily couldn't afford it all – and teenage boys, wow, they ate a lot! So the bank it was, and she had to make do with some windsurfing every now and then. And now, with all this going on, it was time to stop dreaming once and for all, Zoe.

She'd have to borrow it, she supposed. How much would that be over a year? Two years? What's that per month? Over a year, one hundred and sixty-six Euros sixty-seven cents a month. Plus interest. Could she get an evening job or work weekends? In a bar, maybe? Could she save on the rent? Probably not, because if she moved she'd end up paying more for the commute. Sharing with Stella kept the rent down anyway. Should she ask her boss? He was a banker after all. She'd been his loyal assistant for years now. But he kept his distance, did M. Bernard. He was very formal, very proper. To admit to having a need, that she was in trouble? It didn't appeal. He liked everything to run smoothly, to be just so. And she couldn't risk this job.

No, she'd say nothing. She'd find another way.

She changed the subject and asked Noah about the football. It took a while but eventually she got him talking. Noah was their best goalkeeper. He and his friends there could be the names of the future, their faces on posters in the bedrooms of the boys of Marseille, and the girls too, hopefully. You had to have a dream to get out of a place like this, to rise above what everyone expected of you. Noah was Zoe's dream as well. It made the rest of it bearable. And bear it she would, because somehow, big sis would always manage things for both of them. Even though, right now, she had no idea how.

Chapter 4

Pippin slipped silently through the streets of the old town. He liked to be invisible. Small and slight, little-boy face, neat hair, round glasses, the gazes of passers by slid over him without registering. That was generally the way, unless he wanted people to see him, of course. Right now he was happy to trot along, looking up, admiring the tall yellow houses with their narrow green shutters, the deep blue sky of Nice filling the gap above his head.

The colours. The colours! That was why so many artists came here to the south of France, why Vincent came here. Something in the light made the colours more intense, more moving. The contrasts resonated and lifted the soul. Vincent would analyse what he saw when he went on his long walks. In his letters to Theo he would describe the landscapes he'd seen, muse on the difference between colour and tone, consider how he would paint what he saw. A small amount of yellow in a colour makes it very yellow, but a blond woman can be shown in a drab grey. Sunlight on a red roof doesn't need vermilion or chrome, but touches of red-ochre on top of a muted shade. Shadows aren't black or brown. They're violet, say the Impressionists. Violet next to yellow makes both sing; they're opposites.

Pippin thought about these things as he walked. Pippin couldn't paint, though. In his hand the brush remained leaden, had never transformed into a conductor of his soul. His strokes never came to life, never spoke for themselves, never became more than simply oil on canvas. No, Pippin wasn't an artist. But he knew what he liked.

He'd seen the antique shop before, dusty windows, wooden furniture piled up outside in the street. No signs, no name, just the product itself, good quality if sometimes worn, retrieved mainly from house clearances, but a hand-written note in the window indicated *Offers considered.* He saw that note when he passed by a few days ago. Now he stopped outside, hesitated, took a long, slow breath, and went in.

A conversation stopped as he entered, two men behind the counter. One of them was short and grizzled with spectacles, the other tall, younger, long nose, high cheekbones, eyes proud, or maybe accusing. The tall one was wearing a waistcoat and a hat, a kind of trilby. The proud eyes followed Pippin as he started to browse, then turned back to the other fellow. They resumed their conversation in a mutter.

Pippin squeezed himself between the clutter to look around. The shop smelled pleasingly of furniture polish. The stock was mixed. Mostly small items, low-value, to tempt the passing tourists, but all a certain quality. Silverware: candlesticks, bowls, jewellery. Tableware, porcelain, sitting on scratched leather-topped tables with carved legs. Glassware, brassware, paintings and prints, clocks, watches, mirrors and toys. Vases, one or two. Nothing special. For the tourists. He looked round. The tall one was still talking to the short one, who was looking at Pippin.

"Are you interested in something in particular?" he asked, bringing the other man's conversation to a halt.

Pippin approached. "I have something..." He reached for his backpack, but paused as the man gave a shrug that shouted indifference. "I don't know if it's the kind of thing…"

"No, no," The man made a grudging beckoning sign. "Let's see what you have. I can't take anything, you know, I have stock, we're full, really. But let's see."

Pippin looked at them both. The younger man was watching, his arms folded. Pippin put his backpack on the counter, unfastened it and drew out an object just under a foot long, wrapped in a towel. He unwrapped it, stood it on the counter and took a step back. He chewed his lip while the old man leaned in for a closer look.

Silence fell in the shop. Outside, a group passed by, their voices echoing in the narrow street. Not much light penetrated the dirty windows, but there was enough for Pippin to see the expression on the old man's face change from indifference to curiosity to disbelief, then, finally, suspicion.

"What is it, Max?" The younger man had seen it too.

Max turned to look at Pippin. Pippin didn't want that. He wanted to be invisible today. But he needed to do this. Max's sharp eyes examined him.

"Where did you get this?"

Inside his pocket, Pippin clenched a fist. "It's been in the family for years. It was passed to me. I don't want to sell it, but – I need the money."

"Max, what is it?"

"Quiet, Gustave!" He waved his hand dismissively at the young man. He kept staring at Pippin. "How long has it been in your family?"

Pippin's turn to shrug. "Many years. I don't know."

"Can you prove that?"

"Prove what?"

"That it belongs to you! You have a receipt, some paperwork? Something that says where it came from?"

Pippin shook his head. "My grandparents had some old files, but most of it was destroyed in a fire."

"Oh, a fire, of course." His voice had a little sharpness to it.

Pippin's fist clenched some more. "Well, if you'd like to make an offer, whatever might be appropriate…I really do need the money."

Max's gaze fell to the object again. His eyes roamed the thin stem and the detailed geometric carvings, then rose up its widening black sides. He reached out and gently turned it on its base, examining all angles. His face was intense, lips pressed together, but finally he sighed and shook his head.

"It's not something I can take."

Gustave's eyes were wide. "Are you sure, Max? It looks old."

"I can't sell a thing like this!"

Gustave frowned at the stress in Max's voice. Pippin stepped up and wrapped the vessel. He had his answer. Max was rubbing his eyes, fingers under his glasses. Gustave watched Pippin pack the object, making him fumble. He just wanted to be out of there now.

"Sorry to have troubled you," he muttered, and tried to slip out of the door, but he pulled instead of pushing. Outside, the fresh air greeted him and he walked away fast, looking up again, getting comfort from the blue sky, the sun on his face, the yellow and green. It was over at least.

He didn't turn back. He didn't see Gustave come out, watch him walking away, and start to follow him.

Chapter 5

Since Salisbury had so reluctantly given the green light, Rose wasted no time flying out to Nice and establishing herself and her team there. She didn't want anyone changing their minds. Now she was video calling Walter from the team HQ, a spacious holiday apartment in a suburb of Nice. Outside the window the sun blazed onto a large balcony which looked out over a nicely tended tree-studded garden. Their beach towels were hanging out there to dry.

"Are the others there already?" asked Walter.

"Yes. Yvonne drove down from Paris. Ollie flew in yesterday."

Rose's team consisted of two people plus herself, but they were good people. Yvonne was half-French and on loan from Paris Station. Ollie, drafted in from Vauxhall Cross, was young but already had an impressive record in the field.

"You flew there together?"

"No, separately. He had his windsurfer sent over. It's a good time of year for it, apparently. Yvonne's rented a moped. She's keen on them. The three of us are going to have a great little holiday."

"How do you know each other?"

"Work. We're accountants."

"Accountants on holiday?"

"It happens."

"And why Nice?"

"Most tourists don't stay in Monaco because it's so expensive. They stay somewhere in France and go there for the day."

Crammed into the hallway was a collection of Ollie's water-sports gear, taking up a lot of space. Yvonne's crash helmet sat on the table along with a collection of spirits bottles, mixers and glasses. The place had a real holiday feel to it, three youngish Brits enjoying the late summer sun. But Rose was working hard, and the other two were out on surveillance, keeping discreet tabs on their target informant.

"So did you speak to Hong Kong about Alastair?" she asked Walter. The screen showed his age; he looked pale and thin against a washed-out background that gave nothing away.

"No can do, I'm afraid. I think he's genuinely unavailable. On loan somewhere. Special assignment. Need to know, and so on."

He gave her a regretful smile. Rose thought it unlikely Walter couldn't find out what a certain officer was working on if he wanted to. Walter was one of the MI6 old school that wasn't supposed to exist any more: avuncular, faded around the edges, softly-spoken. But behind his flowery language lurked a dangerous sharpness; Walter knew what was what. Clearly he wasn't going to give her any more on Alastair. Her attempts to make contact with her friend had failed, so she had no trouble believing what Walter said, as far as it went.

"So we'll need to look elsewhere," he said. "It's all a bit chummy, the fine art market. With all the regulatory tightening that's going on post Panama Papers, terrorists and other criminal types have fewer and fewer options for getting their grubby fingers on their ill-gotten gains. But the art world is all still rather informal – a gentleman's word and all that. Art dealers promise to protect their clients' privacy, as they see it, and don't do all the checks they should be doing."

"Well, that was certainly the case for the Van Gogh." It just so happened that the piece of art they'd associated with one of Grom's companies, a previously-discredited Van

Gogh, had recently become the most expensive painting ever sold at auction. It had achieved some notoriety. "If Grom was the buyer, it would explain why he paid so much for it. It was a way to get money out of Russia quickly. And it also explains why no one knows for sure who owns it despite all the speculation. So we need someone who's familiar with that world."

"Yes. Even better, someone who can credibly move around in it."

"You mean as an operator?" Rose had been thinking about an adviser.

"Well, it would certainly be useful, wouldn't it? At the moment, you're working on a way of discovering Sutherland's Monaco ID. Once you've got it, what then?"

"Plan the next stage. With the name we should get an address, data on other assets, hopefully a link with the Freeport."

"There's a Freeport connection?"

"That's where we think the painting is. You know, these bonded warehouses that are becoming specialised in storing fine art."

"Yes, indeed, they're a money launderer's dream, I'm afraid," said Walter. "No declarations of ownership required, as long as the goods stay within the Freeport. Perfect for holding financial assets in secret. And avoiding tax. And hiding stolen artefacts, for that matter."

"They're often found at airports. Monaco's too small to have an airport, so it's near the heliport. It sounds quite modest compared to some of the new ones springing up – Luxembourg, Singapore and so on. But it's just as opaque. We'll need access to it, or at least some way of verifying our painting is there and keeping track of it. That's going to take some doing."

"Well, this is exactly where an inside man might help. You probably won't welcome this suggestion, Rose, but hear me out."

"Go on." Rose had a feeling she knew where this was heading.

"John Fairchild has Monaco residency. He also owns a company in Monaco that lets and manages luxury apartments. I can see that being useful. He's also the owner of a number of pieces of fine art and is very knowledgeable on the subject. You know how he can absorb information on seemingly every topic. With the right kind of incentive, he might be persuaded to place one of his own pieces in the Monaco Freeport. That would give him a way in."

It was what she was expecting, and she wasn't having it.

"John Fairchild isn't someone MI6 is supposed to be associating with. His loyalties have come into question more than once. Plenty of people have a problem with him. Including Marcus Salisbury."

"Yes, well, Salisbury can be kept at arm's length, my dear. I'm happy to take any flak that comes from that quarter. In this instance, our interests and those of John Fairchild are aligned. Fairchild would be delighted, would he not, to finally track down the man who had his parents killed?"

"I expect he would, Walter, but what would he do then? He's too involved. It's personal for him. As well as his own motivations, in Russia he made a promise that he would kill the man. If we invite him in, what's to stop him walking all over our operation to satisfy his own thirst for vengeance? We're trying to learn something here, about how Grom operates, who else he's in touch with. For us it's about neutralising a threat to British security. Fairchild doesn't give a stuff about British security. He's only in it for himself."

"Well, he may need some management, but I have to say with his credentials and standing in the region, he is someone who could help you get a result."

"Of course we need a result. Salisbury made it very clear he'd close us down if we weren't getting anywhere. But involving Fairchild could jeopardise that. Walter, I know you feel responsible for the guy."

That touched a nerve. Rose recognised that particular tiredness on Walter's face from previous conversations.

"I get the blame for him, certainly. His parents were working for me when they vanished, but nothing I did made them more exposed to our friend Sutherland. They did that themselves. I regret that I couldn't keep Fairchild on board when he was a teenager. I should have shared more with him earlier, I realise that now. He should have found out they were intelligence officers from me, not elsewhere. And yes, I didn't tell him about Sutherland's existence. That was for his own protection, to stop the boy trying to go after him."

Interesting that Walter referred to this man they were pursuing as Sutherland, while Rose called him by his street name. *Grom* was the Russian word for thunder. Back in Russia, Grom was a menacing, powerful force. Rose had felt that force even though she'd never met him. She'd only ever seen him from a distance, once in Moscow and once by Lake Baikal, where his presence even far away sent a chill down her spine. He was much less powerful now, but that emotion stuck, and so did the name.

"But now he knows," said Rose. "He discovered that six months ago in Russia. He actually met the guy. At the time you thought Grom might try and recruit him. Play on his bitterness with MI6 and try to bend him to his own cause, whatever kinds of acts of revenge that might entail. Wouldn't it be a mistake to run the risk of bringing them together again? A master manipulator, that's how you described Grom. Much like Fairchild, in fact. Bringing him into the mix sounds dangerous to me."

"The chances of Sutherland actually showing up in Monaco are tiny. He's in hiding. He's going to be in some place that has no links at all with any of his former FSB personae."

"You can't guarantee that. The whole reason for this operation is that we don't know what his Monaco identity is. He may know that. He may be counting on it. He may be there already. Monaco may be where he's hiding out. We have to plan for all this, Walter. And we will. But John Fairchild isn't what we need."

She was making a solid rational case, but the rational was only one part of it, she was uncomfortably aware. Her reinstatement in the Service and posting to Moscow, both brought about by Walter, were in large part due to his view that Fairchild had developed feelings for her. While this may be true – though nothing had been said – it wasn't something Rose welcomed, and besides, her experience of Fairchild had taught her that he was perfectly able to set his feelings aside when it suited him. But Walter had no qualms about using her to try and keep tabs on his errant erstwhile ward.

Rose hated that her career success was based on such a thing, even if it were only one part of the story. And she hated that despite all of this, when she and Fairchild worked together she also felt a connection with him. Despite their different perspectives they had a lot in common. For all these reasons, she was determined that Fairchild would play no role at all in their operation, and, ideally, in her life. That had been the case for the past six months and she intended to keep it that way.

Walter gave her a meaningful stare over the top of his glasses.

"Well, that's my view, Rose. Fairchild could be very useful."

Rose held her hands out. "And you know my view. Fairchild is too big a risk. He's a wild card."

"It sounds a little to me, Rose, that you're saying you can't manage him."

Walter's turn to touch a nerve.

"That isn't what I'm saying. The man won't be managed. He'll do his own thing."

"Unless he's persuaded otherwise. In which case he'd be extremely useful."

"But Walter, there must be someone else. Some rich guy with a painting or two who'd do MI6 a favour. Jet down here for a couple of days, breeze in to check the place out, find out who's who. We can wine and dine them. I bet you know a dozen people like that, friends of the Service."

Walter gave a slight shake of the head. "None that spring to mind. Besides, persuading Salisbury to give you more resources might start to get tricky. Fairchild, on the other hand, we can manage his expenses a different way I'm sure. It doesn't have to go through the books."

"It can't go through the books. Salisbury would blow a gasket."

"Quite. But, as I say, we can manage that. It's really the only option, my dear."

They both knew full well Fairchild wasn't the only option. Having regrets about the past was understandable, but Walter insisting on bringing Fairchild in on a live project where he had a clear personal interest was folly. Did Walter know more than he was saying? Did he have some ulterior motive? It wouldn't be the first time with him.

"I think it would put the whole op in jeopardy, Walter. I really do."

"Oh, I don't think so, Rose. Not at all. Not with you in charge. You should have more confidence in yourself."

"And besides, I have no idea where he is and no contact details. Last time we parted, we were both in a bit of a hurry, to put it mildly." By that she meant that they were under fire from Russian agents, fleeing on a motor boat across a freezing cold Siberian lake. "We didn't really have time to exchange numbers."

On screen, Walter's expression remained unchanged, his gaze steady.

"You'll think of something."

Chapter 6

After the call with Walter finished, Rose wandered out onto the balcony and stood in the sun, feeling the heat warming the soles of her feet. Southwards, the town spread out below, red and green with a distant glimpse of a glistening blue sea. The drying sand-encrusted towels gave off a faint smell of the beach. The only sounds were birdsong and the low hum of traffic.

This operation needed to succeed. In his usual gentle manner, Walter had pushed her into a corner. Reluctant though she was, she wasn't in a position to refuse him. She collected herself, went inside and did a little desk research on the internet. Getting up to go, she thought about the hot car, sitting in traffic on tarmac, the glare of the sun through the windscreen. Her eye fell on Yvonne's crash helmet.

A few minutes later she was on the moped, the wind in her face, the road passing just beneath her feet, the engine loud in her ears. She could see why Yvonne was so keen on the thing. She headed straight for the seafront at a steady pace, turning into the curves and weaving past slow-moving cars at junctions. The roads were quiet, the moped responsive, the sun warm, her journey short. All good.

But not quite. Something was wrong. She slowed, travelling on an open stretch of road with no other traffic. That sixth sense, the one that came to be tuned to perfection in Moscow with FSB agents in constant watch, was suddenly awake and shouting in her ear. She kept going, all senses on high alert.

There! In the mirror, another moped came into view round the corner, the rider in a black leather jacket, a man, she thought. The rational part of her brain was asking her what the problem was. Other people rode mopeds. If he's coming the same way as you, it doesn't mean he's following you. Then why did she suddenly feel so cold, even in this heat? Trust your instincts, that was what she'd learned. She kept a steady pace, but slow enough that he would have to either pass her or deliberately hold back. He came past. She glanced across. Dark jeans with turn-ups, big boots, black helmet, stubble on his face. She tried to record all details in her head. In front, he turned right at traffic lights which then changed as she approached. She came to a halt at the junction. He'd disappeared up the road on the right. Gone.

Probably nothing, Rose. In this game you could see things that weren't there. She was approaching the seafront now and the streets were getting narrower and busier. Another set of lights stopped her. She relaxed, waiting, admiring the blue sky and the sea up ahead. A moped turned out of the side road in front of her. Dark jeans, black leather jacket. It was the same guy. He was riding away in front of her. The lights changed. Rose set off, all her focus on the rider ahead. Stay behind and follow, or overtake to check? They were almost at the seafront. She sped up and moved out beside him. She went past, looking across. He caught her eye just for a second, then looked away. It was definitely the same guy.

What to do now? She'd reached the seafront and had to go left or right. Her destination was left. She went right. It was busy here, people enjoying the *Promenade des Anglais*, meandering, eating ice cream and gazing out to sea or at the chalk-white frontages on the other side of the road. Rose glanced in her mirror. No sign of the other rider. Strange. He must have gone left or right as well, but he wasn't behind her and he wasn't visible going the other way.

A movement in front caught her eye. Someone was in the road. She jammed the brakes on hard. The front wheel skidded, the rear wheel veered out to the side. She lurched to the left but somehow stayed on her feet. In the road, inches in front, stood a woman in a flowery dress and a straw hat, facing the other way. A hand reached from the pavement and pulled her off the road, accompanied by a tirade in some European language. The woman turned and her mouth opened seeing Rose.

"Désolée!"

She was dragged into the crowd and disappeared.

Heart thumping, Rose set off again. It took a few seconds to regain her alertness. The moped was gone. Not just gone, but disappeared. Could it already have passed beyond her mirror sights by the time she looked? She glanced again at the mirror. The promenade stretched back in an elegant curve, visible for quite some way.

So where did it go? There was no other turning before the seafront. The only other explanation was that he suddenly stopped before reaching the junction. He must have been pretty quick about it and there was no particular reason to pull in there, no shops, no parking bays. And there was something about the way he had looked over at her.

Trust your instincts. But instincts tended to assume everything was about you. Probably, it was just some guy going about his business. Maybe his phone rang or something. Still, Rose carried on going west, and went on an extensive tour of the outskirts of the town before double-backing and arriving from a different direction at her destination, which was the Hotel Negresco.

She parked and sauntered into the lobby of Nice's most famous (and expensive) hotel. She invented pretexts to hang around for a while – reading a restaurant menu, texting on her phone – until the person on the front desk was one of the older members of staff, most likely to be a manager. She caught the woman's eye and strolled over, an envelope in her hand.

"Oh, excuse me. I have a message to deliver to one of your guests." She placed the envelope down. "Mr John Fairchild. I believe he's staying here."

The manager's eyes rested on the name, written on the envelope, for slightly too long before she looked at Rose again.

"I can check to see if we have a guest of that name staying here."

Three taps on the keyboard.

"I'm afraid not. This is not one of our guests. I'm sorry."

"Well, I'm sure he is intending to stay here. I don't suppose – if he does check in – you could let him know that Rose Clarke left a message for him?"

"Rose Clarke?" she repeated.

Rose got out a business card with her contact details on it. "Yes. Just in case, you understand."

The woman took the card and the envelope, saying nothing.

"Thanks." Rose walked away.

She'd heard all kinds of rumours and second-hand reports about John Fairchild's global network and the reach it gave him. Within a few days she would find out if any of them were true.

Chapter 7

The Trade Winds Cafe in Los Angeles was one of Fairchild's more recent acquisitions. Or rather, it was an acquisition approved by him as controlling shareholder but proposed by his very capable manager, a Filipino woman by the name of Carmel. When Fairchild bought the Trade Winds chain a few years ago, Carmel was a mere assistant manager in the Manila outlet, but he soon put her in a role more suited to her skills. Trade Winds then was a pretty successful chain across eastern Asia, but it had become more global since. This was to Fairchild's advantage, but not Zack's, who didn't hide that he thought the places were overpriced and over-rated.

"A lot like you, Fairchild," he said grumpily after his usual rant about the menu. They were sitting at the bar, each with a nautically-themed cocktail in front of them. "Not exactly a great result. Our agent was dead by the time we got to him. But they took their time over it. He was alive for several days. Seems they had a doctor standing by to make sure of it."

"Nice." Fairchild sucked on his straw.

"And Quesada is nowhere. Disappeared into the blue. Took off from that secret runway and never came down again."

"There are dozens of places he could be."

"Yeah, thanks for that."

"Well, it's true, Zack. You had an opportunity to nail him and it went wrong, probably because someone in the local police has been terrorised into informing for him. If any of us had known about the airfield we'd have planned things differently. But if you didn't know about that one, how many others could there be?"

"Yeah, believe me, I've made that point to my superiors."

Who exactly Zack's superiors were was something of a mystery, but they were pretty high up inside the CIA or some military intelligence outfit, and that was all Fairchild felt he needed to know. As long as the guy paid up, it didn't matter to him.

Zack sat back and stared around the place, his trademark mirrored shades not hiding the disapproving look on his face.

"You ever thought of ditching all this junk and just running a bar?" he asked, looking at the fake paintings of sailboats, the plywood tea chests, the vaguely Asian-looking ceramics in every corner.

"It's the theme, Zack. Trade routes, adventurers, east meets west and all that. It's quite a successful chain, you know. One of my more profitable investments."

"Yeah, well, good for you."

Maybe bragging about his business ventures wasn't especially tactful in the circumstances.

"I'm sorry about your man," Fairchild said. "I wouldn't wish that on anyone. The worst possible outcome of an undercover exercise gone wrong." Fairchild had almost been there himself often enough to know. "At least you found the pot farm. That's a few million less profit in the wrong hands, maybe a few thousand lives not ruined by drugs on the streets."

"You think? Hell, this guy will just move production somewhere else. He's got people everywhere. The stuff just keeps coming. Doesn't matter where the guy is hiding out. He can do everything through intermediaries. His name is on nothing. He's got chains of operations, shell companies run by trusts run by nominees, yadi ya. All over Mexico, Colombia, the Caribbean, the world. No one knows what anyone else is doing. They can all claim they didn't know what they were a part of. He even ran it all from prison for years."

"You need to get into his business affairs. Track down his money. Get hold of his assets and squeeze them dry."

"Good idea! Not so easy to do with all these offshore jurisdictions setting up sham companies then refusing to cooperate with law enforcement about who really owns them."

"You mean like Delaware? Isn't Delaware one of the biggest centres in the world for setting up anonymous companies?"

"No, I don't mean Delaware, I mean Panama, Cayman Islands, the Bahamas, places like that."

"Places like the Seychelles? Though didn't the CIA block investigations there? Almost like you have secrets of your own."

"Hey, the reason why the CIA needs anonymity is to nail all those other anonymous creeps. Like the ones selling drugs and recruiting terrorists. And the latter gets more attention than the former. Meaning Quesada has probably gotten away with it because he isn't high enough priority to pursue."

"Why is this your area anyway, Zack? You're not DEA."

"That agent was on loan from the CIA. I knew him. Former marine. Makes it personal."

"Fair enough. But to be honest, Zack, the USA has been losing the war on drugs for decades."

"Tell me about it. But this Quesada guy isn't someone I'm going to forget about any time soon. He may be in the wind now but I'll find him some day. I'm happy to bear a grudge. Don't tell me you don't sympathise with that, Fairchild."

Being the closest thing Fairchild had to a best friend, Zack knew all about Fairchild's discovery of the existence of Gregory Sutherland, otherwise known as Grom, who had

Fairchild's parents killed thirty years ago. Finding this out ended Fairchild's decades-long search for the truth about what had happened to his parents. The truth ought to bring closure, so Fairchild had expected all this time, but somehow it seemed only to lead on to other things.

"Yes. But don't hold your breath for a quick result. I've been chasing down Sutherland for six months and haven't seen or heard anything. I expect he'll come looking for me at some point."

"To kill you? Glad you can be so cool about it."

"That's why I'd prefer to find him first. But he's hardly the only one, is he? Quite a lot of people wouldn't mind that, including Quesada now."

"Why? You got away, didn't you?"

"Only just."

"Only just is where you live, Fairchild. Come on, you love this stuff. Admit it."

Fairchild wasn't so sure. Even to a friend like Zack he hadn't confessed how much he'd thought about packing in the intelligence game and doing something normal. Those thoughts piled in on him more and more often, ever since he first met Rose Clarke, in fact. Soon after that he realised that she was, basically, all he wanted in life, despite this complicated edifice of businesses and private informants he'd set up across the world. Unfortunately, Rose Clarke wasn't interested in him – didn't even like him that much – and was much more motivated by her career in MI6. He couldn't blame her for that. He should really stop thinking about her so often.

"Well," said Zack, after sucking up the remains of his rum cocktail, "Now I have to go lobby for more money to pursue this guy. Your last invoice practically cleaned out the US Treasury. Want to keep on Quesada's tail?"

"Maybe."

"Maybe? You got some other plans?"

"I just like to keep my options open. I don't work full time for the US government, Zack."

"Okay, okay! Go spend your money! Go sailing! Relax on a beach for a while! Get laid! That's what I'd do, if I didn't have to go and explain myself to someone in Washington."

"Sure."

"Or," said Zack, reading his long-time friend with some accuracy, "carry on searching for this Grom guy even though you've done that for six months and not found a trace, and are pretty sure he wants to kill you. Do you actually know that he's still alive, by the way?"

"I guess not."

Zack was looking at him carefully. At least he probably was, but it was hard to tell with the shades.

"Does any of this searching involve that British intelligence officer who keeps showing up wherever you happen to be?"

Fairchild tried to sound casual.

"Keeps showing up? Hardly."

"Really? Hong Kong? Beijing? Tibet? Then Moscow all of a sudden?"

"They were assignments. She was doing her job."

"And it had nothing to do with you? She's bad news, Fairchild."

Zack made no secret of the fact that he had very little time for Rose Clarke. What Zack didn't know was how damaging Fairchild's involvement in Rose's life had been for her. It was because Grom had learned of Fairchild's feelings for Rose that the man had tricked her into getting caught in the middle of a particularly horrific siege, part of Russia's recent abortive invasion of Georgia. Very few people, possibly nobody except Fairchild himself, who was there, really understood how affected she'd been by it. So no way was he going to drag Rose Clarke into anything relating to Grom. Or indeed anything at all. She was much better off without him.

"Whatever, Zack," he said. "If you get clearance to go after Quesada, let me know what you need and I'll think about it."

"Oh, you'll think about it, great. Listen, Fairchild, I want you on this. I want that bastard Quesada for what he did. Will you take it on? For an old friend? I mean, assuming nothing better comes along, that is."

It was gratifying when the CIA begged you for your time. Fairchild was about to say something reassuring when his phone rang. He looked at the display. It was an international call from the Hotel Negresco, Nice, France.

Chapter 8

M. Bernard had clients. No, these people were more important than clients. They were potential clients. Mr and Mrs Howard, from Iowa. Zoe showed them in, gave them her friendliest smile, sat them down at the big polished table in M. Bernard's office, and brought them coffee.

"Of course it's not just about the tax benefits," M. Bernard was saying as she set out the espresso cups. "Monaco offers fantastic quality of life. It's a beautiful place, yes?"

"Oh, yes!" The Howards nodded enthusiastically.

"The mountains, the port, the coast, France and Italy right here. Very good infrastructure, healthcare, transport links. Of course there's the food, too much temptation sometimes!"

He smiled and patted his stomach. The Howards nodded along and chuckled, though it was only ever a half-smile with M. Bernard.

"Zoe, can you stay for this?"

Zoe stowed the coffee tray and got out her notebook so her boss could fire off instructions. This was where her languages came in useful – fluent English as well as Italian. Not that she'd be doing much of the talking.

"So, you're yet to fully explore the option of residency?"

"Oh, that's right!" said Mrs Howard. "Actually, we're on vacation! We're on a cruise, aren't we, Hector, and just love the place so much we started thinking about retirement. We've always loved France!"

"And Monaco," corrected Hector. "So we're not at all prepared, you see. We just walked in."

Who walks into a bank when they're on vacation? Well, maybe in Monaco. M. Bernard nodded gravely.

"Well, one of the criteria for Monaco residency is to demonstrate liquid assets of at least five hundred thousand Euros."

He didn't want to waste time with tourists. But Mr Howard gave a quick nod.

"That's okay."

"In fact, our clients are generally wealthier than that. The cost of living here, it's not insignificant. Thirty percent of the principality's population are millionaires. It gives the place a certain feel, a certain – rarity."

The Howards nodded again. Mr. Bernard became a little more focused.

"So, may I ask what kind of business you're in back home?"

"Vacuum cleaners!" Mr Howard sprang to attention. "Hector Howard Vacuums is the biggest retailer of vacuums in the Mid-West! 'Let Hector clean your home!' That's on the billboards. It's a household name, isn't it, Pearl?"

"Oh, yes! Forty years selling vacuums. Every home needs one! Always will, whatever happens."

"It's all going online now," said Hector. "Things have changed a lot. We got a buyout offer. It's time to move on with our lives, isn't it, Pearl? Cash in."

"That's right. We've worked hard, and we deserve it."

"I see," said M. Bernard. "So you might have a substantial lump sum to invest?"

"No 'might' about it! That's our life's work, we built it up from scratch," said Hector.

"So we'll definitely be joining your thirty percent here," confirmed Pearl.

They all laughed. That was what M. Bernard needed to hear.

"Well, in that case, I'd suggest that Monaco offers some strong advantages over our neighbours, including zero income tax for residents, as you may know."

"Yeah, we heard something about that." Hector had done a bit more research than he was letting on.

"And as a bank which is specialised in wealth management services to foreign residents, we can offer you plenty of guidance in terms of investing your money efficiently. That might be – interesting?"

"It might be, don't you think, Pearl?"

Pearl agreed.

"Well, first, we can assist with a residency application itself. There are some forms, of course, you know how it is, and you need an address here in the principality."

"An address?" asked Pearl. "So we have to live here all the time? Not that we don't love it, but – we want to do some travelling, don't we?"

Hector agreed.

"Well, the rules state that to retain your residency you have to spend three months in every twelve here in Monaco," said M. Bernard. "But – as you've seen, we have no border checks! So nobody can really know whether people are here or not. We come and go as we please. It's how it is here."

They seemed happy with that. Well, thought Zoe, living in a luxury flat in Monaco for more than three months out of twelve could be pretty burdensome.

"Then, of course, you'll need a Monaco bank account for your personal use," said M. Bernard. "Now, if you have funds that are surplus to your everyday needs, we can help you to manage that, and transfer the funds you require into your ordinary account as part of our seamless client service."

"When you say 'manage'," said Hector, "what do you mean by that?"

"There are plenty of options open to you, but one might be to consider placing it offshore. That would put it beyond any domain that demands a tax contribution."

"That would sure be useful, Hector," said Pearl. "I really don't see why we should give up so much of our money to the government, do you? I mean, it was us who earned it."

"Indeed," agreed M. Bernard. "And if you value privacy, these things can be set up in a way which distances you. If you wanted to – be discreet about what you were worth."

"We'd certainly like to keep our personal business that way," said Hector. "When people find out what you got, they all seem to want a slice. Family, friends—"

"Ex-wives," said Pearl. Howard gave her a sharp look.

"A common problem, I'm afraid." M. Bernard was full of sympathy for the plight of the super-rich. "I should explain that Monaco is not in itself an offshore jurisdiction, but many residents live here on a tax-free basis. And there's no bar on setting up a foreign offshore company in a location such as Panama, or the Seychelles or the British Virgin Islands, and managing it through a fully authorised company here in Monaco. There would be no corporation tax." The Howards were following every word. "We have no concept of 'mind and management', the idea that tax should be paid in the domain where the decisions are made. We have no double taxation agreements, no central registry of foreign offshore companies, and a banking system which is totally confidential. There is little to engage the nosey bureaucrat here."

"That's interesting, isn't it, Pearl?" said Hector.

M. Bernard ploughed on. "And if privacy is important to you, I would recommend setting up these corporations with nominees as officers. That way, your name won't appear on any public record of the company, regardless of jurisdiction. The association between yourself and the company will remain private. For even more discretion, you could choose the option of bearer shares. That means that no name appears on the shares, and the only record of ownership is on a register in the company's domain which can be kept confidential. The shares would be stored in the vault here, to avoid anybody – finding them."

Finding out about them, was what he meant. Hector had a question.

"These nominees? Who are they, exactly?"

"They can be whoever you want, but the most straightforward approach is to use members of my staff here at the bank. That way, when you require any changes made, we'll be able to action them straight away without having to pass on instructions to a third party."

"Now, wait a minute," said Hector. "If I put all my money into an account that's in your name, aren't I just handing you all my money? I'm not sure I like that. I'm old-fashioned about these things, aren't I, Pearl?"

"You sure are, honey."

"Of course," said M. Bernard. Zoe had heard this conversation a hundred times. "You must be absolutely sure you're in control. So, we would draw up a management agreement which details exactly what powers you want to give us and what you want to retain for yourself. We would be able to convene company meetings and sign legal agreements, but only under your instructions. You have just as much control as you would as named directors or shareholders. But the instrument of control is a contract agreed between us, which remains confidential."

"A binding contract?" asked Pearl.

"Absolutely."

"A secret contract?" asked Hector.

"A private contract." M. Bernard pursed his lips. "Confidential. Perfectly legal."

"And what about these shares?" Pearl asked. "How can we control them if they're locked in a vault here?"

"If you wanted to sell them or pass them to someone else, you would simply do that through a change to the share register at the company office. The shares themselves don't need to move. Think of them as a commodity that can be bought and sold. Like gold. All cash started out as promissory notes in place of gold, didn't it? It wasn't necessary to pass the gold from hand to hand. It could stay locked in a bank and the cash did the work. As long as the gold remained safe, it could be traded over and over again. Of course, banks no longer work like that. But the general principle is similar."

He waited. They were looking a little tired. M. Bernard was thinking about bringing things to a close.

"We will be your servants in all matters." He was doing his half-smile again. "I've built this company over many years. Like you, I'm proud of its success. Your business is vacuum cleaners, and mine is trust. If you can't trust us, our relationship cannot work. That's why we provide every reassurance through contracts and paperwork, ensuring that you know that you remain in control. If we didn't honour these contracts, our reputation would be ruined and our business could not continue. I like my work here. I want to keep doing this. As an added assurance, you may wish to have all our arrangements checked by an independent third party. Many of our prospective clients do that."

They were both looking dazed.

"I see I've given you a lot to think about. We will send you some materials. Zoe!"

He gave Zoe instructions for things to send, and Zoe took their contact details. Handshakes, thanks, goodbyes, come back with any questions. Zoe took them down in the lift and called them a taxi. They chatted while they waited.

They were a nice couple. Ordinary. Down to earth. She kept telling herself that, but the truth was, all she could think about now was the money. All that money they had and didn't even need. How did people do it? It seemed impossible.

They may look and sound ordinary, but the Howards were like all their clients. They came from a different world.

Chapter 9

Pippin had some warning, at least. Mme Boucher, his ever-present landlady, made some protestations downstairs, but the hearty male voice and fast heavy steps drumming the stairs told him she had relented. So the first rapping on the door of his room didn't make him jump. He got up off the bed and opened it.

Gustave, from the shop. Pippin stared.

"I was hoping we'd run into each other again," said Gustave. "I think we might find we have a lot in common."

"How did you know where to find me?"

"I followed you." He didn't look at all abashed. "From the shop."

Pippin frowned. "I went for a walk."

"I know."

"A long walk."

"I know! All the way along the promenade. You made my feet ache." His expression was amused.

"I was enjoying the sunset. The colours, they were…" The words went out of his head, but he could see it in his mind. The Mediterranean wasn't blue, it was green sometimes, or violet, a tinge of rose or grey in the changing light. The colour of mackerel, Vincent said.

"I understand. We're lovers of art, the two of us. We appreciate these things. We see what others don't see."

He was carrying something, a tube wrapped in brown paper.

"I have something I want to show you. I'd like to know what you think of it."

Gustave wanted to come in. Pippin's heart thumped, his mind picturing the walls of the room behind him.

Gustave waited, eyes on him. "That vessel," he said. "The one you brought to Max's shop."

Gustave had a naturally booming voice. It echoed down the stairs. At the bottom of the stairs was Mme Boucher's lounge, where she would be sitting quietly. Mme Boucher was a lady who took an interest in things. Pippin stood aside and beckoned Gustave into the tiny loft room, shutting the door behind him.

Gustave seemed to fill up the space, ducking under the low ceiling. The room had two chairs, wooden, upright and rustic with woven seats. Pippin sat on the bed, a narrow cot with a red counterpane. Next to him the lead-lined window was open, letting in the sounds of the old town below. The floor was plain floorboards, a washing bowl and jug sat on a square table in the corner and a towel hung on a hook next to it. But Gustave wasn't looking at any of this. He was looking at the walls. Pippin watched the man's eyes roam the heavy frames and their eclectic contents, one by one, large and small, the detailed pencil drawings, the bold abstract shapes. Pippin felt himself shrinking into the corner.

Gustave's eyes stayed on a large piece hanging above where Pippin was sitting, an Impressionist study of a woman and child bathing by a river. Slowly, he raised his finger and pointed.

"That one. I've seen it before. Where is that one from?"

Pippin swallowed and fiddled with the counterpane.

"Was that in the family too?" Gustave's tone changed from curious to knowing. "Belonged to your grandparents? The paperwork all destroyed in the fire?"

He sat on the chair, legs wide, and folded his arms. "Max told me that vase of yours is stolen. Lifted from a museum in Rouen."

Pippin's mouth was dry. "He's wrong. It belonged to my grandparents."

"He says it's very old. Chinese, twelfth century BC. Worth a lot of money."

"He's mistaken. It's just a trinket. A family heirloom."

Silence. Gustave was examining him. He leaned forward.

"I don't know your name," he said. He had an expectant manner, as if he didn't question that people would tell him what he wanted to know.

"Pippin," said Pippin eventually, his voice cracking.

"Just arrived in Nice?" He looked round the room as if its modesty answered the question in itself.

Pippin shrugged.

"Why did you come here?" asked Gustave.

"The light, the colours. Lots of people come here for that."

"You're an artist?"

"No. But I – like beautiful things. Beautiful places. I move around. Sometimes I just have to—"

"Get away?" It was an accusation.

"No." He sounded too defensive. "I go where I feel like going."

"A free agent, eh?" Gustave was grinning. "You follow your soul?"

"You could say that."

"Well, Pippin of the Soul," – his eyes were moving over the walls again – "I think there's another reason why you move around so much. I think you're a thief. I think all these works are stolen. I think if I went downstairs and expressed concerns to your landlady, you may get a visit from the police. You may have to move on again. You may," – his mouth twitched – "find that your soul takes you elsewhere once more. I expect she's already curious, when she comes in here to nose around. She does that, doesn't she? What must she think, looking at all this stash on the walls?"

Something in Pippin burst.

"What's the harm? What problem are they causing in here? At least they're appreciated. Not packed away in some store room, or in the east wing of some ignorant millionaire's mansion, sitting there as trophies of wealth, no one even caring what they're saying!"

He came to an abrupt halt. Gustave was smiling.

"That's more like it! That's the most honest thing you've said so far! So you liberate art, that's how you see it? Free it from the prison of private ownership? You should put all these on display, then!" He opened his arms expansively.

"I'd like to. But…"

"Of course! You'd end up in a prison yourself. That's the world we live in these days. The laws serve the privileged and leave the rest of us paupers. Spiritual as well as financial. Deprived of even the sight of works which encapsulate the pinnacle of human expression. In this world, Pippin, feeding the soul is exclusively for the rich. You agree?"

Pippin eyed him carefully.

"You still have that vessel?" asked Gustave.

Pippin tried, he really tried, to keep his eyes directly in front, but something must have given him away. Gustave jumped up and opened a cupboard door. With no embarrassment he rifled through Pippin's clothes and drew out the vase, still wrapped in the towel. He held it up to the light.

"How did you get this?"

A pause. "I stole it."

"Yes, but how?"

"I grabbed it."

"From the museum? How?"

"I just picked it up."

"You broke in?"

"No, it was during the day."

"The museum was open?"

"I knew the vase wasn't alarmed. The security guard was looking the other way. I picked it up and put it inside my coat. Went straight out to the exit. I was outside in the street before they realised anything was gone."

Gustave was transfixed. "But they must have been looking for you!"

"No one saw me take it."

"Surely they had CCTV. They'd have gone through it."

"I – looked different."

Gustave's eyes were bright. "You were in disguise?"

Pippin looked faintly ashamed.

"Even so, to just grab and go! Anyone could have stopped you." Gustave was bubbling over.

"They didn't. They don't, generally. It's a talent I have."

"A useful one. But why rob a museum? Museums make art available to the people."

"It was only on loan. Due to go back."

"Back where?"

Pippin shrugged. "An anonymous owner. Private collection. Back into the darkness."

"Someone's drawer somewhere?"

Pippin smiled, a little sadly.

"Why did you take it?" asked Gustave.

"I liked it."

"That's all? Why did you try to sell it, then?"

Pippin sighed. "It's like I said. I need money. I can't pay next week's rent."

Gustave considered this. He pointed again at the Impressionist piece, the woman crouching naked, dressing or undressing the little boy.

"What about that one? I saw something about it."

"It was in the home of a countess. She lives in a château full of beautiful things that only she sees. I got a casual job there, in the garden. I would take her flowers that I'd picked."

"You befriended her."

"We took tea together. She told me about her life. She was lonely. I could walk around the house as I wanted."

"But you didn't just grab it and run!"

"No. I replaced it with a photograph."

"A photograph? That would never work!"

"It did work. I went to a specialist developer. It had to be the exact size, the exact colour. I had to have two or three made before it was right. It took time and money. One day I hid in the cellar and came out when everyone had gone to bed. I changed them over, and took the original."

"Ha! Never to be seen again!"

"No, I went back the next day as usual."

"Really?"

"I wanted to see what it looked like in situ, during the day." Pippin nodded to himself. "It looked good. I moved on a couple of days later. It was three months before she noticed. Three months! The theft was reported, but not the method. She was too embarrassed."

Gustave stared again at the painting, and the other works. Pippin could tell the story of each one. But Gustave moved on.

"What are you really here for? In Nice?"

"There's a lot of art here. A lot of money. The two go together."

"And you're into the art, not the money."

It was Pippin's chance to explain what he was about. One artist epitomised this, one artist whose life would serve as an example.

"Van Gogh only sold one painting during his lifetime. He lived in poverty, writing to his brother when he didn't have enough to eat. He hated the commercial side of art. He lived for the expression, the colour, the composition. Now his paintings are priceless. What does that mean? It doesn't mean anything. I could steal to order. Most people do. But I take what I like. Every now and then I sell something to get what I need. I don't think these pieces belong to me. They don't belong to anyone."

"They belong to everyone." Pippin could see Gustave's mind working. "You like to liberate, set things free? Let me show you something."

He took the wrapped cylinder and pulled something out of it, a canvas. He unrolled it on the bed. The canvas was nearly the width of the bed. Gustave turned to Pippin.

"What do you think?"

Pippin moved to see it in the light. "I don't know this artist. Is it contemporary?"

Gustave didn't answer: some kind of test.

"If it is, it's in an old style. A homage, maybe." Pippin's eye roamed the expanse of vivid colour. "Oil, of course. It's a landscape but oriented like a portrait. A church, on a hill overlooking a city. The colours are exaggerated. This sky, it's the colour of blood. The sea is like Prussian blue, so dark. The size of the cross up here, it's huge. Symbolic. Crowds of people. A crucifixion? But is this fire?" He circled with his finger a mass of orange and white, suspended in the air, it seemed. "Martyrdom? Burning at the stake? It's like Chagall, only Christian."

Gustave was gazing at it now, distant. "Their souls were liberated through the flames. That's what the martyrs thought. The soul would fly up, while their flesh melted."

Pippin shuddered inwardly. Then his eye fell on the signature in the bottom left. *G. Fournier.*

"This is your work?"

Gustave straightened, still looking at the canvas.

"Derivative. Unoriginal. Backward-looking. Lacking in strength of concept. Unpopular. Unpopular! See, Pippin, if you're not one of the handful of darlings they all run after, you're nothing. Either it's worth millions or it's worthless. That's the art market. What about a range of tastes? What about paying an artist the cost of their time, something real? With a reasonable mark-up for making the sale? But no. Nothing's real to the gallery owners, the art dealers. Nothing's reasonable. They want to sew up the market. Keep the prices high, but make plenty of sales. Greed, Pippin, greed. It's all artificial, controlled."

Gustave was lost in the painting, deep in his reflections.

"Where did you study?" Pippin asked.

"Paris. *Beaux-Arts.* For what it's worth. I learned a craft. It took years. But the product is valueless."

"Is that why you left Paris?"

That brought him back. He turned from the painting to look at Pippin.

"Not really. That interests you, does it?"

"Well, you asked me the same question." Pippin met his gaze.

Gustave laughed and swept his hand over the canvas. "Keep it!"

Pippin shook his head, taken aback.

"No, I want you to have it. It's worthless, anyway. See, here?" Gustave touched his signature. "If that said Chagall or Vincent Van Gogh, what would this square of oil and canvas be worth? It's vanity, Pippin. But you know that, I think."

He moved to the door. "I'd like us to meet again." He didn't phrase it as a question. "There are some matters we could discuss."

"You won't tell anyone?" Pippin could hear the pleading in his voice.

"No, I won't tell anyone. But we will talk more. Look after your soul!"

His boots hammered down the stairs.

Pippin sat in silence. He stared at the painting for a long time. Then he rolled it up very carefully and slotted it back in the tube. He lay on the bed, breathing steadily, waiting for his heart to slow back to normal.

Chapter 10

Fairchild made his way slowly up the steps of the *Colline du Château*. From here he could look down onto the strip along the Promenade and see directly into the balconies of the seafront apartments, each one a little box arranged with variations of plastic tables, sun chairs and plants. Most of them weren't being enjoyed, though the day was warm and the scenery spectacular. He paused at a viewpoint and watched others look out at the orange roofs of the old town and the blue sweep of the bay. Watching, always watching. He couldn't break the habit.

He was stupidly early. There could be no reason why anyone except Rose Clarke herself would know he was in Nice, or even France, but still he double-backed to check for shadows, and surveyed the tourists with their summery dresses and shorts and sunglasses, hard-wired to pick up on anything that didn't fit. He'd already criss-crossed the Château gardens and still had time to kill.

What a ridiculous life he led. These people around him were enjoying time with friends and family, and he was acting like a spook. A spook with no mission or purpose. What he'd said to Zack wasn't the whole picture. For the last six months he'd been torn between wanting to track Grom down and feeling the need to stay away. He was in suspended animation while his feelings oscillated wildly. Hide from everyone for their safety, or go after the man to end it once and for all? In the end, he'd done neither.

By everyone, Rose was of course top of the list. But now, ironically, it was Rose who'd asked him here. The phone call from the Negresco had shocked him. He tried to have eyes in landmark hotels, set people up who could help if he were looking for something or someone in particular. Rose was the first person to use his network the other way, as a means of contacting him.

He couldn't say no. Not if she were asking for his help. He told Zack Quesada would have to wait. Zack was none too pleased. Fairchild would have to make it up to him somehow. But he didn't have it in him to turn Rose down, though he probably should have done. Their history had been brief, less than a couple of years, a handful of encounters. He remembered every detail of every one of them. Theirs was not an easy relationship. Despite all that, he felt the excitement of a child at Christmas at the thought that he was about to see her again.

Their agreed meet point was the fountain, the *Cascade du Château*, and when he sauntered up tourist-style, still ridiculously early, she was already there. Leaning on the wall looking out at the view, she seemed relaxed. He had a few seconds to observe her, her figure trim and shapely in lightweight trousers and a red top that cropped at the waist, hair up off her neck and her skin flushed from the sun. She turned and saw him. What was it about those eyes that affected him so much?

He went over and they managed some kind of awkward air kiss. He caught a smell of musk, or sandalwood. The intimacy they'd shared in Georgia, sheltering in a cellar from the deadly Russian air attacks, had evaporated long ago.

"Good to see you," she said, though he doubted she'd really wanted to reach out to him. They started to walk round into the gardens.

"Last time we met," said Rose, "you jumped out of a boat to swim back to shore and confront Grom. I have to say I didn't expect you to survive."

"I was lucky. His team turned on him while I was there. They let me go and were all set to shoot him. But somehow he managed to disarm both of them and get away. I don't know how he did it but there were police and agents swarming all over the place and he still got out."

"It's something of a trade mark with him. Getting himself out of impossible situations by doing a disappearing act. At least he didn't claim to be dead this time. It wasn't entirely luck, though." Rose glanced across at him. "It was Walter who masterminded the tip-off to Russian forces that betrayed Grom's real identity. That's what made them turn on him. If it weren't for that, you'd be dead."

"I'm sure he had his reasons."

Rose may need Walter's blessing to pursue her career, but Fairchild would never trust the man. Fortunately, she wasn't going to argue the point.

"Did you never get near enough to him to take a shot?" she asked.

Fairchild had been through these moments in his mind a hundred times.

"Yes," he admitted.

"So what stopped you?"

"He did. He – made some persuasive arguments as to why I shouldn't kill him. Well, they sounded persuasive at the time."

"He played you? *He* played *you*? Wow."

She made Fairchild sound like a manipulator on Grom's level. Sometimes Fairchild had to remind himself how much Rose disliked him.

"What did he say?" she asked.

No way was he going to tell her that, confess to the insecurities and touch-points that Grom had so easily smelled out. He changed the subject.

"You got out of Russia without any further trouble, I take it?"

"None at all, and it was only when I met up with Walter that he told me why. The boot's on the other foot now, Fairchild. All the power that Grom had when he was manipulating the FSB inside Russia, those same people are now after him for everything they can get. His life is at risk in any part of the world where there's Russian influence. And that's a lot of places. We don't know where he's hiding out. We know the Russians want his money. He smuggled a small fortune out of Russia during his time there, but a lot of that has effectively been repatriated already. He's in trouble. We have a chance to eliminate his power base entirely."

They were passing through the *Ruines* themselves, on a mosaic path that led through to the side of the *Château* that overlooked the port.

"You said we," he said.

"Grom is my job now. I have a team dedicated to doing whatever we can to disable him. Which includes ridding him of his assets, as much as we can. I'd have thought you'd like the sound of that."

"Would you?"

He stayed non-committal. Rose seemed fired up, confident. In some ways it was a good post for her. He was pleased at least that the horrors of Georgia seemed to be behind her. It was because of Grom that she'd been put through that experience at all, a deliberate act of malice on his part, and borne out of Rose's association with Fairchild. But the fact that Rose had chosen to take this role, to bind her fate to that of Gregory Sutherland, made something inside him ache, the same thing that ached at the thought that six months ago he could have put a bullet through the man's head and ended it all.

"I suppose this task force, and having you head it up, was Walter's idea?" he said.

"And that automatically makes it a bad thing? He got backing for it, though he had to do a lot of persuading that Grom is a threat. Are you going to try and argue that he isn't?"

"A threat to whom?"

"To MI6. To British security."

She sounded like such a Service acolyte. Loyalty to country, unquestioning devotion to the nation that happened by chance to be your place of birth, was something Fairchild couldn't fathom. But she was right that Grom was a threat. He knew as much from what Grom had said to him by that lake.

"No, I wouldn't. He carries grudges for decades and has plenty of reasons to bear one against MI6."

"Right. And he bears one against you as well. Which I think means we're on the same side. Kind of."

"You're offering me an opportunity to help you in your work, then."

"Come on, Fairchild. It's as much in your interests as mine to see this man sent to ground for good. More, in some ways. He killed your parents, others as well, and he tried to kill you. You think he won't try again? He won't let it rest. He hasn't run out of steam. He can regroup somewhere, build support again. He knows how to get people on side. As long as he has resources. With no money it's a hundred times more difficult. The longer we leave him in exile to recover, the bigger the threat he'll become. That's why we're being proactive."

"And how proactive are you really prepared to be?"

They'd stopped at a viewpoint. The rectangular Port of Nice was below them, boats lined up neatly along the jetties, the surrounding streets grid-like in pink, yellow and orange, hills rising up behind the town.

Rose knew what he was asking. "It was difficult enough making the case for going after his assets. There's no way we'd get clearance for that."

She didn't spell it out; they were in a public place after all. Assassination, was what he was talking about. The Service had the capability, they both knew it.

"You know he could come back even without money," he said. "He'd find a way. Only one thing will stop him."

"He doesn't represent anything like a clear and current enough threat. We have rules, Fairchild, criteria. The bar is very high for such things. Besides, it's not as easy as all that to carry out. As you know."

She was having a dig at him, and she was right.

"I wouldn't make the same mistake again," he said.

"I'm not offering you that opportunity. We're not expecting him to be here, anyway. This isn't for you to go your own way, Fairchild. If you want to help us, you'll need to stick to what we agree. We work as a team."

"I see. So I'd be part of this team?"

"Yes. You'd be part of the team."

He looked out over the port before turning back to her.

"Yellow dress, four o'clock," he said. "Shorts and a striped shirt, camera, directly behind us. That team?"

She didn't let her gaze move off his face.

"Very clever. I'm just following standard procedure."

"Standard procedure? You brought watchers along for a meeting with me in a public place. What did you think I might do to you?"

She looked at him blandly. He regretted the question. There had been times, after all, when they weren't on the same side.

"I have no idea who you're working for," she said. "You might be working for him, for all I know. You two had a nice chat last time you met, and then he got away. Or you could be working for the Russians. You're a mercenary, Fairchild. You go where the money is. Don't be surprised when people treat you like one."

"I can't be a part of a team if you don't trust me."

"I needed to take some precautions. There's a lot at stake here. I'm asking for your help, Fairchild."

It must pain her to ask him for anything. She had to be desperate. Or being leaned on. Walter, probably.

"Why are you doing this, Rose? Of all the postings, all the places you could go, after what happened in Georgia, why take this on?"

She tensed at the mention of Georgia; she didn't want to think about that, but he needed to ask. He carried on.

"You don't want to work with me. You never did. I was a means to an end, that's all. After Russia you could have gone anywhere, taken the opportunity to make a clean break and hear nothing about Grom again. Or me. But you didn't. You chose to go after him. The man who did what he did to you, quite deliberately. Yet when it's all over and he's in the wind, you turn round and start hunting him down? What is it that you want, Rose?"

He'd said far too much. They set off back through the gardens, walking in silence. Eventually she spoke, her voice husky, holding back.

"I was asked to do this. I'm well placed to do this. And I will do it, for the Service and for my country. And yes, for my career as well. I'm not the kind to go and hide somewhere. I wouldn't be in this job if I were. We have a choice here. We can all pretend he doesn't exist and wait for him to regroup, or we can take the fight to him and do what we can to prevent it. Which is it, Fairchild? What are you going to do?"

She stood to face him, colour in her cheeks, eyes accusing. So much anger and passion but controlled, withheld. For good reason. While he'd been prevaricating and rudderless, she'd thrown herself in, directing her energies fearlessly at the person who'd probably caused her more hurt than anyone else in her life. Fairchild would never deserve her.

And he couldn't refuse her, either.

Chapter 11

"So what is it you want?"

How grudging he sounded. He couldn't even bring himself to be gracious.

She started them walking again. "We think Grom has a Monaco residency permit under a false name. We're working to get the name. It must have an address associated with it, in the principality. I understand you have interests in real estate there."

"If it's a property my people manage, that will be straightforward." He was assuming Rose was asking for access to search the place. "If it isn't, that will be more complicated. But not insurmountable."

There was more. Rose's voice was flat now, the energy gone.

"We also think he owns a piece of art that's being stored in the Monaco Freeport. Quite a special piece of art. You've heard of the *Portrait of Theo*?"

Fairchild turned to her. Everyone had heard of the *Portrait of Theo.*

"Walter tells me you know a thing or two about art," she said. "I know what's in the public domain. If you can enlighten me any further…"

Oh, she hated asking for his help. But he did know something about this.

"I was at the auction, as it happens," he said.

Her eyes widened. "*The* auction?"

"I was in New York at the time and heard all the hype, so I went along. But I can start at the beginning, if you want."

She shrugged. They turned for another circuit of the garden. He began.

"Vincent Van Gogh came to the south of France when he was around thirty-five years old. Another of the sudden changes of direction that characterised his life. He was headed for Marseille but had to make an unscheduled stop in Arles and ended up staying over a year. While he was in this part of the world he painted prolifically, inspired by the light and the colours. Lots of landscapes but portraits and interiors as well. Still lives – the famous *Sunflowers* dates from that time. Almost as soon as he got here he started talking about setting up an artist commune. It was a dream of his, to live with other artists and spend time discussing the finer aspects of their trade. We know all this because of the letters he wrote to his brother Theo. They were close for the whole of their lives. They formed this plan to invite Paul Gauguin to live with Vincent. Gauguin seemed to take some persuading, but was penniless himself so eventually agreed."

"Theo was in Arles as well?"

"No, he lived in Paris with his family. But Vincent relied on him for money, supplies, all kinds of things. Anyway, Gauguin arrived and they lived together in what Vincent called the Yellow House. Unfortunately, it didn't go to plan. Gauguin, according to Van Gogh's surviving family, was a dominating character, and their frequent disagreements pushed Vincent into serious mental illness, resulting in the infamous ear incident."

"Oh, that."

"Yes, that. Gauguin left Arles shortly afterwards. But before all of that, their artistic discussions included the merits of painting from memory compared to painting what's in front of you. Gauguin was keen on the former. His work was a step towards Expressionism, the artist using images and symbolism to express an idea or emotion or abstract concept, while Van Gogh was more about trying to encapsulate the essence of what he saw with his eyes. Under Gauguin's influence, Van Gogh apparently tried painting from memory, but soon abandoned it."

"And this is important because?"

"It's important because the painting we're talking about is a portrait by Vincent of his brother Theo, painted in Arles. It couldn't have been painted from life because Theo didn't visit Arles, except briefly when Vincent was in hospital suffering from severe blood loss, after the ear incident. And it didn't date from that time. It was earlier. He must have painted it from memory. This is why it wasn't considered a genuine Van Gogh for so long. It's also atypical in style, freer than the work he did before or after. So throughout its history it was treated as a fake and valued accordingly."

"So what changed?"

"What changed is that the Van Gogh Museum in Amsterdam devised a trusted method to determine what's a real Van Gogh and what isn't. Often, authentication's a pretty subjective process, with different so-called connoisseurs having views based on their 'reading' of a work. There's analysis of materials and so on, but it's not always conclusive. The Museum's new approach is generally trusted, and they've pronounced a number of works genuine that were previously thought to be fake."

"Including this one."

"Including this one. Following a house clearance it passed into the hands of a couple of dealers who thought it was worth a try. I was told they paid a thousand dollars for it."

"For the authentication?"

"No, for the painting."

"Each?"

"Nope."

"Christ."

"Yes. They got it assessed, claiming it could be an experimental piece Vincent did under the influence of Gauguin. Which would make it a one-off, a rarity even among the rarities that are Van Gogh originals. The Museum backed them up."

"Wow. That must have made their day."

"It made them multi-millionaires overnight. If they could find a buyer."

"Well, they did."

"But they weren't in a hurry. They went round the globe hyping it up as much as they could. They showcased the verification methods, they even made a film about it, the artist, his relationship with his brother, the influence of Gauguin and Arles, the painting and what's different about its style. What they wanted was to make it notorious and prompt a bidding war. And when they eventually passed it to the auction house in New York, that's exactly what they got. The auction house went full out. They produced a lush catalogue purely for this one item. It detailed the provenance, which no one questioned, the authentication, which no one questioned either, and its significance, which, in the story of modern art is pretty high. They sent the thing on tour across the globe, and fifty thousand people went to look at it. They got shots of celebrities standing in front of it looking emotional, and stuck it all on YouTube. They played on the relationship between the two brothers, and made a whole soap opera out of it, how close they were, how Theo was devastated when Vincent took his own life and died himself shortly afterwards. All that. They milked it for all it was worth, literally."

"I remember this. It was a year ago now, wasn't it?"

"Nine or ten months. Even big art sales don't usually get into mainstream media, but this one did. The coverage was intense. There was nothing the owners or the auction house didn't do to talk it up. I also heard a rumour…"

He broke off. He was doing a lot of talking. But Rose was taking it all in.

"Go on," she said.

"The auction house wanted to place it in a contemporary art auction, not an Old Masters category. That's where the trophy works sell, where the high rollers and billionaires splash out. But they needed a reason to do that. So they commissioned a very well-known Chinese artist to create an original work on the theme of 'Brotherhood'. This was all through an intermediary of course. The connection only came to light afterwards. The intermediary put it on the market straight away, so they placed the two items in the same category and branded it with the Brotherhood theme."

"They commissioned a new painting purely to inflate the price of an existing one?"

"Well, they deny it. They simply said it was a happy coincidence. But even if *Portrait of Theo* had sold at the estimated price of two hundred million, they would have earned twenty-five million in fees. And as we know, it sold for a lot more than that."

"And you were there." She almost sounded impressed.

"The auction lasted half an hour. That's an unusually long time. The auctioneer made it pure theatre. Long dramatic pauses, meaningful gestures to lighten the atmosphere, drawing out the bids."

"So who was bidding?"

"Hard to be sure. Most buyers aren't there in person, they have an agent in the room with a mobile phone. Some people are bidding from the sky boxes on the upper level overlooking the auction room, but they're behind smoked glass. I was told two of the bidders represented the governments of Saudi Arabia and Qatar. There's a huge rivalry between them. The increments were staggering – twenty, thirty million a time. It's as if it's not real money."

"But it wasn't either of them who bought it."

"No. A late bidder came in and trumped both of them. The last bid was four hundred million. The new bidder offered five. An increment of a hundred million dollars."

"That's crazy money."

"And it brought the auction to an end. Then people started speculating about who it was, and didn't get very far."

"We were approaching it from the other way. One of the shell companies we associated with Grom paid money into the fund from which the painting was purchased. So at the very least, he contributed to it. Then we heard a rumour that the portrait had been moved to the Monaco Freeport. That tied in with our theory that he has assets there. The Russian government and their international operators are slowly closing off his other holdings. This painting is becoming more and more important to him, as his other assets fall away. But we need to know for sure that it's in there. We're checking paperwork, but that may only get us so far. We need access."

"And then what?"

"First we find out if it's really there, and if it's really his. Then we plan our next move."

Clearly she wasn't going to share everything with him.

"You do know how secure Freeports are, don't you?" he said. "They hold hundreds of billions' worth of assets."

"I'm aware of that, thank you. We need to see inside, but you can't just walk in. You have to go in with a clearing agent. We need a pretext. Like a client who has an item stored in the Freeport and wants to view it. Maybe they want to get it valued for a potential sale, something like that. The places have viewing rooms for the purpose. You own a number of pieces of art, I'm told." Walter again. "How feasible would it be to get one of your pieces moved into the Freeport?"

It wouldn't be difficult," said Fairchild. "But it's not necessary."

"Why not?"

"Because I already have something in there."

Chapter 12

Zoe was pretty good at faces. Your clothes, your hair, what you did, what you wore, that could all change, but a face didn't. Windsurfing last weekend on the beach at St Laurent du Var. The woman had been messing about with a couple of friends. Last night at Villefranche in the bar, after Zoe and Stella had gone for a swim. The woman was there, sitting on her own that time. And now, Zoe was out during her lunch break in the Casino garden, sitting on the concrete wall looking out at all the yachts, and she was there again. On her own again. Looking Zoe's way again. Zoe hoped she wasn't sending off the wrong vibe. Then the woman got up and came over. It seemed she'd soon find out.

The woman sat down at the other end of the bench, not looking at Zoe to start with. What was that about? She stared out to sea. Blond hair, blue eyes. In her thirties, maybe. Intelligent-looking. She turned to Zoe as if surprised Zoe was staring at her. But why wouldn't she?

"It's a nice spot," she said. "Good place to see how the other half lives. But that's Monaco, isn't it? One half living the jet-setting life, the other half watching them doing it. Funny, they all look the same after a while. You know Somerset Maugham?"

Zoe didn't say anything.

"'A sunny place for shady people'. That's how he described Monaco. Would you agree?"

Seriously, did she think Zoe was going to just make conversation?

"Are you following me, or what? If you're some kind of weirdo, I'll call the police."

She didn't look too bothered.

"This is a public place. A lot of people come here to visit."

"You're just a tourist, are you? Come here for the day?"

"Sure. Just looking around. The casino, the yachts, the cars."

"And Villefranche yesterday, by the harbour?"

"Enjoying an evening swim." She had a slight accent, too faint to place.

"And the other time? At St Laurent du Var with your friends? That's just a coincidence, too? You think I'm stupid, or something?"

"No, Zoe, I don't think you're stupid at all. Quite the opposite."

Zoe stared at the woman.

"How the hell do you know my name?"

She didn't answer straight away. Stared out to sea for a bit. Then:

"You're right. It isn't a coincidence. I'm not here on holiday. I'm here to work. My job is to track down people who've done bad things."

"What, some kind of police?"

"Yes, I suppose so."

"Well, you don't act much like any police I know."

"What are you expecting? Someone running around in uniform blowing a whistle? The kind of people I'm after, that won't work for them. These kinds of criminals are subtle. Clever. Intelligent. Secretive."

"So you're a kind of sleuth? An investigator?"

She thought. "You could say that."

"And what do you want with me? You don't think I'm some international crook, do you?"

She smiled. "No. But you know a few."

"What are you talking about? I don't know any criminals. What do you think, if I'm black I must be in some gang or something?" It was unfair, but the woman riled her.

"That's not what I mean. You're the personal assistant to the director of a Monaco bank that provides wealth management services to foreign residents."

Zoe really didn't like how much this woman knew about her.

"So?"

"Your clients, Zoe. Why do you think they're so shy? Why do they squirrel their money away in offshore accounts that don't even bear their name? Create trust funds to manage generic-sounding companies that don't really do anything except sit on a lot of money?"

"To avoid paying tax."

"Sure, some of them. In part. What else?"

"For privacy. Keep their business to themselves."

"I don't need to spell this out, do I Zoe? You're not stupid, as you said. Millions of dollars are generated worldwide from criminal activity. Drug dealing. Smuggling. Extortion. Corruption. Trafficking. Intimidation, violence, murder. Where does all the money go? There's no benefit in doing all those things if the perpetrators can't spend the proceeds."

"Our clients aren't drug dealers." Zoe thought of Hector Howard, the vacuum king of the Mid-West.

"Not all of them. But if they were, they're hardly going to walk in and say so, are they? Quite a lot of them don't walk in at all, I'll bet. It's all handled by intermediaries, who deal with yet more intermediaries, and more, and more, so the person behind it all is completely obscured. My job is to follow those money trails. Trace them from country to country, from entity to entity, so we see where it all ends up.

Because no matter how clean it looks sitting pretty in the Seychelles or wherever, that's dirty money that came from dirty business."

"We don't break any laws."

"I know. Everything you do is legal. You simply enable criminality. Make it worth people's while. I say you, but you're just the PA, of course. You just do as you're told. That's all that's expected of you. All that you're capable of, so they think."

Zoe still felt some instinctive need to speak up for her employer.

"M. Bernard wouldn't take on a client with those kinds of – problems."

"Not if he knew. Not if he absolutely, explicitly, undeniably knew about them. But does he really want to know? Does he systematically lift up every stone and explore all possibilities? Or is he happy with a piece of paper that lets him off the hook? A signature to say that the checks were done. A declaration. A letter of indemnity, maybe. Due diligence and he's happy. Criminals need people like M. Bernard. That dirty money has to go somewhere, if it's going to turn into things people want, like real estate and planes and cars and yachts. A grubby pocketful of cash exchanged on a city housing estate eventually turns into a Ferrari. M. Bernard is on the path between the two."

She paused, waiting for Zoe to say something, maybe, but Zoe kept quiet. The woman gazed out to sea, recrossed her legs and carried on.

"Think about it, Zoe. The layers of secrecy you provide. The sums of money involved. They're all for legitimate reasons? Do you ever look at these accounts, I mean really look at them? Consider the sums involved? Where did it all come from? How could it possibly all be legitimate?"

Zoe wasn't enjoying this. "I still don't see how—"

"Those people your brother knows. The gang that has its claws in him."

Her stomach turned over. The woman kept talking.

"All the stuff they do. Drug-running, pimping. Where does the money go? Away, somewhere. But it comes back. Through banks just like yours, all over the world. They ruin people's lives, Zoe. Young people like Noah get pulled in and coerced. They lose control. Dreams are destroyed. Lives go wrong. Some lives are lost entirely. Amongst the little people, anyway. The people who don't matter."

This was really not funny now.

"My brother has nothing to do with my job. You need to tell me who you are and what you want. You need to do that now!"

The woman was so serene it was frightening.

"My name's Anna. I work for the British government. I'm here to ask for your help. You can help us track someone down. Someone who isn't very nice. Who's done some bad things."

Her face changed, just for a moment. Some memory that hurt.

"He did bad things to you?"

She snapped back, icy cool again. "To lots of people. He's callous, and a traitor, and a thief. And he'll keep on going if he has access to what he's stolen. We know about some of the companies he's using here. The beneficial owner, Zoe, on those contracts you have, those agreements that govern how the companies are run, you have a record of whose money it is. You forward their mail. You know who they are. You know where they live."

Zoe thought through what she was saying, pictured the files on her computer.

"You want me to pass you names? That's confidential. I could get fired. I need this job. I can't take the risk. And I don't even know who you are!"

Anna took an envelope out of her bag and put it on the wall between them.

"I can give you some credentials, if that's what you need. This information is worth something to us, Zoe. We can do things with it. The right things. Knowledge is power, it really is. And we will pay you for your trouble. We don't want you to take risks. We absolutely don't want to see you get fired. We want everything to carry on just as it is now. We just need you to do a little piece of investigation for us, a one-off. Take a look."

She nodded down at the envelope. Zoe hesitated.

"Don't worry," she said. "There's no one watching us. No one who minds, anyway."

"What does that mean?"

"My people are here, keeping an eye on us."

"Where?" She looked around.

Anna kept her gaze on Zoe. "Don't try and spot them. They followed you out here from the bank. Just to make sure no one else is taking an interest."

"Like who?"

"Have a look in the envelope, Zoe."

Zoe picked it up and peered inside: a stack of hundred Euro notes. She did a quick count. Twenty of them. Two thousand Euros. Two thousand, exactly. She took a breath.

"How did you know?"

"It's enough to get him out of trouble for now, isn't it?" said Anna. "And if you can help us, I'll give you the same again. Just a name, Zoe. That's it. It will end there."

Zoe looked up. "Is this legal? What you're asking me to do?"

Anna paused, preparing an answer.

"There's probably something in your contract about breaching confidentiality. But think of this. The agreements you offer those people, guaranteeing anonymity to drug barons and embezzlers, those are legal. You said that yourself. But does it make it right? The law can be used for very different things. When you started working at the bank and signed that contract, what did they tell you about the clients you'd be serving, about where this money you'd be handling was coming from? What are they telling you now? Legal doesn't cover everything. And no one will know. We'll make sure of it."

Anna stood.

"My business card is in there too. It's down to you now. Your decision."

She paused. The envelope was heavy in Zoe's hands.

"If I say no," Zoe said, "I'd have to give you this back."

"I'm afraid so," said Anna regretfully. "But if that's what you want, fine. You can walk away. I keep my word, and I think you do, too."

She turned away.

"He was doing it all wrong," said Zoe.

Anna turned back, frowning.

"Your friend. At St Laurent du Var. The one who was teaching you to windsurf. His knees, how he positioned his feet. His technique. All wrong."

Anna smiled.

"I'll let him know."

She strolled off down towards the waterfront.

Zoe sat, looking out at the yachts, the envelope in her hand.

Chapter 13

Pippin came back from *Carrefour* with a baguette, a packet of sliced ham, two large tomatoes and a bottle of rosé wine that cost three Euros. When Pippin could find a buyer for a twelfth century BC Chinese bronze vessel, maybe he would dine out on lobster, but this would have to do for now. It could be worse.

He closed the door behind him, opened the screw cap of the wine and drank a swig, put everything else down on the bed and opened a small drawer in the washing bowl table. This was something he always did when he returned to his room. Inside were a few personal objects carefully arranged, including his *Carte Nationale d'Identité* that showed his full name. His real name. This was still carefully arranged, almost exactly how he'd left it. But not quite. It was a little out of place. Someone had come in here and poked around. He could think of only two suspects.

As if summoned by Pippin's thoughts, a banging on the door below set Mme Boucher in motion, then, after some dialogue, his name was called out and he opened the door, wine bottle in hand, to see his landlady staring up at him alongside his other suspect.

"Let's go," said Gustave.

"Go where?"

"I want to talk to you about something. Come with me!"

Gustave waited expectantly. Mme Boucher stared up at Pippin. He put the bottle down and followed Gustave out.

Gustave took him to a long dark bar with a green ceiling, red walls and low hanging orange lamps that cast deep shadows. A pool table sat in the middle, but no one was playing. The handful of customers sat at the surrounding tables in tired, furtive groups. The place smelled of bleach. Their footsteps were loud on the plain wooden floor. Gustave led Pippin down to a table where two men sat, one small, one big. They were introduced as Henri and Clem.

"This is the one I was telling you about," Gustave said to them. They both stared at Pippin. Pippin didn't know what to say.

"So!" said Gustave, "we are four now. Can we do it? It's enough, I think."

This seemed mainly directed at Henri, who was the only one of them in a jacket and tie. Office clothes, though his shirt was creased and frayed at the cuffs.

"Well, it depends, doesn't it?" said Henri irritably. "On what everyone can do. I mean, you need a plan. You can't just walk in there, I told you that."

"Walk in where?" asked Pippin politely. The two new men turned to him with disbelieving eyes, then back to Gustave.

"You haven't told him?" asked Henri. "He doesn't know?" His eyes narrowed. "Where did you say you found him again?"

Someone came over with a tray and put a drink in front of each of them, a cloudy glass smelling of liquorice. They left again.

"We can trust this guy?" That was Clem, in a low, gravelly voice. Taken together with the man's shaved head, thick neck, solid torso and battle-scarred face, it was a voice that people would generally listen to.

"I told you!" said Gustave impatiently. "This guy has a room full of stolen art. You could go up there and see it! It's just hanging over his bed!"

That's fine, Gustave, Pippin thought to himself. Just invite the whole world into my room to take a look, why not?

"He's done it all, I tell you," Gustave was saying. "Smash and grab, inside job, this one's a pro."

Gustave had been doing his research. He'd uncovered some of the stories behind Pippin's precious objects. Where had he heard this? Max, who wouldn't touch the vase, Max might have heard some of those stories.

"You said we need two people inside," Gustave said. "A dealer and a customs officer."

"He'll be a dealer?" Henri eyed Pippin doubtfully.

"Of course not!" said Gustave. I'll be the dealer. He'll be the customs officer."

Henri's expression remained sceptical.

"You still haven't told me—"

"What's your name again?" Clem's heavy words cut Pippin off.

"Pippin," he said.

"That your real name?"

Pippin's gaze slid to Gustave, who picked up his drink without looking at him directly.

"What if it isn't?" he asked.

"Hey, come on Clem, we all have things to hide," said Gustave. "We could all sell each other out if that was our game. Go to the authorities and put the boot in. What would that achieve except make losers of us all? Let's be better than that. Let's use what we have to fight back! Make a statement!"

Clem smiled, not pleasantly. Henri smirked.

"Well, you make your statement, Gustave," he said. "You know what I want out of all of this. A hundred thousand Euros and a one-way ticket to Mexico on a clean passport. That's my price. You take the loot. I've no idea how you're going to shift the kind of stuff we have in there, but that's your business. Make a statement, sell it, hang it over your bed, I'll be on the other side of the world! A long way from my debts, and my ex-wife, and you. That's my price, like I said before."

"Relax, Henri, I said we could do that," said Gustave. "Clem can handle the ID, right, Clem?"

"Sure, easy."

"Now, the money," continued Gustave. "Of course we'd have to sell something to raise that kind of cash, but your fee would be the first thing covered."

"No! No! That's not what you said, my friend!" Henri, red-faced, was pointing at Gustave. "Up front, you said! I need my fee! I need my fee, you understand, before any of you, any of you, set foot in that Freeport!"

The room went cold.

"Freeport?" The word came out of Pippin's mouth as a whisper. The argument carried on.

"Without me you don't even get through the door. I'm the inside guy, remember? The clearing agent! You need me, and I'm telling you there's no plan unless I have my cash in advance. That stuff in there, it's worth millions. You put something up front, Gustave, you show willing here, or the project goes nowhere."

Gustave held his hands up.

"Okay, okay. I mean, Henri, do any of us look like millionaires? I'd sell one of my paintings to get you the dough, but current fashion has determined that it isn't worth anything! If I had something else, something like the stuff in Pippin's room…"

He gave Pippin a sideways glance.

Clem looked thoughtful.

"What's he got in there?" he asked Gustave.

"A Swedish Impressionist painting of a nude woman and child. The artist is Anders Zorn, says Max. Lovely piece of work. Worth a few million at auction. Of course it will probably never get to an auction. You know someone who might be interested?"

Clem shrugged. "I might. For the right price."

Pippin had a sip of his drink. It was *pastis*, strong and sweet.

"You're not seriously thinking about a Freeport, are you?" he asked. "Even the big guys haven't tried that. Those places are fortresses. You're up against state-of-the-art technology, twenty-four hour armed security. The value of what's inside, I mean…"

He trailed off, six eyes boring into him. Henri turned to Gustave.

"I thought you said this guy was a pro."

Pippin answered him directly. "I do small town museums, private homes. I work on my own. This is like walking into the Louvre! You don't even realise what you're up against. If you haven't spent your whole lives working heists on this level, forget it!"

An awkward silence. The three of them exchanged glances.

"Well, that's a blow," said Henri. "We can't do it without him, can we?"

"No, we can't," said Gustave. "We need an agent and a customs officer, Clem is the delivery guy and Henri gets us in. It's a four-man job. We can't do it with three."

"Listen to me," said Pippin, not feeling at all sure they would. "There are plenty of takings round here. Those villas along the coast, top of the range real estate. What do you think is inside those places? And they're empty a lot of the time. The towns round here are stuffed with museums. There must be twenty at least here in Nice. And all the art galleries on top of that. You want to steal art, you can steal art, but a Freeport? Do you know the kind of people who use Freeports? These are the richest people in the world. In the world! They won't just shrug and walk away, and neither will their insurance companies."

It was the most he'd said to anyone in a long time. Another silence, then Gustave.

"You're forgetting we have someone on the inside. He's going to lead us right in."

"And then what?" asked Pippin. "He'll persuade the armed guards to let us walk right out again carrying whatever we want?"

"We'll be equipped to handle the armed guards," was Gustave's response. "Right, Clem?"

"Not a problem," said the gravelly voice.

Pippin felt his jaw go slack. "Guns? You're going in there with guns? A stick-up? You're all mad!"

"You know, you should be more ambitious, Pippin," said Gustave, his lips thin. "Swiping candlesticks and chatting up old widows is all very well, but what does it change? This is on a different scale. It's an opportunity to do something big, something glorious. This will be the biggest heist of your life. You'll be making history. And getting a message out there. Yes, you're right, we're no professional outfit. But imagine the reaction when a bunch of people like us break apart one of these bastions! These prisons, where the human spirit is locked away for the benefit of a tiny elite! We can do this. Who are you to say we can't? You've been under the thumb for too long, creeping about, hiding away in attic rooms. I bet the people who run these places are arrogant. I bet they're not prepared for a bust like this."

"It's true," said Henri. "There are holes in the system. For sure."

He looked serious. So did Clem. So did Gustave.

"And don't forget, Pippin," said Gustave. "The police might be interested in seeing some of the stash in your room. And to know your real name. The one that's on your identity card."

They stared at each other. There was anger in Gustave's face, intransigence, passion, bitterness, determination. He wasn't going to let this go. He wasn't going to let Pippin go. Pippin was trapped. His stomach flipped at the thought.

Like it or not, he was going to rob a Freeport.

Chapter 14

M. Bernard was in his office with the door closed. That meant he was doing something important that Zoe wasn't needed for. Zoe didn't much care, and anyway she had a stack of paperwork to sort out. Something else as well. Another small task which might save everything. Ruin everything, if she were caught.

There wouldn't be a better time than this. The girls she shared an office with were out. M. Bernard was behind a door. If he opened it, she had two or three seconds to clear her screen. It was enough. She went into the customer database and clicked on Search. Anna had given her the company name, Smart Russia Holdings, Inc. She typed it in and waited.

It was there. It was a corporation based in Monaco. She scrolled through the record. The bank had set up a number of offshore companies for this client, associated with the company. Vanuatu. Cyprus. Seychelles. All channelled through the Monaco entity. But that wasn't what she needed. Who controlled the company? She clicked through to the incorporation details. The company director was M. Bernard. The company secretary was Zoe. That wasn't unusual. She'd signed hundreds of those declarations. It was just a formality. The legal agreement set out how the company was managed. That spelled out what they as nominees could and couldn't do.

The legal documents were on another drive, but Zoe had access. Zoe had access to most things. Their workstations were tracked; people could look up what she was searching for. If they did, they'd want to know why, but she had a couple of excuses lined up if that happened. She found the right date folder and did a search. What she wanted was in the top ten results. She opened and scrolled down. Pages of legal speak. She skipped to the end. There was the name! Igor Yunayev. The beneficial owner. That was it. Mission accomplished. But the name told her nothing. It was just a name. His Monaco address was there too, a penthouse near the Casino. There was another forwarding address – a company in Zurich. That was where they'd send any mail they got from the offshore domains. They had a process for that: put the mail inside a brown envelope with a fresh address, and send it on. So the offshore accounts couldn't be linked to him except by whoever opened the envelope.

She got a notepad and wrote it all down. She closed all the files and slipped the note into her bag. Job done.

She looked at the notepad on her desk. What if they did that thing where they rub something across it to read what was written on top? She had no idea who would do that, but she'd seen it on crime shows. What if she got mugged when she went to meet Anna? What if someone found the note in her bag? She'd get fired. Maybe even arrested.

Now she couldn't think about anything else. She threw the whole notepad into her bag, picked it up and went to the ladies' room. Inside the cubicle she sat and got out her personals bag. She tore the wrapper off a tampon, pulled out the tampon and put it in the sanitary bin. She took the paper with the name and addresses, rolled it up and put it inside the applicator, the waxy tube. She stuffed some toilet paper down each end and put it back in the wrapper, back in the bag. No mugger was going to look in there. She took the top two pages of the notepad, tore them up and flushed them down the toilet.

She went back to her desk. Nobody was back yet. She sat and smiled. That was kind of fun. Now for the paperwork.

This included the forms for Hector and Pearl, the first stage of their investment of their vacuum cleaner fortune. But her mind went back to Igor Yunayev. He'd done bad things, Anna said. Zoe started to wonder what kind of bad things.

There was still no one about. On her phone she searched the internet for his name. Nothing of note. She went back to the company database. This time she searched for Yunayev himself, not the company. The results included Smart Russia and a bunch of other entities as well. She looked at those, and the corporations linked with each. Quite a few. She picked a company in the Seychelles that had been established for a while and checked out its bank account details. Because she was a nominee, she could access the online account and had a record of all transactions. As one of the nominees, she would in fact have to authorise any transaction, following instructions from the beneficial owner or someone on his behalf. Though to save time, the paper trail for these authorisations was often created using blank pre-signed forms. She'd signed thousands of blank forms over the years, to speed up processing. It was the kind of thing they did every day. She looked up the current balance. The company account contained just over eleven million US dollars.

Before that conversation with Anna, those numbers in front of her would just have been dots on the screen. None of her business. She was there to serve the clients and would carry out the task, whatever it was. But eleven million dollars? Where did that kind of money come from, sitting in the account of someone who wasn't very nice? What did that mean? Was it amassed from bribes, was it stolen, was it drug money? She stared at the figure until her eyes went funny. Or it could be, she kept telling herself, that Anna was spinning her a story and it was just legitimate business earnings.

She shouldn't be thinking about this. She should take her four thousand Euros and be grateful. But she started to consider all the other entities that were part of this same web, leading back to that guy. If they were all worth eleven million as well, that would be… she did the sums in her head. A lot. An obscene amount. Hard to imagine how anyone could make a sum like that, then just keep it sitting in these accounts. And why would one client need so many of them? Most of these companies had bearer shares. She knew where all the bearer shares were kept, in the vault. Until now she'd just seen them as pieces of paper, admin, that was all. She'd never thought before about what they were worth.

The door of M. Bernard's office opened. She moved her mouse and minimised the screen. He wanted her to bring him a coffee. The door closed again. She heard voices outside; the girls were back. She closed everything down and went to make coffee. But her mind kept turning it all over.

Back at her desk, finally starting now on the paperwork, her phone vibrated. It was Noah. Everything should be fixed now with Noah, the gang got their money and it was all squared off. Anna's other two thousand she'd keep somewhere safe. But when Noah's name appeared on her screen, she had a bad feeling.

Why was he phoning her now? He should be at college and he knew Zoe was at work.

She picked up.

Chapter 15

It wasn't a very glitzy building, the Monaco Freeport. Shy, in fact. Fairchild knew all about the new Freeport in Luxembourg, its gala opening resembling a high-profile exhibition; these places were positioning themselves as private galleries, museums and exchanges, all-inclusive fine art hubs for the super-wealthy investor-collector. Monaco was not one of the newer state-of-the-art places, but the agent, a Henri Murat, welcomed him effusively enough in the lobby and took him down in the client elevator.

From the outside the Freeport looked just like any other commercial building. Regular offices adjoined it on all sides. A goods entrance had security gates but the facility itself wasn't gated, crammed as it was into the built-up downtown area near the heliport. He remarked on all of this to Murat as they descended.

"Oh, if you have any concerns whatsoever about security, M. Fairchild, let me give you every reassurance," said Murat. "The facility allows only biometric access and nobody can come in unless accompanied by a registered clearing agent. Also, we have CCTV," – he nodded up at the camera in the lift – "recording and monitored live by the security team on the front desk. They always know what's going on throughout the building."

They stepped out of the lift into a clean and shining corridor with white walls and floors and uniform fluorescent light. It stretched away into the distance, heavy fire doors and metal shutters lining each side.

"Video surveillance here as well, twenty-four hours." Murat pointed out the cameras above as they walked. Fairchild took careful note, feeling the man's eyes on him.

"Also, the anti-intrusion alarms are individual as well as collective. Separate vaults with additional security are available for special items or collections, as well as the main warehousing areas. We go this way to the viewing rooms. You know we can custom-fit the viewing rooms to suit – bespoke flooring, wall coverings, lighting and so on. Your personal art gallery!"

Fairchild nodded, examining the substantial metal doors. "Fireproof?"

"Of course. The fire alarms are highly sensitive."

"Sprinklers?" Fairchild made himself look unimpressed.

"Well, as I'm sure you know, the most modern facilities now draw oxygen out of the room instead of applying water, to protect the artwork. We have that in some of our individual vaults, should it be your requirement. It's a new feature we're in the process of installing throughout. As you can see, the floors are dustproof and there's nothing in this environment that would start or spread a fire."

But Fairchild had moved on. "You control the light and humidity, I take it."

"Of course. Temperature and hygrometry strictly monitored and kept constant in all areas. Here's the viewing room. Excuse me."

He placed his thumb on the fingerprint pad and leaned into the retinal scan. The door clicked. He opened it. The room inside was small with white walls, a single picture hanging centrally on the largest wall, tastefully illuminated. Even in this limited space it looked too small, too slight for the setting. A three-seat sofa with thin legs was positioned in front of it.

Fairchild went and stood directly in front of the picture. He knew every millimetre, every colour gradation, every shape on this image. His eye travelled over every part of its surface. The agent stayed back.

"I don't want to see any degradation," said Fairchild. "No fading, no discolouration, no rippling. Perfect condition, front and back."

"Monsieur, we store all works upright in the packaging supplied by the client in the climate-controlled warehouse, as I said. It's not exposed to light, heat or humidity. Of course, if the materials were inferior in the first place, that's not something we can control. Some of the oils used by Van Gogh, for example," – Fairchild turned to look at him when he said the name – "have faded with time, such as the chrome yellow used for his famous *Sunflowers*. But this is different altogether…it's an original?"

Fairchild turned back to the work. "It's a print. A Japanese woodblock print. Many copies are made from the same woodblocks. That's the whole idea. So there's no such thing as an 'original'."

"Of course," said Murat, backtracking, "but what I mean is, does it date from the time of the artist? Those have more value, do they not?"

Fairchild kept examining the print as he spoke. "Eighteenth or nineteenth century. Landscape featuring cherry blossom and a bridge. A little-known artist. Printed from the original blocks with some skill. Printer's name not recorded. But his artistry is just as important as that of the artist himself."

"Is it part of a set?"

"If it is, this is the only piece I know about."

Fairchild sat in the middle of the sofa and contemplated the print, as he'd done before so many times. The agent continued to hover. He gave a low cough.

"We are able to arrange a valuation, if that's of interest?" he suggested. "In fact, I thought – that's often the reason why our clients request to view a work."

"Well, I just wanted to view it," said Fairchild without turning round.

A long pause. Fairchild's eyes traced the shape of the cherry blossom trees, saw those same shapes hanging up in several of the homes he remembered from childhood – there were so many. He'd stared at this print so many times over the years. What was he not seeing?

Another slight cough. "If you're at all interested in selling, that's something else I could perhaps assist with. A sale doesn't necessarily mean the work has to be moved. We can just re-categorise it within the Freeport, if the buyer is happy to keep it here. Such transactions attract no tax, no need to declare —"

"I'm not interested in selling." Fairchild cut him off sharply.

Murat didn't like that. "Well, it's just that these woodblock prints don't carry a particularly high value. A skilful early print from the original blocks might fetch a few thousand if part of a set, but really, the costs of keeping it in a facility like this over time are going to amount to more than the item is worth by quite some margin. Of course it's not in my interests to point that out, but…"

Fairchild finally turned to look at the man.

"That's it, is it? You see nothing here except what it's worth? Dollars, Euros, nothing more?"

Murat stumbled over his words. "Well, I mean, most of our clients are investors—"

"Well, I'm not most of your clients. This was in my family. It was passed to me by my parents. It was important to them. I don't care what it's worth and I don't want to sell it. Now, if you don't want my custom I'm sure I can find some other facility to store it, perhaps one that's a little more up to date."

"Oh, no, sir, I didn't mean…" Murat responded in the only acceptable way, with a torrent of reassurance about how important Fairchild's custom was. Fairchild zoned him out and focused again on the print.

Why this print? In the legal mess during which his parents' assets had eventually passed to him, it came out that they had gone to the trouble of specifically bequeathing this to him on their death, in a letter which only mentioned this one work, none of their other possessions. It was not their most valuable item and Fairchild could remember nothing in particular about it from his childhood, other than it being up on the wall in most of the places they lived. It must have some particular meaning, but he'd never come close to understanding what. In their time at MI6, neither of his parents had worked in Japan or had any particular dealings with the country, as far as Fairchild knew. He took scrupulous care of it, moved it around periodically, carried out detailed research on it, but it was still a mystery.

Or maybe there was no mystery. Maybe they just liked the print. But he wasn't satisfied with that idea. His parents were in the habit of playing games: puzzles, riddles, cryptic messages. For as long as he could remember they made a point of involving him as well, setting him challenges, constantly testing him, as if they were training him for something. This print felt like that. Some message, some meaning lurked here, but he couldn't fathom it. Maybe he never would. But he wasn't ready to stop trying, not yet.

It was probably time to move it again. The facility here was far from impressive; newer Freeports offered greater reassurance. Fairchild had fulfilled the other purpose of his visit today. He knew how Rose and her team could get in and search for the Van Gogh. It would be challenging but possible with the right know-how and resources. Reason in itself to protect this print even more, from theft and damage but also from prying eyes. Until he could figure out its importance, he didn't want anyone else getting close.

He'd seen what he wanted to see, but the money-minded obsequiousness of Henri Murat left him irritated. So he sat for a few more minutes in silence while the agent hung around impatiently behind him.

Chapter 16

On the way home from work, Zoe got off the train one stop early and walked towards the Port of Nice. She found the bar and went inside. It was nothing special, a place like many others round there. At that time on a weekday it wasn't busy. Anna was at the back, like she said she would be. It all seemed like a pointless game now. But she had to go through with it.

She slid in to the seat next to Anna. The woman insisted on doing kisses like they were friends, although who would be watching, and how could it matter? Anna offered her a drink; she asked for a peach schnapps with lemonade.

"So, how are you?" she asked.

"I've got what you want, if that's what you mean." Zoe couldn't find it in herself to be polite.

"That's not what I mean. I mean, how are you?"

"Let's just get this over with." Zoe's bag was on the couch between them, below the level of the table. She got the tampon out of her personals bag and offered it to Anna on her palm, out of sight. Just like she'd give another woman a tampon, like you do sometimes. Anna looked surprised, but took it and put it in her backpack.

"It's in the tube," said Zoe. "In case I got mugged."

Anna nodded. "Good thinking."

The drinks arrived. Zoe took a long swig of peach schnapps. Anna was watching. When the waiter had gone, she said:

"So, now that's out of the way, how are you?"

"What do you care? You've got what you want. Just give me my money and that's it."

"Sure."

Anna opened her backpack and the envelope was there, just like the first one, but she didn't hand it over.

"Any problems?" she asked. "Anyone see you getting the information? Asked you about it? Behaved strangely towards you?"

"No, nothing. It was easy. No one's going to suspect me of anything."

"Why not?"

"Because I'm unimportant. Just a PA. I fill in forms. I sign things. I forward mail. I take notes. I change nothing. I just do as I'm told." Zoe took another swig.

Anna was thinking. Then she asked: "You gave Noah the cash from before? That's all sorted now?"

Zoe put the glass down. She wasn't normally into sharing her problems, but this woman seemed to know everything about her business anyway. So what difference would it make?

"Sure, I gave him the money. And he gave it to them. But now they want some more. Another thousand. They think they're onto a winner now. Ask for two thousand Euros, you get it. So he must be good for another pay-out! Then we give that and there'll be another and another. Never mind it was their money in the first place. Never mind he didn't want anything to do with them anyway. We'll tell the club, that's what they'll say. He'll be labelled a gang member and thrown out. That's what you get for wanting something in this life. For thinking you can break out. They just slam you down."

She felt tears coming. She blinked them back and took another drink. Anna waited. She was doing that thing when people wait for you to fill the gap. Which Zoe did. She wasn't in the mood to hold back.

"What's in there, they'll end up with all that." Zoe nodded down at the envelope. "But there's no more coming. He can't get out of there. He's got nowhere to go. Unless I quit here. Move to Marseille. Get a job there. We can find a place in a different part of town. I won't get a job as good as this one, though. Rents are higher there, as well. And they can still find Noah if they want. They could just hang around near the academy. Shit, this is so rubbish!"

Zoe drained her glass. Anna sipped on her wine.

"Well, we don't want that, do we?" she said.

"What does it matter to you? You've got what you want. It's over now. That's it, finished! That's what you said."

"And it is. But it's kind of useful knowing you're there. In case we ever needed to come back. I'm not saying we would. But just in case."

"You said this was a one-off."

"And it is. But I also said, didn't I, that we didn't want you to lose your job. Look, don't do anything straight away. Give me a bit of time. We'll see if we can help with this. You've done us a big service here and maybe we can help you out."

What could the woman really do? It sounded like just a load of big talk. Anna could see what she was thinking.

"We all have our fields of expertise. You know about money and accounts and corporate entities. I know about bully-boy gangsters who coerce teenagers. You leave them to me."

She got up. "Go home. Have a nice evening. Go to work tomorrow. Stop worrying. It'll be fine. And thanks."

It was only when Anna reached the door that Zoe remembered the money. She jumped up to go after her. Then she realised that the envelope was already in her bag.

Chapter 17

All three of them went over to Marseille the next morning, Ollie and Rose in the car and Yvonne on the moped. They needed to wait, in any case, for the FININT team to run Grom's Monaco identity through the systems before they could do more planning. Rose had passed the name on as soon as she got it from Zoe. She'd also given Grom's principality address to Fairchild to see if he could get them access to his penthouse. Fairchild had reported back on his visit to the Freeport. Last night they'd thrown some ideas around for getting in there, some of them more credible than others. But a few days' prep would sort it, especially with Fairchild playing the role of client. Rose wasn't at all happy with how much they seemed to rely on him. But she was just following orders. If it went wrong, no one could claim she hadn't warned them.

It didn't take her long to justify this excursion to Marseille as mission critical. Strictly speaking they were finished with Zoe, but what if FININT needed something else, some further detail? Knowing what she now knew made Zoe a potential vulnerability to the team. They had to watch their backs, particularly if the Russians showed up. That was why Rose used a pseudonym with the woman. But if they could get this right, Zoe was also a resource that others could call on. Once you'd had some involvement with secret services, it was never really and truly over. Zoe wasn't an asset but she was a name, a contact, someone who could be approached. A friend, maybe. It was always good to have friends. If things went smoothly in Marseille, they could become pretty good friends.

She'd made it clear to her team that Fairchild wasn't to be a part of this little trip. There was no reason for him to know anything at all about their informant. Besides, Fairchild was busy trying to get access to Grom's apartment.

The sun shone as they bowled along the autoroute past shopping malls and business parks and sprawling warehouses. Rose kept an eye on the mirrors. The incident with the moped rider on the seafront still tugged at her subconscious. She hadn't shared the detail of this with the others, but was insisting on their vigilance.

"So he calls himself Epée," she said to Ollie.

"Yep." Ollie nodded as he drove.

"Seriously? 'Sword'? Not very subtle, is it?"

"Subtlety's not his strong point."

They'd formulated a plan last night but it wasn't really much of a plan. It all depended where the *Pirats* were hanging out when they got there.

"Where shall we start?" asked Rose. "What's their most likely activity of a late weekday morning?"

Ollie had spent several days watching them and their interactions with Noah.

"There's a park near one of the schools. They wait for the kids to come out and trade cigarettes. Amongst other things."

"And it was definitely them that took the cash?"

"Oh yes. Different people of course, but once they'd laid into Noah, beat him up a bit and emptied his pockets, they went straight back to Epée and handed it over. Minus a small fee. It was all pre-arranged. They knew he'd have it on him."

"Something neat about it, isn't there? Give a guy two thousand Euros, rob him to get it back then persuade him to repay you anyway. A one hundred percent profit."

"One hundred and fifty, if they get the extra thousand as well."

"They won't."

Ollie glanced over at her. "You're not worried about them carrying? I said they might."

"I have excellent back-up."

Ollie smiled. He was better at this than windsurfing.

They tried the park first but no luck. They made a plan to split the estate into east and west and meet back at the park, keeping in touch via mobile. Rose and Ollie were back there first. After a few minutes Rose called Yvonne. No answer. A cold feeling spread up her spine.

"What's she doing?" she muttered.

"Probably just in traffic," said Ollie.

"She's got a hands-free. Why isn't she using it?"

Ollie looked at her curiously. Her phone rang. It was Yvonne.

"Where are you?"

"A street away. Police patrol cars pulled up. I gave them a wide berth."

Rose breathed out. It was a good move. The last thing they wanted was to be on the radar of the local police. Yvonne's moped rounded the corner in front of them. She pulled in but didn't acknowledge them.

"I just found them, anyway," she said through her hands-free. "Hanging around a bench near some shops."

"Great work."

Yvonne gave some details of the layout and they came up with a plan. Nothing too dramatic: they were going to do a little leaning, nothing more. A nudge, as some liked to say. A gentle nudge. They got into position.

Ollie and Rose were watching when Yvonne walked across the middle of the square towards the group of three.

She was dressed for the part: skin-tight leather trousers, three-inch heels, a plunging lacy blouse and a short leather jacket. She was intending to be noticed and she was, by the three of them and any number of passers-by. As with so many French women, there was something naturally stylish about her shiny straight brown hair, the subtle make-up on her face, and the pink scarf tied so casually around her neck which covered up so very little.

She addressed them, standing in front of them, legs apart. All three were taking a good look. The guy sitting on the bench stared at her face before his gaze moved back down to her crotch. He was thin, white, muscular. The other two were bigger, but this one had more purpose to him. Of the other two, one was black and the other white; clearly the *Pirats* didn't discriminate in terms of who they drew in to their world.

Neither Rose nor Ollie could hear what was being said, but Yvonne was managing to make some kind of point, as they were spending more time listening to her and less time looking at her body. Yvonne nodded towards a corner hidden from view, a gap between the back of some shops and a multi-storey car park. Eventually the guy on the bench got up and gestured at Yvonne. She led the way and the other two stayed behind. Rose, viewing all of this from the second floor of the car park, descended into the alleyway and was waiting there when Yvonne arrived. Ollie, she knew, was somewhere behind her.

Yvonne gestured for the guy to go in first. He did, but stopped when he saw Rose.

"What the hell is this? You said Salvato was here!"

He was speaking to Yvonne who had come up behind him.

"I lied," she said.

"You little bitch!" His hand came up to slap her but it never reached her face. Instead he shrieked as she pinned his arms behind his back. Ollie came forward and frisked him. No gun. Rose watched, arms folded.

"Who the fuck are you?" he said to her. His voice was loud.

"I wouldn't call your friends over," said Rose. "Unless you want them to see you get beaten in a fight by a woman. We just want to talk. You're the person calling himself Epée, I take it?"

"And what do you call yourself, as you're not Salvato? Are you with him? Is he here?"

"I expect he's back on Corsica, continuing to get rich on all your earnings. I've never met him. Just heard the name."

"Heard the name how?"

"Not important."

"So who are you, then?"

"That's not important either. This is what's important: Noah Tapoko. Mean anything?" She kept her language plain and formal; she wasn't posing as one of them.

"The footballer? Guy's an idiot. Lost our money."

"He was mugged. It was stolen from him."

"Yeah, he said that."

Rose stepped forward and slapped him in the face, same as he wanted to do to Yvonne earlier. That drew a string of expletives. Yvonne's grip tightened as he struggled.

"He said that because that's what happened," said Rose. "And those muggers were working for you. As soon as they got their hands on the cash they brought it to you and handed it straight over. You set it up. You recruited Noah, loaded him with cash, had him beaten up then leaned on him to double your money. Then you went back for more! What a little dirtbag you are."

A key part of Rose's preparation for today was getting Yvonne to list the most suitable French insults. Epée had stopped struggling.

"How do you know all this?"

"We know a lot of things. All your dirty little secrets."

"Well, how?"

"Because we're clever. Cleverer than you. You should remember that."

He looked round at all of them. "If you're not with Salvato, who are you with?"

"Someone bigger than that. Much bigger. Much better. Much wealthier. Whoever you think you can buy or intimidate, we can do more."

His face widened into a grin. "Oh, you're scaring me! What is this bullshit? I've never seen you before. You're nobody!"

Rose stepped forward and stamped on his foot. He shrieked and doubled up, or would have done if Yvonne had let him.

"I'd be quieter if I were you," said Rose. "Or your two friends might make an appearance. You wouldn't want them to see you like this, would you?

"Whatever." It was just a mutter.

Rose leaned in closer. "I'll tell you something else you don't want them to see. And that's how much you're skimming off the top without them knowing."

He took a sharp breath and looked at her.

"It's meant to go three equal ways," Rose continued. "Isn't it? What you make from the drug runners in this area. And so it does. Except for the runners who only come to you, the loot that you pocket without anyone else seeing. Except for all that."

His mouth curled in contempt. "They won't believe you."

"Oh, you think we can't prove it? You see, this is what I mean, Epée. You need to revise your view of us. Wherever you're thinking of going, we got there first."

She turned to Ollie, who stepped forward and showed him a series of photos on a mobile phone that he'd taken during surveillance. Epée twitched and slumped.

"It's very easy," said Rose. "All you have to do is remember this. Noah Tapoko is one of us. Anything that happens to him, it'll be like you did it to us. And we will turn it right back on you. Only ten times harder. And we will know. If you speak to him, we'll know. If you go anywhere near him or his home, his college, his club, his family, we'll know. If you lay a finger on him, we'll know. And you'll make sure everyone else keeps away from him as well, because we won't buy it if you say it wasn't you. If Noah Tapoko does so much as trip in the street or knock his head on a lamp post, we will come to you."

"That's not fair! I don't control everyone."

"Don't you? Certainly looks like you do to us. Fair or not, Noah's wellbeing has become very important to you, M. Epée. And as long as Noah's okay, you and I are okay. If he carries on with his life, you can carry on with yours, and your greedy little side scams will remain our secret."

She backed off two or three steps. "Don't think we're going anywhere, Epée. We'll be right here, watching you."

She looked at Yvonne, who released him. Epée lurched forward. Rose stood, arms folded, as Ollie stepped in. He dodged Epée's ill-aimed fist and landed a knee and a punch where it would most hurt. Epée fell to his knees and Ollie kicked him in the ribs to make sure he stayed down. Rose stared at Epée as he gasped for breath.

"I hope you've learned something today, Epée. Because if you haven't, your life here is over. Simple as that. You won't get a second chance."

She walked away, out of the far end of the alley, and the others followed. Epée stayed curled up on the ground, quietly groaning.

Chapter 18

Henri was waiting when the two of them pulled up together in a taxi. Gustave was pale, and had said few words on the journey. He was dressed flamboyantly, a purple waistcoat visible under what looked like a dinner jacket. Steel-rimmed glasses and a waxed moustache finished off the look. Pippin didn't know many art dealers who dressed like that, but no matter. Pippin himself was in a standard suit and tie. Nothing eye-catching. It was how he liked it.

Playing the part, Henri came forward with a polite smile. Pippin shook hands, introducing himself. Gustave was wooden, leaving the other two to exchange pleasantries as if nothing were strange or different. Just a regular visit to the Freeport, that was all.

Inside, Henri leaned on the reception desk and pushed the visitor book over to them.

"If you wouldn't mind, gentlemen. I can vouch for you both, of course, but just for the records."

Henri stepped back to make room. Gustave produced an expansive signature, a pre-agreed name. Pippin stepped forward and wrote neatly. The guards sitting behind the desk watched.

"You're Customs?" asked one of them.

Pippin nodded.

"I'll need to see your ID."

Henri was over by the lift.

"Hey, guys? Is this working properly?" He was pointing at the biometric security unit. "Never seen it do that before."

"Do what?" One of the guards got up and went over.

Pippin reached inside his jacket pocket. He pulled out a wallet, and at the same time a folded handkerchief wrapped in film.

"Just one moment, please," he said to the other guard, while at the same time pulling the handkerchief away from the film. He didn't break eye contact as his hand reached out lightning-fast and grabbed the guard's neck, pushing his face forward into the handkerchief.

"Hey!"

The other guard turned back to the desk, but Henri and Gustave were on either side of him holding him back by the arms. Pippin felt the body under his grip slacken. One second of struggling: two seconds and he was already starting to slump.

"You can't do that! Let me go!"

The other guard was close to breaking free. He had a gun in his holster. But Pippin was there already and clamped the cloth over his mouth. The guard fought for a few agonizing seconds then went limp. They dragged him behind the desk and laid them both out of sight, on the ground underneath the row of CCTV monitors.

"Very smoothly done," muttered Henri. He stepped over and bolted shut the reception doors.

Pippin shrugged. "Two more, you think?"

"A warehouse operator." Henri pointed at one of the monitors. "There should be another guard somewhere. I can't see him."

"Well, come on then!" Gustave was finding his voice again. "Let's get on with it. We'll be in trouble if someone else shows up."

Henri activated the lift with his thumb and retina, and they got in. Pippin caught sight of himself in the mirrored wall of the elevator and rubbed his thumb through his ginger beard. Pippin wasn't looking like Pippin today.

Henri sniggered. "Fine job with the hair dye there. Nice and subtle. You've put on weight as well!"

Pippin was pleased with his padding but looked at Henri anxiously.

"Don't worry, no microphones in this place. Only cameras."

There was a camera in the lift, they all knew, and had managed to avoid looking into it. Henri turned to Gustave.

"You think you're unrecognisable like that, Gustave? You look like you're appearing on stage. Should have asked your friend here for some help."

Gustave looked disdainful.

"Unless you're planning to come to Mexico, like me?" said Henri. "No point me hiding my face, they'll know I'm involved. That's why I need that passport."

"Well you've got the passport, and the money," said Gustave casually. "So if there's any trouble, you're the one who won't be getting out of here."

Arguing wasn't going to help matters. Pippin tried to wrap it up. "The van's already here," he said. "I saw it on the monitor."

The lift opened and they walked the length of an underground corridor, Henri leading the way. It was brightly lit and smelled of paint. At the far end another set of Henri's biometrics let them into a spacious warehouse, aisles separated by wide shelving stacked with packages. Footsteps approached on the polished concrete floor, a man in a sweatshirt with a radio on his belt.

"Good afternoon." Henri stepped forward with his authorisation note. "Item to be moved out. The van's here already, I think."

"Let's see." They went over to the far end and the others followed. The guy hit a release button and the shutter started to lift. The van was there, backed up and ready for loading. Clem was standing next to the driver's door looking suitably vacant.

"Can I see that?" asked the warehouse guy.

Henri handed over the chit and the guy went off into the aisles with it, looking for the reference number. But he never found it, because Clem ducked in under the rising shutter and followed behind him, bringing him to the ground with a couple of hard punches. They all gathered round and stared at his prone body. It didn't move.

"Just as neat as your cloth up the nose," said Henri to Pippin. There it was again, that conspiratorial look.

Pippin shrugged. "Same result."

Gustave was getting impatient again. "Well, let's move, then! Henri, you and Clem find the other guard, Pippin and I will load up the van."

"No, I think it's best if Pippin comes with me," said Henri.

Everyone stopped.

"That's not how we planned it," said Gustave.

"I know, but Pippin looks the part. If the guard catches sight of Clem, he might get suspicious and raise the alarm before we can take him out."

"You're saying I look like a criminal?" Clem stood up straight, his muscular form towering.

"Well, no offence, but…" Henri didn't need to finish. "Besides, Pippin's trick with the cloth was pretty good. No need for fisticuffs, eh? And you and Gustave can get more loaded between the two of you."

Gustave was hesitating.

Clem didn't mind. "What do we take?" he asked.

Henri thrust a piece of paper at him. "Those are the highest valued ten items in the main warehouse that I know of. The serial numbers. After that – whatever you like! Let's move, shall we, before this guard finds us."

Pippin could feel Gustave's eyes on them as they walked off. Henri led him down another corridor identical to the first. He stopped by a door, glancing over Pippin's shoulder to check they were alone.

"You'll want to see this," he said.

The door had a code of its own as well as the biometrics. Henri punched it in.

"Aren't we going after the other guard?" asked Pippin.

"There is no other guard. During the day there's two on the front desk and the warehouse guy. That's all. They rely on the technology to do the rest."

"Two guards and a warehouse guy?"

"These places are all hype. I told you. Come on!"

He pulled Pippin inside. The room was small, a storage vault. A stack of shelves was empty except for one item, a picture in a frame wrapped in padding and brown paper. Henri picked it up carefully by its edges.

"Want to guess what this is?"

Pippin shrugged.

"Well, let's take a look." Henri started to unwrap the paper.

"What are you doing?" said Pippin. "We don't have time for this. We have to get back."

"Just enough to check." Henri was fumbling like a child unwrapping a birthday present. "A little corner, that's all. Ah! Here!"

He tore along the top of the packaging enough to pull the top of the frame out by a couple of inches. It was an oil, yellows and browns. The brushwork. The brushwork! Pippin would know it anywhere. His heart started to pound.

"Come here! Take a look." Henri was beckoning him closer. Pippin peered inside the packaging. There was enough light to see that it was a portrait. A portrait of a man with a thin face, a moustache, and a cravat. Even in semi-darkness, he recognised it.

"Holy shit."

"Exactly. And I'll tell you what, Gustave isn't getting his self-righteous hands on this little beauty. You and me, Pippin. We keep this to ourselves. I know you appreciate these things. Clem's just a street fighter. You and I together, we form a plan for this particular piece."

Pippin couldn't stop staring at it. Henri carried on burbling again.

"You think I'd pull a stunt like this, put everything on the line, for a hundred thousand Euros? Make a fugitive of myself? Five hundred million dollars you're looking at there, Pippin. Half a billion! Even if we only got a tenth of that, we'd have twenty-five million each. Imagine!"

Pippin felt hot and cold at the same time.

"But what do we do with it?"

"Load it into the van with everything else! You're driving straight to Paris, right? Once you drop me off. As soon as you stop, get it out of there somehow."

"How?"

"I don't know! You'll think of something. You're smart. I've been watching you. There's more to you than you're showing. I think you'll know what to do with this. I want half, though. I'm not greedy, you can keep the rest, but I want my share."

Pippin closed his eyes and opened them again.

"How do you know I won't just keep it all?"

"I think I know enough about you to make your life uncomfortable. You're not like Gustave. You're not making a statement. You don't want to be in hiding after this, but I could make that happen. We could both ruin it for each other, couldn't we? But why do that? Just get me my share. Okay? Come on!"

He didn't wait for an answer. "Bring it!" He was opening the door.

"How will we get it past the others?"

"I'll distract them, you load it on. Come on!"

Pippin picked it up, barely breathing.

"We should take something else as well," he said. "Then we can say that we picked these two up on the way, from another storage room. If we only have one painting, they'll get curious."

Henri thought, and nodded. "This way."

In the corridor they carried on down to another door which he opened with biometrics, but no code. This was a small viewing room with a Japanese print on the wall. Henri took it down without ceremony.

"Out for a client viewing," he said.

"It's not wrapped."

"Doesn't matter. It's not worth a lot. Put it on top. Let's go!"

In the warehouse, Gustave and Clem were carrying some enormous frame. Henri went over to them spouting some story about overpowering the other guard. Pippin slipped the two extra items in. No one was anywhere near the van. The space was filling up, mainly with large frames – Gustave's choices, no doubt. Pippin stood by the shutters while the others approached, one on each end of the frame while Henri talked at them. And it was at that moment that the alarm went off.

They stared at each other. The ringing was loud, almost unbearable. Clem moved first, dropping the frame unceremoniously.

"Let's go. Go!" he shouted, running for the driver's door. "Get in the back! All of you!"

Gustave didn't shift. "What did you do? You two! What did you do?"

"Nothing! I don't know what this is!" Henri threw up his hands. "One of the guards must have come round in reception."

Clem started the engine. Henri stepped towards Gustave.

"Get in, for God's sake!" he shouted.

Gustave stood like a rock. "No. No. You're not coming with us. You did this, I know it."

"Gustave, come on, you can't leave me here, you know that! Stop messing around and let's just go."

It was too fast to see. Gustave, somehow, was pointing a gun at Henri's head.

"You're right!" he shouted above the noise. "We can't leave you here. But you're not coming with us, either."

He pulled the trigger. The sound was barely audible over the alarm. Henri fell to the ground, his head a mess of blood and bone. Gustave turned to Pippin and fired. Pippin ducked and turned. The bullet passed him. He darted out towards the van. Gustave was walking towards him. He fired again. Pippin got round the front of the van and threw himself to the ground. Under the van he could see Gustave's feet coming towards him. He needed to make a run for it, back into the warehouse. He rose to a crouch. The feet came closer. But then they stopped.

"Drop the gun, Gustave!" Clem's voice boomed out over the alarm. "Drop it or I'll shoot you in the head."

Pippin circled the van and peered round the back. Clem was aiming his gun straight at Gustave. A siren started going off in the street, not far away.

"Now!" Clem shouted. Gustave dropped the gun.

"Kick it over here. Do it, now!"

Gustave did. Clem picked it up.

"Get in the back. Both of you. Now. Or I go without you."

He stepped forward and got into the driver's seat. Pippin scrambled into the back. The engine revved. The sirens got louder. Gustave climbed in. The van lurched forward before the doors were fully shut. They swung open and everything slid backwards. One of the packages bounced off and hit the ramp as the van sped up through the gates. Pippin and Gustave clung on and reached out for the doors. Pippin could only just touch the door with the tips of his fingers. He strained further. It took several seconds to get a good enough grip to pull it towards him and slam it shut. Gustave pulled the other door shut just as they reached the main street and Clem accelerated. The force threw them both back against the doors. Pippin's face hit the metal catch, hard.

The van screeched round corners, tossing them from side to side. The sirens faded. Pippin's cheek throbbed. Wherever they were going, they were in Clem's hands now. The package containing the portrait slid and rested against Pippin's foot. It didn't look any different from the others, but he couldn't stop staring at it. He sat silent, holding on, not looking at Gustave, who had his head back and his eyes shut.

Gustave, the man who'd just tried to kill him.

Chapter 19

"Well, I was right," said Rose. "I didn't think we'd be the only people interested in that Freeport."

She took a swig of gin. All four of them had long pink gins in front of them, but their focus was elsewhere. They were sitting round the table at the Nice apartment, coming together for a rushed brainstorm as soon as the news broke. A dramatic Mediterranean sunset was in progress outside the window, but all heads were down looking at screens, following the coverage of the theft on laptops and tablets. The TV was showing CNN, which had picked it up as well.

"Yeah, interested," said Ollie. "We weren't going to rob it, though."

"True. We just wanted to poke about. That'll be all but impossible now. They'll tighten up their security to ridiculous lengths."

"They may even close the place down," said Fairchild. "Ship everything elsewhere. Though moving stuff out of Monaco would be pretty difficult because of all the tax complications."

"How can we find out what they've taken?" asked Rose. "If they have the Van Gogh, the Freeport's no longer of interest to us anyway."

"With a lot of difficulty," said Fairchild. "Nobody really knows what's in there. This is why it's such an insurance nightmare. One firm could have millions of dollars' worth of liability within a single building and not even know it. This, or a fire, could wipe out an entire company."

Fairchild was looking irritatingly relaxed, in a designer shirt, branded chinos and a navy jacket that looked custom made. Understated yet expensive. Very Monaco. Rose turned to Ollie and Yvonne.

"Are they saying anything at all?" Each was monitoring media reporting of the theft, Yvonne on French media, Ollie internationally.

"A lot of speculation," said Ollie. "Basically, no one has a clue what was in there, so they're padding things out with lists of anything that's changed hands recently, or anything they know is owned by someone who lives in Monaco. They've had Christie's on, Sotheby's, lots of commentators taking guesses."

"Are they talking about the Van Gogh?"

"Oh yes." Both of them nodded.

"The police are surely going to know what was taken," said Rose.

"Absolutely," said Fairchild. "The question is whether the Freeport management company will want that made public or not. On the one hand they'll be shining a light on the holdings of their clients, something a user of a Freeport is not going to welcome. For every item, there'll be endless speculation about who owns it, which could be embarrassing for some of them. On the other hand, publishing the list of stolen items will make it much more difficult for the thieves to sell them on. Although, they may well have their buyers lined up already."

"Stealing to order?" asked Rose.

"Sure."

"They would have needed to know what was in there," said Rose.

"They did," said Yvonne, staring at her laptop screen. "They've just announced the identity of the man who was found shot in the warehouse. He was an employee at one of the clearing agents."

"So he was working with them?" asked Rose. "The inside man?"

"What was his name?" asked Fairchild.

"Murat. Henri Murat."

"That's the guy who showed me round."

"So how did he end up dead?" asked Rose. "That couldn't have been part of the plan. Not his plan, anyway."

"Could he have been abducted or forced by the thieves?" asked Ollie. "Maybe they got in under false pretences and put a gun to his head to get to what they wanted."

"Could be," said Fairchild, "but that would have made stealing to order more difficult. Without a willing participant on the inside, they wouldn't know what was there in advance. Even if they did, it's not that easy. There are half a dozen clearing agents in Monaco. They'll know what their own clients have deposited, but none will have a complete inventory of what's in the place. Only the management company will have that, or possibly customs."

"That means they might not have had any idea what was in there beforehand," said Ollie. "Just taking pot luck."

"But why risk so much when you have no idea of the value of what you'll end up with?" said Rose. "Besides, they managed to rob a secure facility in the heart of a built-up area during the day. And got away, which does suggest they knew what they were doing."

"Not all of them," said Yvonne. "One of them is dead. And I'm seeing reports that an alarm was sounding. They must have had to leave in a hurry."

"We don't know for sure that they're in the wind," said Fairchild. "We only know what's been released to the press. The police may be closing in already."

"They might not have planned to shoot the clearing agent," said Ollie. "Maybe something went wrong."

Maybe, maybe, maybe. Rose was getting agitated. This theft was a surprise. She didn't like surprises.

"There must be CCTV inside the Freeport. Also of the surrounding streets, the major roads, routes out of the region. Analysis of the bullets as well. I assume they're no longer in Monaco. Will the Monegasque and French police work together on this?" The question was addressed to Yvonne.

"I expect so," said Yvonne. "They have all kinds of protocols, since Monaco is basically surrounded by France. I can contact Paris Station and find out what I can."

"Tell them as little as possible," said Rose. "We're meant to be low-profile. It doesn't help that the place we were the most interested in is now featuring on CNN."

"There's a possibility that Sutherland might have engineered this," said Fairchild.

"Why would Grom steal his own painting?"

"Because he knew the Russians were after it. It's one of the few assets he has that's still out of their grip. Maybe he wanted it to disappear altogether."

"Well, it's only worth something if he can sell it," said Rose. "It's a pretty notorious painting. Even more so, if it was part of today's stash."

"It's possible if you know the right people. Selling stolen art is always more difficult than stealing it, but it can be done. I do have a few contacts in the less formal sphere of the art world."

"Why does that not surprise me?" said Rose.

"Maybe it was the Russians," said Ollie. "Stealing the painting to get it away from Grom. We know Russian crime syndicates are active all over the Riviera."

"Or it could be completely unconnected," said Yvonne. "Remember, we don't know if the Van Gogh was stolen. We don't even know if it was in the Freeport at all."

"Right, so it was Grom, or it was the Russians, or it was some random group," said Rose. "We kind of need to know a lot more than this."

"I could go back to the clearing agents," said Fairchild. "I'm a client. I can legitimately ask some searching questions about the security in there and how this came to happen. Maybe we can figure out how they did it, which would tell us a lot more about who they are."

"Good idea." Rose was grudging, but it would probably help. "How are things going with Grom's apartment?"

"We should be okay. I'll have some news imminently."

"What kind of news?"

He held her gaze. "Good, I hope."

"We don't have all the time in the world, Fairchild."

"I appreciate that. This is the property market we're talking about."

In the corner of her eye she saw Ollie and Yvonne exchange glances.

"Anyway," said Ollie. "If these thieves are just some third party and they did take the Van Gogh, I don't envy them. They're going to have some pretty determined people on their tail. As well as Grom and the Russians, their insurance investigators, the police—"

"Anyone else whose stuff they took," said Fairchild. "Which could include me."

"And us," finished Rose. "I don't much fancy their chances. But if they've got the Van Gogh, we need to find them. Before anyone else does. So let's get moving."

Chapter 20

It was Clem who knew about the lock-up. A row of garages in an out-of-the-way estate where no questions would be asked, no cameras recording. It was after dark by the time the van pulled up. When Pippin and Gustave climbed out, they had no idea where they were.

Clem told them.

"Jesus Christ!" said Gustave. "We're back in Nice? We've been driving for hours! I thought we were heading for Paris!"

"Too many cameras," said Clem. "Too many toll roads. We went west, then I double-backed and brought us east again on a different route. Smaller roads. They won't expect that."

"But this is the last place we should be!" Gustave was pale. "The police have our faces. People might recognise us!"

"Then we don't go where people know us," said Clem. "Hole up somewhere. Don't go out at all. Pippin's okay. No one will recognise him."

Pippin would be okay once he ditched this disguise. Even so, knowing they were back in Nice made his palms sweat.

"I can't believe it! This wasn't our plan at all." Gustave was blustering. "Paris, that was the plan! I've got contacts there! We could get help! Not this tiny gossipy little town right on the doorstep! We're wanted by the police, Clem! For theft!"

"And murder," said Clem. "That wasn't part of the plan either."

That silenced Gustave. Clem lifted the up-and-over door of the lock-up, climbed into the van and reversed it in. Gustave and Pippin stood in the yard side by side. Pippin couldn't bear to even look at Gustave. Gustave fidgeted but said nothing. Clem closed and locked the up-and-over and put the key in his pocket. They stood, the three of them, looking at each other.

Gustave was calmer now.

“Okay, well, we need a new plan,” he said. “I admit, it shouldn’t have gone like that, but it did, and now we all have to stick together and trust each other. I know people in Marseille. There are some possibilities there. We meet here in twenty-four hours. That’ll give me some time to check them out. We stay hidden till then. And Christ, think, we did it, didn’t we? We robbed the place! Think of what’s in the back of that van!”

A silence. Pippin had to give the guy some credit. Shocked, subdued, cornered, he still assumed he was in charge, was still trying to give them a pep talk.

“Stay strong, both of you,” said Gustave a little awkwardly. “Until tomorrow.”

He walked away. Clem and Pippin exchanged a brief glance, then Clem too paced off. Pippin watched their backs disappear in different directions before sloping off another way.

In some shadowy corner he jettisoned his facial hair and padding. He stood looking up at the colours of the night. Vincent would see a troubled sky, every shade of violet, blood-red purple to ashen, pale sulphur and malachite. It was a sky under which one could ruin oneself, Vincent would say. Pippin already had a plan. Gustave was arrogant and unstable. He also seemed to be overlooking the fact that Clem had the keys to the van and the lock-up. What neither of them knew was that Pippin didn’t always need a key.

After an hour he came back via a different route and watched for a while. The place remained deserted. He believed Clem about the lack of cameras. But either of them could come back at any time. His only cause for hope was that despite Gustave's motivational words, neither Gustave nor Clem had any idea what was in the back of that van.

The up-and-over lock he picked easily. Inside he closed the door behind him and got out a torch. The van doors took longer but he had the right gear with him. He only wanted one thing from the van. He fumbled and rearranged the other stuff, the bigger, grander stuff, but none in the same league as the modest package he eventually laid his hands on.

There was barely space on the floor of the lock-up to lay it straight. He had to do this very carefully. Tensed for the slightest noise, he slit open the packaging and slid out the Van Gogh, his trembling hands making the torchlight wobble.

Don't look at the painting. Turn it over. Do what you have to do, Pippin. On the back he prised off the tape and worked the frame loose. None of this cutting pictures out of frames. That was hooliganism, not theft. Eventually, the frame came loose and he could pull it away and turn the canvas over. He allowed the torchlight to rest on the portrait for a second. In that light it looked colourless and bland. Just a bit of oil on a piece of canvas. Half a billion dollars. Half a billion! Sitting there in front of him. He shook himself out of it and rolled the canvas up, barely breathing. Using tape discarded from the frame he secured it and put it in his backpack, inside a plastic *Carrefour* bag. He reconstructed the frame and put it back inside the packaging, back inside the van with everything else arranged just as before.

As he lifted the up-and-over, Pippin half-expected Clem to be standing there in front of it. Why wouldn't the man come back now and make off with the lot? After what happened, he didn't owe Gustave anything. Clearly he knew how to sell the stuff. Or maybe Gustave himself would be there, wandering around the place with his purple waistcoat and his fake moustache and his bitterness. But no one was there and Pippin sloped off again, as Pippin liked to do, leaving everything looking just as it did before.

He went back to his room and stashed the painting under the bed. Well, Clem was right. No one would expect the thieves to still be around here. No one had seen Pippin's face. No one would look under Pippin's bed for a half-billion-dollar painting.

He splashed water on his face, got into bed and didn't sleep at all.

Chapter 21

Noah phoned early, when Zoe was on the train to work. She let it go to voicemail then called him back while she walked from the station to the bank.

"Hey, Noah!" She tried to make it sound bright. No need for little brother to know how much she'd been worrying.

"Hey, sis! You all right?"

"Yeah, I'm all right. What's new?" It was the wrong time of day for a social call.

"So, it's all cool here. The money and that, it's fine. Don't worry."

That sounded fishy. "What do you mean, don't worry?"

"I mean, don't worry. Epée is cool about it. He spoke to me."

"He spoke to you? When?"

"Last night, after football practice."

Zoe's heart sank. "Oh, man."

"No, seriously, Zoe, it was fine. He said forget about the money, we're all square. It wasn't serious anyway. Just a couple of his people playing a joke."

"A joke?"

"Yeah, I know. But that's what he said. And if any of his people caused any trouble I should let him know. You still there?"

Zoe had taken ten steps without saying anything. "This was Epée himself?"

"Yeah. Epée himself. I think it's okay, sis."

Zoe wasn't so sure. "It's not some big game they're playing?"

"There's a rumour going round that Epée got a visit from some shit-hot woman from Paris who knocked him into line.

But he's too embarrassed to admit he was pushed about by a woman."

"A woman?"

"Yeah. Or maybe a couple of women. But whatever."

She remembered Anna's words in the bar the other night. *I know about bully-boy gangsters. You leave them to me.*

"This woman, what was she like? Black, white, French, something else?"

"Hey, I don't know! I just heard a rumour, that's all. Some hard-ass tart with her own crew got him into an alleyway and bent his ear. No one knows exactly what about, but he's as meek as anything now. He's gutted. He knows people are laughing behind his back."

"Yeah, well that doesn't matter to you, does it? Long as you're out of their sights they can laugh at each other all they like."

"Sure, but like I said, Zo, it's cool. I want to meet this woman, though. She sounds like she rocks. You should be into that, sis. You're always on about girl power."

Noah was right, Zoe thought, as she sat at her desk that morning. She did go on about girl power. It must have been Anna. Couldn't be a coincidence. Wow, what a result! Those gangs bled people dry once they got hooked in. But one visit and everything seemed reversed. How did she do it? Not just intimidation. That would only work if you were there all the time and built a gang as big as Epée's. She must know things. Found something out. Had something on him. Knowledge is power. She said that herself, didn't she?

Zoe rifled half-heartedly through the paperwork in front of her. Their clients. Criminals. Not all of them, but some. Most, maybe. Men like Epée. No, not like Epée. Like the people who pull Epée's strings, the people he takes his money to, the people who supply him with the drugs and whatever else, the shady people who don't hang around in the *quartiers nords* but set it all up, keep it going, push the product and take the gains and see it stack up and up in these accounts where it disappears and comes back again as yachts and apartments and Italian clothes and vintage champagne. Respectable people in their fast cars, important people. Criminals. And here are all of us, servicing their every need, clinging to them because of the money they have, or else falling into line because we don't feel we have a choice. But do we? They're powerful and we're powerless. That's right, isn't it?

But maybe not. Maybe if you have a little knowledge, if you know one or two things, you have power. Anna changed everything almost overnight. She wasn't afraid. She knew these people, she said. And she proved it. Zoe opened the file again and turned the papers more slowly. Zoe knew things. Zoe knew how this all worked.

On her computer she looked up the name again, like she had before. Igor Yunayev. Igor was a bad man, so Anna said. She said it with some emotion too, like she'd met the guy or something. Zoe accessed the bank account for Smart Russia Holdings, the Monaco entity at the heart of his network. But this might not be the only heart. He could have networks like this in a dozen other places. Even just this one was worth tens of millions.

She scrolled down the list. All these transactions were authorised by herself and M. Bernard. That just meant that their signatures were on the blank forms that got printed up with all the details and put in the file. Money in, money out. Big money. Where did it come from? Where was it going? Most of the payees and donors were generic company names like this one. Money going round the world, hidden away. Private. Secret. Enabled by people like M. Bernard. And her.

She looked again at the Monaco address for Yunayev and checked it out on the map on her phone. A penthouse right in the heart of Monte Carlo, one of the most sought-after addresses. Non-citizens working in Monaco could only ever dream of living in a place like that. She knew how much it cost; the rent payments came out every month. Smart Russia was paying the rent. Smart Russia had signed the contract. Smart Russia was the tenant. It must have been set up by someone here at the bank. With her authorisation. She stared at the photos of the building on the street view map. It was five, maybe ten minutes away from where she was sitting right now. An idea started forming in her mind.

Chapter 22

The concierge on duty at one of Monte Carlo's most prestigious apartment buildings was nudged out of a long boring afternoon by an attractive young black woman claiming to need access to the penthouse. To measure up, she said. For new curtains and upholstery. Nothing wrong with the old ones, he just got bored of them. That sounded about right for a Monaco millionaire. He said the concierge would let her in, she said. Well, it was the first he'd heard of it. Strange, she said. She was told the man himself wasn't going to be there but the concierge had keys and would know about it. It would only take a few minutes. Well, there was no need anyway, the concierge said, because he's in. He's upstairs at the moment. Really, she said, looking surprised. He was sure, though, because the penthouse had its own lift. Only goes up to that floor. So he remembered the guy coming through, especially as he'd never seen him before. A bit of an absentee, so the others said. What a waste, having all that space up there and never being in it.

Anyway, the concierge called up, even though she tried to stop him, saying she didn't want to interrupt. But the guy answered straight away. No problem, he said, after a slight pause. Send her right up. So the concierge pointed her over to the lift and she seemed very unsure, but in she went. You see all sorts in this job. These millionaires are all over the place. Makes you wonder how they got so rich to start with.

Zoe stood in the lift as it raced upwards. Fool! The last thing she wanted was to come face to face with Yunayev himself. She needed to slope off before getting to the apartment door and make a sharp exit, but this damn lift only went to that floor. There must be some stairs and a service elevator, but where? How would she get out of the building without passing the concierge desk? This game was way more complicated than she thought. You had to plan for everything. Anna would have done that. She'd have had a backup plan, a way out.

The lift arrived and the doors opened with a *ding*. She stepped out, already looking for a fire door or discreet service exit. But too late. The guy was already standing there, at the door of the apartment, waiting for her to arrive. Tall, well dressed, brown hair, grey eyes, younger than she'd pictured him, he seemed amused at her arrival. She stood and faced him. Well, there was nothing else she could do.

"So," he said, folding his arms and looking down at her. "You've come to measure the curtains, I understand."

She met his gaze and smiled politely.

"Yes, that's right."

There was a long pause.

Chapter 23

Fairchild had only been there a few minutes when the concierge called. New curtains? Pretty unlikely, but he allowed the woman up anyway. He needed to know who else apart from him was sniffing around the place.

They stared at each other. She seemed as curious about him as he was about her. Youngish, under thirty for sure, dark skin, dark eyes, lively. Scared yet fearless at the same time.

"I know full well you're not here to measure curtains," he said.

"Do you? Well, I know full well this isn't your apartment."

He wasn't expecting that.

"Really? How so?"

"Well, you just don't sound like an Igor Yunayev to me."

They'd been speaking French. She didn't have an accent and he liked to think he didn't either. He certainly didn't have a Russian accent. But where did she get that name from?

"Well, you're wrong," he said. "This is my apartment."

She smiled in surprise. "Oh yes?"

"Yes. Yunayev may be the tenant, but he doesn't own it."

"And you do?"

"Yes, I do."

"Since when?"

"Since yesterday."

"You bought the place yesterday?"

"Effectively. The sale is in progress. But my company now manages it. I made the owner a very generous offer. My company holds a number of property interests in Monaco."

"Very nice." She sounded impressed, but also slightly amused as if she were humouring him. He held up the set of keys he'd collected from the previous agent earlier that day.

"Which is why I know that no one has asked for new curtains. We'd be aware if they had."

"And does Mr Yunayev know about this sale?"

"He'll have been notified as a sitting tenant. Nothing changes from his point of view. It doesn't matter who owns the place as long as he can claim to live here and have use of it."

"So he wouldn't have a problem with you coming up here and walking about as if you live here?"

She seemed to be enjoying this.

"You think he wouldn't have a problem with you coming in here either, on some pretext?"

Her chin came up.

"In actual fact," she said, "this is my place."

His turn again to be surprised.

"Is it now? How do you figure that?"

"The tenancy agreement is with a company called Smart Russia Holdings. The company pays the rent. I'm the company secretary. I'm one of the people who authorises the payments. Basically, I'm paying the rent here."

The penny started to drop. Rose Clarke had been in the process of acquiring Grom's Monaco identity. This woman must be involved in some way. From the moment he'd picked up the call from the concierge, Fairchild had a suspicion that MI6 had a hand in it somehow. And yet she wasn't acting like a spook, and didn't even seem to have a particular reason to be here.

An informant, then. She must be Rose's informant.

"You work for a bank?"

"I might," she said. "What's it to you?"

"Well, this is awkward," he said. "Given we can both claim to be the hosts, should I be inviting you in? Or should it be the other way round?"

She laughed.

"Well, you were here first," she said. "After you."

He led the way, and turned to watch her as she stepped into the main reception room. Her eyes travelled from the dripping diamond chandelier to the vast sofas as wide as they were long and piled with cushions, over the expanse of velvet-soft carpet and out to the wall-to-wall sliding doors to the balcony with its view of the perfect horizon of the sea.

"Wow." She walked in slowly, staring at everything. "I mean, wow."

"Take a look around," said Fairchild. "It's on two levels. The terrace is very impressive. You appear to be here to sightsee, after all."

She gave him a playful look but didn't contradict him.

"Yeah, I will, then."

He fixed a couple of drinks while she wandered, and took them out to the terrace. He found a table and sun loungers in a chest, and got them out. He was sitting comfortably enjoying the view by the time the woman appeared again. The terrace was suitably private for the shy millionaire; no one could see them from below, but they could see out, over the top of the Casino Monte Carlo, the gardens, a broad sweep of Monaco with its glittering high-rises lining the hills, clusters of white boats in and around the harbour, and the sea beyond. He handed her a drink.

"Gin and tonic. I found ice, too."

"Thanks."

Finally, a shadow of doubt crossed her face.

"You don't think Igor Yunayev would mind us helping himself to his drinks like this?"

"I think he'd mind very much. But I don't think he's going to find out."

Fairchild's agency was due to come in after him and do a thorough service of the place. They'd put everything right. Besides, Grom wouldn't show up in Monaco. With the Russian state after him, he'd be crazy to make an appearance in any place where he held significant assets. It worried Fairchild more that the Russians would track this place down.

"I don't think we've introduced ourselves," he said. "My name's John Fairchild."

"Well, I'm Zoe Tapoko," she said. "Very nice to meet you. Hell of a place, isn't it?"

She stretched out in the lounger. The sun was warm but a breeze kept the air fresh and cool. Faint sounds of the city rose up from below.

"What a life. Imagine living in a pad like this," she said. "But I guess you do live in a pad like this."

"Not exactly. If it's not a rude question, what are you doing here?"

She looked sideways at him.

"Well, I could ask you the same thing, couldn't I?"

"You could. I may even tell you. But you go first."

"Me first? Can't I just enjoy the sun a little?"

"Aren't you at all afraid?" asked Fairchild.

"Of what?"

"Of being in a place like this with someone like me, when you've no idea who I am?"

"Do you think I should be afraid of someone like you?"

"Yes," he said. "You should. Not everybody like me is as nice as me."

She sat up, more serious.

"You mean this guy, don't you? Yunayev." She held up her drink to acknowledge him in his absence. "I heard he's not nice at all. Who is he? You met him?"

Fairchild's mind went back to a freezing lakeside in Russia, a figure on a bench, a man who twisted words and played on your desires and talked himself out of a bullet through the brain. Then to Dimitri, the former gangster who had helped Fairchild, and his horrific death at Grom's hands. Then to Rose, almost certainly Zoe's source of information about Grom. But the Rose who suffered at Grom's hands in Georgia, that was surely a different Rose from the person Zoe would know. That Rose would show only a professional exterior and almost certainly use a false name. Zoe had picked up something from her, though, about Grom and his nature. Something had shown through the mask. Zoe must be perceptive. But she couldn't know how reckless she was being.

"He's been many things to many people," said Fairchild. "He's tricked and deceived all his life. He manipulates, and when that doesn't work he tortures and kills."

A silence.

"You didn't know that?" Fairchild asked. "That he was a murderer?"

She shook her head. "A criminal. A bad man."

"And who told you about him?"

Zoe's face turned neutral. She'd been sworn to silence then, about her involvement with Rose, and was keeping it to herself. Good for her.

"If you're not afraid of him, you should be," he said. "You should be glad if he doesn't know your name and has no idea who you are. That's the way it should be."

Her smile disappeared.

"The way it should be? Yeah, I know all about that. The guys with the money and the power, the people who decide how it's going to be, and then people like me. Invisible. Unimportant. Just there to do a job, measure their curtains, move their money around. Well, what if that isn't the way it has to be? Who says I'm not one of you? Who says I can't call the shots? Tell people what to do? Live in a place like this? It's all pre-determined, is it? People like you and people like me? Well."

She drank her drink and stared moodily out to sea.

"That's not exactly what I meant," said Fairchild. "There's a lot to be said for not being on the radar of people like Yunayev. Do you want to be constantly looking over your shoulder? You have a good life, don't you? Okay, no penthouse suite, but you've got a job, friends."

"I work in an office that's a five-minute walk away from here. I handle the money of the people who live in apartments like this. But I've never, in my life, ever, been inside a place like this. Why don't I get this? I'm not a criminal. I'm not a bad person."

Something had got to this woman, got her questioning things. Or someone.

"I'm curious. Why did you come here today?" he asked.

"I wanted to see. I wanted to see for myself the lives these people lead. This apartment I'm paying for, apparently, with someone else's money. My name's on the lease and I've never seen it! What's with that? It doesn't make sense."

She was looking out to sea again, rattling the ice in her drink.

"Are you sure that was all there was to it?"

"Sure, that's all." A little too casual.

"Well, I wonder if you were trying something out. Just seeing how far you could get with a little bit of information and some face. And it worked. You talked yourself into a penthouse apartment you had no business being in. But it's a dangerous game to play."

"Well, you're playing it. Others play it."

"I've been playing it a very long time. And I spend a lot of time looking over my shoulder. And I'm not sure I had a lot of choice about it."

"Really?"

She was interested in that. Could he stand to tell her his story? He'd told plenty of other people, if he trusted them, if his instincts permitted him. He liked this woman, had a good feeling about her. But it wasn't right to lead her into the forest of intrigue and betrayal and secrecy which he inhabited. She was better off out of it. And besides, was it true? Did he really have no choice? He could have walked away from all this at any time, couldn't he?

He'd piqued her interest, though.

"So, you're not a criminal?" she asked. "A bad man?"

"I don't think I'm bad, but not everything I do is legal."

"Huh." That seemed to remind her of something. "So what are you about?" she went on. "What's your story?"

"What's yours?"

"You don't want to share, then?"

"Happy to, but you go first."

"Okay." She sipped and looked out. "I'm a simple girl. I like the sea. I love my brother. I'm cleverer than people think. I'm fed up of doing what I'm told by people who don't deserve what they have. Yeah, I guess that's me. Your turn."

"Okay, well, I don't think I'm very simple, but maybe I overcomplicate things. I don't have a home. I travel around all the time."

"That's sad."

"It's not sad. It's what I want. I'm a wealthy person. I guess I have a lot of freedom, but I haven't used it well. I can be a little – obsessive."

A short pause.

"And Yunayev?" she asked. "What's he to you? He must be important for you to buy this place."

"Yunayev is none of your business. You don't want to know anything about that man."

She sat back, deflated.

"Well, I don't. I mean, there's nothing in this whole apartment that says anything about the guy. Except that Japanese thing in the bedroom. Everything else looks like it came from a hotel."

"What Japanese thing?" Fairchild hadn't even been into all the bedrooms.

"A picture. Blossom trees, mountains, that kind of thing. Quite nice, kind of out of place. What?"

Fairchild was already on his feet. He found it in one of the smaller guest rooms, hanging in an alcove. Zoe was right that it didn't fit. But it matched exactly the style and period of Fairchild's own print.

He lifted it off the wall, but it was framed so he couldn't see the back of it. He replaced it and stood staring. Zoe came in behind him.

"Does it mean something to you?" she asked.

"Yes. Well – I have one just like it. I – it's important to me. I didn't know there were any others so similar."

"Where's yours, then?"

"Good question. It was in the Monaco Freeport. Right now, I'm not sure."

He hadn't even been told yet whether his print was part of the stolen stash. Awaiting full analysis, was the stock response from the clearing agent. He stepped even closer to the print, eyeing every detail, just as he'd done to his own a few days earlier. Seeing this hanging here made the skin on his neck prickle. It must mean something but he had no idea what.

"You know, you never said what you were doing here," said Zoe, who was watching him. "I told you, but you never told me."

"I wanted to check it out," he said. Before Rose arrived with her troops, he added internally. But he didn't say that part.

"It's personal, isn't it?"

"What is?"

"You. This Russian guy. He did something to you, didn't he?"

Yes, he did something to me, thought Fairchild. He killed my parents. He took my life. Now he's on the run and I should have the upper hand. I made a promise to end him and I will. But why do I still feel that he's a step ahead?

He tore his eyes away from the print to look at Zoe.

"Yes," he said. "It's personal."

Chapter 24

Even teeming with visitors, the courtyard had a serenity to it, a symmetry that calmed the soul. Pippin paced its cloister, looking through the regular archways at the ornamental central garden with its tinkling fountain, visitors posing for photographs in front of stonework painted sienna and white.

Did Vincent wander here too? Was he rendered serene by this neat, pleasing outdoor space? He painted it numerous times during his stay here, those haunted weeks, trying to find solace, coping with blood loss and whatever hideous monsters inside his head turned him inside out. He'd stayed in one of the upstairs rooms. It wasn't a hospital any more, of course. You could tell where he painted the courtyard from. It wasn't open to the public, that area. But Pippin could find a way up.

For now he stood, taking in the colours, the blue of the water, shades of green – jasper and emerald – lush in the garden beds, darker where the ornamental trees bushed out. A delicate scent of flowers reached him, and the sun warmed his face. He closed his eyes. A moment of peace. Then onward.

He had to meet the woman in a cafe. He would have liked to sit outside. That was what he imagined when he suggested it. They could gaze at passers-by, take in the air, imagine a night sky above them full of stars bursting like fireworks, but the woman was already inside, in a corner. Always in corners, they met. He was tired of it.

"Why Arles?" she said. "There are safe houses, places closer than this. You getting paranoid?"

Pippin shrugged. "Maybe." He wouldn't be able to make her understand. It was a homecoming, a resting place. It just felt right. It was the kind of thing Vincent would have done. Though he would probably have walked, wearing out the soles of his shoes, sleeping in hedgerows, energised by the ever-changing countryside around him, the colours, the light, the sky.

"So what the fuck happened?" she asked. He almost flinched. Such ugly words, such harshness, such anger. He didn't want any more ugliness. He wanted to live within beauty and peace from now on. Maybe that was all he'd ever wanted.

"Well?" The woman demanded an answer.

"Gustave," said Pippin. "Gustave happened. Gustave had a gun. That's what happened."

"Where did the guns come from?"

Pippin sighed. "Clem."

"Didn't Clem have a gun?"

"Yes, but Clem isn't Gustave."

"I'm aware of that. You're not explaining yourself very well."

He looked at his orange juice, wishing it was wine. "Clem got us out of there. Gustave is a menace. He got suspicious and rounded on Henri and me."

"Why?"

"Because he's unstable. Unsafe."

"That's not what I meant. What happened to make him suspicious? What was going on in there?"

"It was just a big mess. A bad idea from the start."

Her eyes narrowed.

"Is there something you're not telling me?"

"No, there isn't. You're seeing things that aren't there. You think there was a plan and there wasn't. It was just chaos."

She looked at him as she drank her espresso.

"You'd better be telling me everything, *Pippin*." She had a particular way of saying his name.

"It's time for *Pippin* to leave," said Pippin. "Things have got out of hand. Pippin needs to disappear."

"No," said the woman. "Not yet. We need to find out what Gustave is planning. His contacts. Who put him up to this."

"Nobody did. It was his own stupid idea."

"You don't know that. He's naïve, certainly, but people like that can be manipulated by others. We need to know who's pulling his strings. Who's behind all of this. What's the plan now?"

The woman's face required an answer.

"Not Paris. The journey is too dangerous. Gustave said something about Marseille. He claimed to have contacts there."

"Well, there you go! In Marseille he could link in with anything. Crime rings, smuggling, radicals in North Africa, this could easily be part of something bigger. You have to stick with it. It's important."

"It's dangerous. They have guns. Gustave tried to kill me. He shot at me. Why wouldn't he do that again?"

"Well, why would he do that again?"

Pippin had an answer to this, but he wasn't going to share it with the woman.

"You need to rebuild that trust," she said. "Take things back to how they were before. And stick with it. I know you can handle it. When the others said you couldn't, I spoke up for you, you know. They thought you wouldn't see it through but I said you were tougher than you looked. That you'd do the right thing. That you'd realise what was at stake."

On the face of it, she had a misplaced faith that there had to be a plan, motivation, logic. What Pippin had realised, lying awake in his tiny bed with half a billion dollars rolled up underneath him, is that there was no plan. Gustave was chaos. Gustave was a force of nature. Anger and drama and statement and rebellion. Violence, yes – he remembered the man's gun pointed at him. He would kill and destroy, but for nothing. Because there was no purpose to any of this, no carefully-considered exit, no endgame.

The woman left. Pippin left. He watched her walk away. But he didn't follow her, not this time. He didn't need to, because he already knew what he needed to know.

Pippin liked to be clean. When he slipped away he didn't leave a shadow. This woman did. When Pippin disappeared, he was gone, invisible, no trace, just thin air. This woman left a mark, a wake that someone like Pippin could travel in for a time, to discover her secrets, other corners that she'd frequent, other conversations that she'd have, and realise that there were things he couldn't tell her. There were things he couldn't tell anybody.

He looked up, and imagined a night sky above the cafe full of stars bursting like fireworks. He realised he was crying.

Chapter 25

They were in the car on the way to Monaco when they heard the news.

"Here we go," said Ollie, sitting in the back. Yvonne was driving and Rose was in the front. "The Freeport has released the entire list of stolen items. Reported online in the last five or ten minutes."

"Put us out of our misery, Ollie," said Rose. "Is it on there?"

A brief silence as he read, then: "Yup. It's there. *Portrait of Theo* by Vincent Van Gogh. Latest sale value five hundred million dollars. That's a lot of zeros."

"What did they take, anyway?" said Yvonne, glancing at Ollie in the mirror.

"All sorts." He scrolled down the list. "A real mixture. Some high value items, but others aren't worth a lot at all. If it was a theft to order, it was a hell of a complicated order."

"They hit the jackpot, though," said Rose. "They must have known the Van Gogh was there."

"Must they?" asked Ollie. "They couldn't have just lucked out?"

"It would surely have its own security in there, wouldn't it? Be in a separate vault or something. Not just in a warehouse with everything else."

"I guess. So maybe they took the Van Gogh, then just filled up the van with whatever else they could grab."

Does that sound professional to you?" asked Rose.

"They robbed a Freeport, though," said Yvonne. "And they got away. That's not easy."

"With someone on the inside," said Rose. "You can get into almost anything if you have someone on the inside."

"You know something," said Ollie. "The Van Gogh is worth fifty times as much as the rest of the haul put together. If they intended to steal it, why bother with the rest? Wouldn't it be cleaner just to go straight for the portrait and take off?"

"This could have been the Russians," said Rose. "Some local thugs with their strings pulled by the Kremlin. They lifted the Van Gogh for their Russian government friends, then picked up some other stash for themselves."

"So what about our target?" asked Yvonne. "How's he going to react?"

"Badly," said Rose. "He was counting on that painting. If he's lost it, financially that's really going to hurt."

"It could still have been him behind it," said Ollie.

"True," said Rose. "It could be his way of manipulating things. Steal it before anybody else can, then somehow make sure it's recovered later. Put it on the market then to maximise its value. He's a real game player, is Grom."

"I guess that could work," said Yvonne. "But it didn't go to plan, did it? If it had, one of those robbers wouldn't be dead right now."

The flow of traffic slowed as they entered Monaco. Rose shook her head.

"Unbelievable how a country smaller than Central Park can be so obsessed with cars. I'm amazed it's not gridlocked all the time."

"There's always space for a Ferrari," said Ollie philosophically, as they started moving again. They entered one of the many road tunnels crossing the principality.

"We need to find these thieves," said Rose, going back to their business. "We've got a clear direction now, we need to focus our efforts on figuring out who they are, what they're about and what they've done with the goods."

"We won't be the only ones," said Ollie. "A bunch of people are going to want exactly the same thing. I don't think I'd like to be them."

"You don't want five hundred million dollars?" Yvonne glanced in the mirror again. There was something of a rapport building up between the two of them.

"Not if it gets the Russian mafia on my back," said Ollie. "And Grom. I'll get by without. Anyway, you'd never sell it for that kind of money on the black market."

"Fairchild can help with this, can't he?" said Yvonne to Rose. "He said he knew people in the black market."

"Yes, he did." Rose hadn't been too keen on this option, or indeed any option giving Fairchild centre stage, but they'd have to consider it now.

"This one okay?" They'd emerged from the tunnel and Yvonne was slowing to enter a car park, again underground.

"Sure." They turned and went down the ramp. Rose had been keeping an eye on who was behind en route, but she wasn't taking any chances. "We'll get out together and separate in the stairwell. I'll go in first."

She outlined a route which would give Yvonne and Ollie time to check her for shadows.

"And you check each other, too, before you approach. Clear?"

"Sure," said Ollie carefully. Rose was keeping her concerns about the moped rider to herself, but her caution was causing her young team to pick up on something. No matter: if it sharpened their senses it was a good thing. Hers were maybe a little too sharp.

A few minutes later she emerged alone at street level and made for the centre of Monte-Carlo.

Chapter 26

Rose brought her entire posse with her. But they didn't arrive all at once. Rose buzzed first and came up in the lift alone. She stopped before entering the penthouse itself.

"Do we know it's clean?"

"I swept the whole place. It's clean." Fairchild had spent a while working round the apartment with a bug checker. Apart from the print, there was nothing here of real interest. Rose stepped inside and looked round the grand reception room. She wasn't as impressed as Zoe had been.

"It seems like his kind of place," she said. "He isn't someone who shies away from making a statement. Any idea what it's worth?"

"I know exactly what it's worth."

She looked at him. "You bought it?"

"I made an offer. The opportunity arose."

"Seriously, Fairchild? Wasn't that a bit provocative?"

"He won't even know. It's through the company. Nothing's in my name. The tenancy carries on uninterrupted. As far as he's concerned, it's simply a change of management agency. And why would he care about that? He's not going to show up here, is he? Especially now."

The intercom buzzed. Rose checked the camera and took it upon herself to let them in. Fairchild watched her as she surveyed the place.

"Someone comes in to clean" she said. "No dust."

"Of course. It's fully serviced. That'll be my people from now on."

"Well, that might be useful. Hello!" She'd noticed the two washed glasses draining in the kitchen. "Someone had company."

"That was me, I'm afraid." Fairchild wasn't going to mention Zoe to her. That woman was getting herself into enough trouble without Fairchild making it any worse.

Rose looked at him quizzically. "You're helping yourself to the guy's drinks, now? And inviting people round? Is that normal practice for your letting agency? I must remember to avoid it."

"It'll all be put straight."

Fairchild was on edge today and her presence wasn't helping. She was being managerial, part of the establishment, the same establishment that had been so indifferent about the fate of his parents, hadn't felt it was judicious to lift a finger to try and find out what happened. Yes, he loved the woman, loved who she was. But he didn't love *what* she was.

The others were at the door now. He let them in, eyeing the equipment they were toting.

"There's no point setting up bugs in here," he said to Rose. "It's an empty flat. Waste of time."

He sat on the sofa and stretched out. Rose's foot soldiers looked to her. She'd certainly bounced back all right. In fact she'd done very well out of Grom. She'd seen an opportunity and taken it. She was ambitious after all, he'd always known that. If she weren't, they'd never have met. Who was he to have a problem with it? He could be single-minded. So could she. He just didn't like what she was single-minded about.

Rose considered. "Well, we're here now and we've got the gear, so we may as well make use of it."

She nodded to them, and they busied themselves appraising lampshades and air conditioning grilles. Spooks. He hated them sometimes.

Rose wandered off, looking round the other rooms. He lay on the couch and stared at the ceiling. Rose returned and sat down on the other end of the couch. She was some distance away.

"You've seen the news, I take it," she said.

"I have." It was why he was in such a foul mood.

"Did they steal your piece?"

"Yes, they did."

"Is it worth a lot?"

"No, not really."

He could sense her looking at him.

"What is it, exactly?"

He sighed. "It's a Japanese print, very similar to the one that's hanging up in the bedroom upstairs."

"Oh."

He heard her get up and leave, then return and sit down again.

"Very pretty."

He didn't dignify that with a response.

"So what do you think they're playing at, these thieves?" she asked. "What's their plan?"

"No idea. Do you have any clever theories?"

He heard her shift on her seat.

"Come on, Fairchild. You've seen the list of what they took. What does that tell us about them? You've been inside the place. You've got an idea of how it operates. What's your impression?"

Reluctantly, he put his feet on the floor and sat up to look at her.

"They must have known the Van Gogh was there. Something of that value would have had stand-alone security in a separate vault. They must have had a specific plan for that item, and access to its unique security codes."

"What explains the rest of it? It's such a mixture, the values and styles."

"In the warehouse everything is packaged. Unless they're working from an inventory list with reference numbers, they won't have time to open things up and take a look. It's not like raiding a museum or a private home where it's all on display."

"But the Van Gogh alone is worth way more than the rest of them put together. Why bother with any of it once you have that?"

"If you take what something achieves at auction at face value. But values don't necessarily hold. The whole story around that auction was to create a piece of theatre and ramp up the price. On the black market it won't be worth anything like that."

"It's still a Van Gogh. People out there will pay handsomely to possess it, even if they can't show it to anyone."

"True," Fairchild said. What was eating him, he had to admit, was why they felt it necessary to swipe his low-value print when they were already carrying something that was almost priceless. Couldn't they have just left it alone? "Maybe they fell out with each other," he suggested. "One of them ended up dead, after all."

"What do you think they'll do now? If you were in their shoes, if you had all that and you wanted to cash it in, what would you do?"

"Bury it for a long time. Years, even. Break it up. Handle each piece separately. There are specialist fences for particular genres. I'd go international. Smuggle them out one by one. The Van Gogh must have been stolen to order. It could be out of the country already."

A pause. "You said you had contacts. Fences."

"I suppose you want me to ask around."

"If it's not too much trouble. I'd have thought you'd want to anyway, if you care about getting your piece back."

How she hated having to ask him for help. But she was right. They needed each other, in fact.

"They could have gone anywhere. Tell me what you know and what you can find out via Paris Station. The police must have something by now, not least from all the CCTV cameras they have here. Knowing where they were heading would give me a starting point."

"All right. We'll keep you in the loop."

Another pause. Ollie and Yvonne were elsewhere, installing MI6 electronic ears in every corner. Rose stood and walked around the room, opening drawers and cupboards.

"Why do you keep that print of yours in a Freeport, if it isn't worth much?" she asked. "It must cost an arm and a leg storing it in there."

Was this something he wanted to share with Rose? She might run off and relay it all to Walter, he supposed, but then Walter already knew.

"My parents passed it to me. I don't know why. I can't think of any particular reason why they would bequeath that print to me in particular."

"And Grom has one just like it? How similar are they?"

"Very similar. Made by the same artist and probably the same printer."

"What does that mean, Fairchild?"

"I've absolutely no idea."

"You need to investigate that. Put them both in front of an expert."

"Yes, that idea had occurred to me. Two slight problems, though. One of the pieces has just been filched."

"All the more reason for you to get on the tail of these robbers."

"And the other doesn't belong to me."

"The one upstairs? Take it. Grom probably stole it himself. The guy's a thief on a grand scale. Besides, it'll take him ages to find out. He's not about to show up here."

He'd already had the same idea. In some ways, he and Rose did think alike.

The two youngsters reappeared. Rose and Fairchild made some arrangements for staying in touch. After they'd all gone, Fairchild went back to the guest bedroom, removed the print, rolled it and stashed the frame in an empty cupboard. He took one last look around the sumptuous apartment, MI6 now recording every whisper, and left.

He wouldn't come back here again.

Chapter 27

Pippin was lying in bed staring at the ceiling when Gustave hammered on the door below. A quick shouted conversation seemed enough for Mme Boucher to let him up the stairs. But maybe he'd managed to get his gun back and was waving it about. Pippin didn't move. If Gustave was going to shoot him, he'd prefer to be comfortable while dying. He tried to still his heart. It wasn't as if he didn't know this would happen. He had to steel himself and get through it; he had no choice. But even so, when the door flew open, his gut did a somersault. He stared up at the fury and angst that was Gustave's face.

He saw surprise there too. Despite the dramatic entrance, Gustave wasn't expecting him to be there. Pippin had hoped not to be there, but it didn't work out that way.

"You think you're such a clever little operator, don't you?" Gustave said. "Did you really think you'd get away with it, you and Henri? I should have shot both of you."

He filled the tiny room, but he wasn't, as he had been in all Pippin's imaginings of this moment, carrying a gun. Pippin didn't respond. Gustave sat on the chair, just as he'd done the first time he'd barged his way in there.

"I didn't know about it," said Pippin. "Henri and I didn't stay together inside the Freeport. He disappeared somewhere. He must have taken it then. I didn't see what he had. It was packaged."

"You think I'm STUPID?" Gustave's shout bounced off the walls. Mme Boucher would have heard that, even if she wasn't listening. "Henri's dead, if you haven't forgotten! He never made it out of the warehouse! So how does a priceless portrait, which it turns out we stole, end up disappearing into thin air?"

"I don't know what you mean," said Pippin.

"Christ's sake, you moron, it's not in the van! I checked as soon as they released the list. No sign of any Van Gogh! You took it." He pointed a long finger at Pippin's face. "You did. You went off with Henri in the Freeport. I could tell you were up to something. Then it disappears and you don't show up at the rendezvous. Did you think they weren't going to publish the list? Well, they did. So now I know what a double-crossing little shit you are. You used all of us!"

Pippin should stay calm. Pippin tried his best.

"Clem must have taken it."

"Clem? How would he even know it was there?"

"He must have been in on it with Henri. They planned it together and after you shot Henri he thought he'd take it all for himself."

"That's ridiculous. Clem?" Gustave snorted.

"Or you," said Pippin blandly. "You could have gone through the haul and found it in there, taken it for yourself."

Gustave's face moved from astonishment to contempt. "Why would I come here looking for you, if I had it already?"

"You shouldn't have come looking for me. Mme Boucher reads the news. She could recognise your face. She could be phoning the police right now, sending them your way."

Gustave flicked his head dismissively. "So why are you here? Why did you come back here but not show up at the rendezvous?"

"I'm out. I don't want anything more do to with this." Somehow his voice remained steady. "You and Clem are welcome to what's in that van. I never wanted to do this in the first place, remember? You threatened to sell me to the authorities if I didn't. Now you've got your stash and made your statement, you and Clem can do what you like with it. I'm out."

"You think it's that easy? That you can just walk away? We're all part of this whether you like it or not. You're just as guilty as the two of us."

"But my face isn't all over the news," said Pippin. "I thought ahead. I changed my appearance. I did a proper job of it. They can't link me to it."

"Rubbish. They know there's a third person, and they know you're a thief. Even the police will work that out."

"Who says I'm a thief?" asked Pippin.

And it was only then that Gustave looked around. He stood up and turned a full circle. The walls were all bare except behind his chair, where a large lurid oil painting hung in a simple frame.

"I don't steal anything," said Pippin. "People give me things, sometimes. Like a *Beaux-Arts* trained painter with a liking for symbolism."

Gustave's painting had, by some symmetry, exactly fitted the frame vacated by the Swedish Impressionist work Clem sold to finance Henri's cooperation. Gustave stared at it for a moment. Who knew what was going through his head? Who cared?

"Besides," said Pippin, "you can inform on people anonymously. A lead to you would be valuable regardless of its source."

"You got rid of all your stuff?" Gustave seemed almost impressed. That annoyed Pippin.

"Because I had to. Because of you. Because your stupid, ill-conceived, clumsy mess of a heist got us all dirty! I was fine before. I did things my own way. Now I'll have to start again somewhere else. And you won't leave me alone! You and Clem, you could have gone together, but you had to come back for me!"

"Of course I did!" said Gustave. "You disappeared with the most valuable piece of the lot. More than the rest put together!"

"I thought money didn't matter. I thought that was all bourgeois exploitation."

"And it is! But that's what makes it so powerful! A bunch of nobodies steals the most valuable painting in the world? It's amazing! It's heaven-sent! Or would be, if you joined us. Imagine the message we could send to the establishment with a coup like that."

"You're asking me?" Pippin couldn't quite believe it. "You're asking me to come back? You tried to kill me! You fired a gun at me! Why on earth would I want to have anything to do with you? Besides, I don't have it. You should be saying all of this to Clem."

That set Gustave on a different train of thought.

"Where is it? Where did you hide it?"

"I told you, I don't have it!"

But Gustave was scanning the room again.

"It's in here, isn't it? I think you've done with the Van Gogh what you did with yourself. It's hiding in plain sight."

His eyes travelled round the bare walls. He stepped forward, lifted his own painting off the wall and turned it. Nothing was attached to the back of the canvas, nothing was on the wall.

"Would have been a nice bit of symbolism," muttered Gustave, "but no."

He opened the cupboard, pulled out drawers and flung their contents on the floor. The drawer in the wash stand yielded nothing either. He turned and considered Pippin, still lying on the bed, then his gaze travelled down. He dropped to the floor and scrabbled under the bed.

"I told you," said Pippin. "I don't have it."

Gustave resurfaced empty-handed. He stood and stared down at Pippin.

"Are you satisfied now?" said Pippin. "I'm worth nothing to you. I just want a quiet life. We can go our separate ways. I'll say nothing if you just walk away. Keep the loot. It's yours."

Gustave's next move, a hand inside his jacket then out again, proved that Pippin had been wrong earlier.

He did have his gun, after all.

Chapter 28

It was several years since Fairchild last visited the quaint and unworldly antique shop in Nice run by Max, a sometime arranger of dubious sales of artistic objects, and former thief himself. Max smiled warmly when Fairchild entered the cluttered little shop. They shook hands, old friends.

"So how have you been, stranger?" asked Max. "I thought perhaps one of your tricky situations had been a little too tricky."

"So far, so good," said Fairchild.

Max gave him a searching look. "Your enquiry? Anything new come to light?"

Max was one of Fairchild's network, one of the people Fairchild had shared his story with. Max had agreed to help if he ever heard anything about the mystery of Fairchild's parents. In return, Fairchild had done Max a few favours over the years. Max was a solid guy, trustworthy amongst thieves. More trustworthy, for sure, than some of the people whose job was to go after the thieves. Fairchild updated Max on what he now knew of the fate of his parents, and the even bigger issue to emerge, his discovery that their killer was still alive.

"He's thought to be the owner of *Portrait of Theo*," he said.

Max's bushy eyebrows rose. "Well, he won't be very happy at the moment, then. Unless it's insured of course. In which case why would he mind that it's been stolen by a troupe of chancers who have no hope of selling it? He has his money. That's all it was to him."

"It's unlikely to be insured for five hundred million dollars," said Fairchild. "That's a speculative price, probably a one-off. And besides, this fellow takes things personally.

He has some grudge against me, so it seems, for what my parents did before I was even born. I can't imagine him being satisfied with an insurance pay-out when what's probably his biggest investment has been swiped by a bunch of amateurs. I imagine he'll go after them."

"A lot of people will go after them," said Max. "It shows what fools they are. The hotter the property, the more difficult it is to fence, the bigger the gap between its supposed value and what you'll actually get. Stealing and selling art is a very poor investment strategy, my friend. I know. I did it myself for many years."

"So you've become legitimate?"

"You buy, you sell, you make a little money each time. It's a living. There's a lot to be said for that. No ladders in the middle of the night, no masks, no panic every time you hear a police siren. I'm an ordinary citizen now. I recommend it."

Fairchild could see the attraction. But his life didn't seem to work out that way.

"Surely the police still consider you a person of interest in a number of significant heists?"

"They gave up on finding enough evidence long ago. We have stalemate now. They won't lay those things on me. In the meantime, I spent years learning the hard way that art theft doesn't pay. So now the authorities and me, we muddle along, on speaking terms mainly."

"These Freeport raiders still have this lesson to learn, it seems."

Max gave him a knowing look. "You have some active interest in the matter too?"

"You mean, apart from the fact that their most valuable trophy was owned by the man who killed my parents? You're right, Max, as ever. It turns out that they swiped something that belongs to me while they were stumbling about in there. It's not worth a lot, but I want it back."

"Well. You will have some competition to get to them first."

The bell dinged and a young couple came into the shop and browsed for a while. Fairchild and Max chatted about politics, mutual acquaintances and wine until the couple left empty-handed.

"So, what do you know, Max?" asked Fairchild. "With your credentials in the black market, I'm sure you would've heard something."

Max shook his head. "I've made it clear for many years now that stolen goods aren't my area. Full provenance is what I need. Then maybe I can help. I know one or two collectors after all."

"So you have no idea about any of the people who were involved?"

Max looked wistful. "People don't come to me asking for advice, you know. Besides, if they did, I would advise them not to do it. Now if I had to put money on it—"

The bell dinged again. It was late morning now, and the tourists were starting to appear in the streets, meandering after long late holiday breakfasts. It was a while before the conversation could continue. Max even made a sale. Eventually they were alone again.

"So tell me, Max," said Fairchild. "Who would your money be on? I have great respect for your financial decisions."

"You've seen the photos that have been circulated. One of them looks familiar to me. And it fits, the element of theatre about the whole escapade. An artist called Gustave Fournier has been hanging around here a lot. Likes to sound off about the commercialisation of the art world."

"Well, he has a point. But why would that make him want to rob a Freeport? He's proving that he's just as financially driven as anyone else, isn't he?"

"He'd do it as some kind of statement. Or that's what he'd say. The word is that in Paris he was involved with some group of left-wing extremists. Anarchists, basically. Blow up the establishment, that kind of thing."

"What's he doing down here?"

Max shrugged. "Maybe Paris got a little hot. I get the impression he was trying to create a similar cell here, but with a focus on the art world. He was wasting his time with me, of course. None of this is new, though. The police must surely have him in their sights already."

"Okay," said Fairchild. He paused. Max must have some reason to mention Fournier above and beyond all that.

"Not long ago," Max said, "Gustave was hanging around in here and a guy came in. Very unassuming, didn't say a lot. Had something to shift."

Max paused. He was milking Fairchild's interest, as he liked to do.

"What was it?" Fairchild asked.

"It was a Chinese bronze vessel dating from the twelfth century BC."

"That's very precise. Wouldn't you need more time to verify that?"

"Not in this case. I recognised it. It was stolen from a museum in Rouen a few years ago. It never resurfaced. Not amongst any of my people. No approaches of any kind. And some nobody walks in here trying to get a few Euros for it. Intriguing."

"So did he get a few Euros for it?"

"Not from me. I told you, dealing in stolen artwork is a bad idea. But what he did get was a lot of interest from

Gustave. In fact, when this boy made a sharp exit, Gustave went after him."

"And then what?"

"No idea."

"Gustave knew the vessel was stolen?"

"I may have mentioned that to him, yes."

"So Gustave was interested in an art thief?"

"Well, however that boy got his hands on it, it wasn't legitimate. That was Gustave's interest."

"This guy, did he give a name or say anything about himself?"

"No. He was a careful person. Very careful." Max's eyes rested on Fairchild.

"Description?"

"Young-looking, thin. Glasses. Small. Nothing noticeable. The opposite of Gustave, who can't blow his nose without making a speech."

"You think this man is involved?"

Max paused. "I think there's more to him than on the surface. I think he's interesting. That's all."

"It couldn't have been the one who got shot?"

"Oh no, it wasn't him. There were photos of the man who was killed. If this boy was involved he's still out there. But like I said," finished Max, as more customers came in, "a lot of people will be interested in these thieves. It wouldn't surprise me if they all ended up getting shot."

They shook hands. Before Fairchild was even out of the door, more customers had come in and Max was in a conversation about some trinket or other. A legitimate businessman doing a legitimate job, having left the murky waters behind him. Fairchild walked out into the sunshine and crowds, suddenly envious of his old friend.

Chapter 29

Zoe was doing a lot of thinking. In particular, she was considering Anna's comments about right and wrong. She decided to finally accept an invitation to lunch from Laurence in their legal team. He'd been trying it on for weeks.

"So what do you think?" she asked him in a playful tone, as they sat on the terrace of an Italian restaurant in front of dessert. "If something is legal, does that make it right?"

"Ha! Not necessarily," said Laurence, who, all the women in the bank knew, was handsome, attentive and married. "You've got criminal law, which governments make, and those laws are to promote a decent society where people don't go round stealing and murdering. So, you could say, breaking criminal law is generally wrong. But, some defendants might argue it isn't a good law, or they had mitigating circumstances."

"But not all law is criminal, is it?"

"No, you have civil law, where cases are brought by individuals who feel wronged by someone. And maybe there's compensation, but no prison. That's there if you choose to use it, but of course a lot of the time it's not used, even when it could be. Otherwise people like me would be very busy!"

"So why is it used sometimes and not at other times?"

"Well, okay. So, today, I invited you for lunch. What if after our meal I decide to run off and leave you to pay the bill? That wouldn't be very nice, would it? Would you think of taking me to court?"

"Of course not! I'd come back to the office and get the money out of you!"

"Precisely. You have no need to involve lawyers because you can right the wrong yourself. But also, you would have trouble making a case as I could deny that I invited you to lunch at all, or I could claim that you invited me. Also, the costs of hiring lawyers and the time involved are simply not worth it for the price of a meal. A judge might decide it was too trivial to be heard. Also, your reputation. It might be embarrassing, no, to expose to the world that you were abandoned like that? And maybe, you would look a fool for being vindictive enough to pursue it in that way. So, better just to let it go."

"So it's not always worth it, even if someone did break an agreement they had with you."

"That's right. Even when the stakes are much higher it isn't always a good idea. There was one case, right here in Monaco. A Russian oligarch decided to buy some pieces of fine art. Spent a lot of money on some very expensive paintings. He had a dealer, a Swiss guy with good contacts, looking out for things and buying the pieces on his behalf. The dealer was making a commission on everything. But he was also selling the painting to the oligarch for much more than he was buying them. Remember the Leonardo they discovered a few years ago?"

"I remember something about it."

"The dealer bought it for eighty million dollars and sold it to the oligarch for a hundred and twenty seven million."

"What? Wow! That's like almost fifty million dollars in profit. That Russian must have been furious."

"He was, when he found out. The dealer kept doing this again and again. Eventually they think he made a billion dollars in profit from the oligarch."

"No! Unbelievable."

"Really. So, of course, the oligarch should take him to court, right?"

"Yes, of course! For that kind of money."

"Well – he did. He filed civil suits in several different countries and in Monaco he also reported it to the police and invited the dealer here on some pretext. The dealer was arrested for fraud and there was a criminal investigation."

"So what happened?"

"Well, of course all of this is out in the open now, so the business affairs of these two gentlemen are on display. And evidence came forward that the oligarch had become very friendly with some of the political elite in Monaco, and also some senior police officers. Lots of gifts, social gatherings, and so on. In the end his case was thrown out and he was arrested himself for corruption."

"No way!"

"Yes. And this is despite the fact that the dealer never denied that he'd marked up the prices. He just said that as a dealer he was entitled to sell for as much as he could make. It's not moral, but it's legal, he said."

"So that was it?"

"It's all still going on in other countries, working through the civil cases. I guess it goes to show that if you don't respect the law yourself, you can't expect to use it to protect your own interests."

Aspects of this story preyed on Zoe's mind. She found herself putting in long hours at the bank, staying after everyone else had gone, looking up names, piecing together the webs of companies and entities, tracing them back to their ultimate beneficial owners. She'd done background reading too, looking up the details of the Panama Papers and the other huge leaks that exposed the offshoring industry.

She could see the same patterns there, how eventually everything would link back to a particular name.

These names, these beneficial owners, the bank's clients, she researched as well. Often she could find nothing online, or nothing untoward. Hector Howard's hoover empire was much as he and Pearl had described it. Others had various news stories attributed to them, certain controversies. A Mexican who'd done jail time for murder. A Russian who'd been accused and jailed then exonerated for ordering a hit on someone. A Korean conglomerate owner charged, but never convicted, of embezzlement. And so on. Publicly nothing was black and white, but with what she knew about their private finances – well, she started to realise exactly what was meant by *knowledge is power*.

If you don't respect the law yourself, you can't expect to use it to protect your interests. You could end up exposing your own secrets. And these people had secrets, that was for sure. Slowly, an idea started taking shape, an idea that began as unthinkable, but as she explored and probed and turned it over and broke it down, became fascinating and terrifying at the same time, so much so that it came to be there in her head day and night.

She often returned to Yunayev, intrigued about his role in the lives of both Anna and that man John Fairchild. Yunayev was her special research topic. Who was Yunayev? Where his money came from she couldn't trace, but she could examine what he spent it on. They had records of every transaction, his financial life here in Monaco. She started following up, going into more and more detail. Yunayev owned property in France, it seemed. And a yacht, berthed here in Monaco. Wow, a yacht! But of course he had a yacht. He was a Monaco millionaire. And when Zoe found out how much he'd paid for it, she knew she had to see it.

Chapter 30

The next day Zoe walked along the quay at Port Hercule staring at the yachts, as she'd so often done. But this afternoon would be different. In the berths to her left floated a line of gleaming white motor launches. Walking by, you got a good look inside. These craft were owned by people who weren't shy of their money. She could see rattan deck furniture, generous white cushioning, an on-deck sauna, an enormous TV screen, counters equipped with coffee machines and huge glass jars and cocktail shakers, magazines laid out on a coffee table like in a waiting room.

These super-yachts would have crews of fifteen or twenty sometimes. But on a motor yacht it was all cleaning and catering, nannying children and serving drinks. The sailing yachts were more her thing. She'd had a lot of fun on those with tanned easy-going crew hands that didn't care where they went as long as they were at sea, and happily worked for a pittance. She could have settled for that but was destined for something better, so she was told. Looking at the deep blue colour of the ocean, seeing the ropes dip lazily in and out of the water with the gentle swell, smelling the salt on the air, she wondered who in their right mind would think that a bank was better than this.

She carried on walking, looking closely at the names. Eventually she found what she was looking for, the *Princess Voyager*. This one looked a lot like all the others, equally sumptuous and grand. A guy was washing the wooden deck. He was crouched down focused on his work and wearing the shortest pair of shorts she'd ever seen on a man. Wiry dark hair. Hairy legs too. Tanned skin. She knew the type.

"Hey!"

The guy looked round and gave her a wide grin. Lovely.

"You one of the crew on this one?"

He stopped washing and came over, drying his hands on a worn old towel.

"Yeah. Can I help you with something?"

"It belongs to my boss. Mr Yunayev?"

She lowered her voice to say the name. The yachts may all be out on display here, but it was still a rule that no one ever revealed who the owners were. She could see that the guy recognised the name.

"He's changed his plans and is coming tomorrow," she said.

"Tomorrow? No way! Does the captain know?"

"I expect so. If he doesn't, someone needs to tell him."

The guy looked lost.

"Well, you can get organised, can't you?" said Zoe. "The crew's on notice when you're shoreside."

"Yeah, sure, it's just getting supplies and doing the rosters and all that."

"Sounds like the captain's job to me," said Zoe breezily. "But I do need to take a look. Make sure it's ready. Mr Yunayev has some important guests coming. They'll be talking business. So he needs to be sure it's all in order. Can I come aboard?"

He hesitated.

"Well, it's not really my—"

"I've got authorisation," said Zoe. "A letter. I'm his secretary, you see. It's all in here." She waved a file of papers. "I'll be really quick then get out of your way. You'll have a lot to do. I'm Zoe, by the way."

"Oh! Freddy."

"That okay then, Freddy?"

Zoe stepped onto the deck. Freddy didn't try and stop her, though she was half expecting it. She gave him a friendly smile. She'd dressed up for the occasion: a little more make-up, outfit a little more classy. This was fun.

"Watch the wet areas, they're slippery," he said a little sheepishly.

"Thanks. Look, don't mind me, I just want to check the cabins, make sure it's clean. But you can show me round if you'd prefer."

"I guess I'd better," he said. "But don't worry, it's clean!"

The stern deck had a set of sun loungers arranged around a low table, a dark wood trim finish and two bay trees in pots, each at the bottom of a set of steps. Zoe followed the guy up to some glass doors leading inside.

"This is the salon." He slid open the doors and they stepped through.

Plush, was the word. Sofas, heavy wooden tables, silverware, carpet. Wow, you could just forget you were even on a boat. It was so huge, wide as well as long. She was used to narrow, something that cut through the water like a knife and heeled in response to the wind. This just sat in the water like an iceberg.

Freddy was looking at her face.

"Not up to standard?"

"Oh!" Don't forget your cover story, fool! She walked around surveying the furniture critically, running a finger along a mahogany bar to check for dust, peering into the corners of the ceilings.

"Seems okay."

"Want to see the upper deck and the sun terrace?"

That was two more decks up. Two more decks! Up there, parasols, beige cushions, immaculately cleaned wooden trim. Zoe inspected it for quality and nodded.

"I think this will be good enough. I'd like to see the sleeping quarters."

"All of them?"

Christ, how many did the place sleep?

"Yes. The master bedroom first."

He led the way. A huge bed with a padded type of canopy, great big decorative vases, long sleek drawer units, a huge TV screen. Roly poly cushions. Like a hotel room! Zoe straightened some table mats and looked into a drawer. It was empty. This space, it was huge, and owned by someone who didn't need it, didn't even seem to use it. That was criminal in itself. As were the roly poly cushions.

"Cinema room here," said Freddy, as they passed a door. "That there is the spa. You need to see?"

She looked at everything, appraising it, finding occasional criticism and managing to hide how completely bowled over she was.

"So what are his plans?" asked Freddy as they went back aft. "Where are we going? For how long?"

"I don't know the detail, sorry. The captain should have been told by now. I'd follow up with him. But thanks for your time. Bon voyage, Freddy!"

She walked off confidently, leaving him looking a bit lost again. They were being watched by a couple of guys on the quayside. Nothing unusual about that. She'd spent a lot of time here at the port doing exactly the same thing.

It was why she was here, in fact. She'd gazed at all these boats so often, and now she'd got a chance to have a good poke about inside. And maybe that John guy was right. She wanted to see if she could talk her way in. But that was all. Just a fun way of passing an afternoon. Nothing more.

But it had been so easy. And that got her thinking again.

Chapter 31

It took a good deal of asking around Fairchild's network to pinpoint Max's elusive vessel-hawker. While Fairchild was at it, a few things struck him as odd. One, if the guy really wanted to get rid of this object, why didn't he try anyone else in town besides Max? Fairchild approached the most likely market stallholders and cash loan shops but no one had heard of the man or the object. Maybe Max's response had scared him off – but if he needed the money you'd have thought he'd try again somehow.

Then there was the fact that he wasn't using his real name. Fairchild discovered this after learning of the quiet unassuming lodger of Mme Boucher, a landlady who didn't require references, only cash, and didn't ask too many questions. She didn't mind answering them, though, when gently quizzed by an old friend of Fairchild, a retired family doctor who knew Nice and how it worked. Mme Boucher happily revealed to the former doctor some interesting detail about her lodger, how recently he'd come to Nice, how he called himself Pippin but that wasn't the name on his ID card, how he was visited more than once by a loud Parisian whose face seemed familiar, that he owned some nice-looking paintings considering how little money he seemed to have. Also, how she hadn't seen him for a couple of days although his things were still in the room, but he'd missed the rent this week.

Fairchild was fully intending to pass all this information on to Rose. But not before he'd had a look himself. It did no harm to stay ahead of the game. It was helpful, in fact, to investigate further and check that this guy was a legitimate lead before wasting Rose's time on him. But he'd have to be discreet. Rose and her gang – which, at times, included him – would probably approach Mme Boucher, which meant that he had to find some other way in. And that was why he was, late one evening, staring out of the window of an empty holiday let in the middle of the old town, looking across the street directly at Pippin's window.

The street was so narrow that if the window had been wide open, you could step across from one ledge to the other and drop straight inside. But it wasn't open, though it was ajar. That made the manoeuvre a little more tricky. Fairchild looked down into the street three floors below. It was not too late for strolling couples and groups to pass by, exploring the restaurants and bars of Nice. He'd have to be quick. Choosing a quiet moment he bent, flexed, used the wall to push himself off and landed on the ledge opposite, grabbing a sturdy-looking drainpipe with both hands. The drainpipe thankfully supported his weight, along with a couple of indeterminate cables, some of which would never be the same again. He balanced himself and let go with one hand to feel for the flimsy window catch. He pulled open the casement and lowered himself silently down inside.

The doctor had told him how sensitive Mme Boucher's hearing was, so he moved around as little as possible. The room appeared to be in use. The bed was made. Clothes hung in the cupboard. A piece of stale bread sat on a plate. An empty glass smelled of sweet wine. On the floor by the bed lay a very worn copy of the *Letters of Vincent Van Gogh*. Fairchild carefully pulled open a drawer under the dresser. A French ID card lay inside. He photographed it and closed the drawer.

In the cupboard he went through the pockets of every single item and found nothing. Nothing at all. Curious. There wasn't a lot of stuff of any kind; Pippin obviously led a very simple life. No twelfth century BC bronze Chinese vessel, or indeed artwork of any kind, except for a rather alarming outsized oil painting in an inappropriately plain frame. Fairchild risked more light and shone his wrist torch directly onto the canvas, moving it around slowly. He stopped at the image of the church, on a hill high above a city with ocean in the background. A bonfire was blazing and people were dying. The colours were deep and saturating; the images disturbing, their features exaggerated. His torch travelled to each of the corners. He found a signature in the bottom left: G. Fournier. Interesting.

A door opened below. Fairchild's torch snapped off. Stairs creaked. Mme Boucher was on the move. Either she had incredible hearing or a sixth sense. Very impressive, but Fairchild didn't wish to make the woman's acquaintance this way. As the creaking neared and a light flicked on, giving the door to the room a sudden yellow halo, Fairchild opened the window, stepped onto the sill and climbed swiftly down the drainpipe. Just under the window ledge he tucked himself in and froze. Above, he heard a muttering. The window was pulled shut and fastened. He waited but heard nothing more. Below, he looked down onto the heads of a passing group of four. Engaged in an animated conversation, they didn't look up. Fairchild quietly waited then climbed the rest of the way down and disappeared into the night.

Chapter 32

They took a soft, friendly approach with Mme Boucher while Ollie kept watch outside. Yvonne led, explaining they were insurance investigators trying to trace a painting, and that there were rumoured to be some upstairs in her lodger's room. If they could just take a quick look, probably nothing in it, but a preliminary check to rule it out would save them having to call the police and get them round. At that idea, Mme Boucher did eventually step aside to allow Rose past up the stairs, closely followed by John Fairchild. Yvonne stayed to chat with the woman and see what she might have to say about Fournier.

It was a tiny bare-floored loft room, only just big enough for the two of them to stand in. Rose closed the door behind them and donned a pair of gloves. Sooner or later, this room would probably be combed by the police and she didn't want them poring over her biometrics.

"Not much of a place," she commented.

"Handy for the old town."

She stepped over to the casement window and glanced down into the street. Fairchild picked up a tumbler and sniffed it.

"Rosé wine, I'd guess." He was wearing gloves too. He tapped the remains of a baguette sitting on a plate. "Left in a hurry."

"The rest of the place seems neat and tidy." Rose opened a drawer and found a few clothes folded into piles. She searched it, then the other drawers.

"Is it just me?" she asked, "or is this room practically devoid of any personalising marks?"

Fairchild opened a small drawer in a table that was being used as a wash stand.

"There's an ID card in here," he said.

Rose stepped over and glanced down.

"Well, so there is."

But her attention was on something else, the choreography of Fairchild's movements.

"You've been in here already, haven't you?" she said.

He looked bland.

"For heaven's sake, Fairchild. We're meant to be working as a team! How am I supposed to trust you?"

He had the grace to look slightly shamefaced.

"I didn't want to waste your time. So I thought I'd check it out first."

"But you could have said something." She thought of Mme Boucher. "The landlady didn't recognise you."

"No, she wouldn't."

"Then how did you get in?"

Fairchild glanced over at the window. Rose looked out at the drop below and the window opposite.

"Really? That's a lot of trouble to go to, Fairchild. Apart from staying one step ahead of me, what did you gain from it?"

"I thought he was interesting enough to investigate further. The room gives very little away, like you said. Even the ID card is on its own in a drawer. Where's his wallet? If he took his wallet, why isn't the ID card with it? It's as if it were deliberately placed here."

Rose opened the drawer to take another look. Her phone rang. It was Ollie.

"What?"

A pause at the other end.

"What is it, Ollie? Have you seen something?"

"No, it's okay," said Ollie. "False alarm."

That cold feeling again, working up her spine. "You thought you saw something?"

"Yeah, but I was wrong. Forget it. All clear."

"Ollie, what did you see?" She could feel Fairchild's eyes on her.

"Seriously, it was nothing. All clear out here. Sorry, my mistake."

"Well, okay. Call if you need to."

She hung up.

"Everything all right?" Fairchild was still watching her closely.

"False alarm."

Her heart was still pumping but she made an effort to refocus on the search.

"These paintings the guy's supposed to have, they seem to be gone. Apart from this one." She pointed to an enormous oil. "What did you make of that, on your previous visit?"

Fairchild ignored the dig. "Nothing notable or well-known. A throwback to twentieth-century expressionism. There's something very Chagall about it, this red sky and the deliberate avoidance of realism."

"Is that a polite way of saying the perspective's all wrong?"

"I guess, but anyone can paint a nice view of Marseille. The point about expressionism is that it's the emotional landscape of the artist, not a literal depiction of reality."

"Marseille? That's Marseille?"

"Sure. That's the church of Notre Dame de la Garde. It's one of the city's most famous landmarks."

"Yeah, sorry, not all of us are walking encyclopaedias, you know."

Ollie had really unnerved her. Fairchild looked amused.

"You know this painting is by Fournier, don't you?" he said.

"Really?" Rose stepped closer. Fairchild pointed out the signature.

"So what does it say about the guy? These people are still very mysterious to us."

"He's a good artist."

"Really? This is good? It looks like something out of Dante's Inferno."

"It's probably supposed to. The crowds, the burning, the suffering. It's dripping with religious subtext. That's why I said Chagall. The intensity of this fire is like purgatory or hell. But the way it's positioned on top of this hill next to the church, that's a statement. A public event. Like a martyrdom, or a bonfire of the vanities. The juxtaposition of the raging fire and the smoke, the cross of the church, and then the city spread out in the background, very recognisable, it's a reflection or comment on society at large. I think the person who painted it has strong views about what's wrong with the world. There's anger here and bitterness. A sense of futility but also wanton destruction. It's understandable."

Fairchild's face was inches away from the canvas as he examined it.

"What's understandable?"

"Well, the value of art is so dependent on fashion and current tastes. If this kind of style were the in thing, Fournier could be a leading light. He's brought something quite new to the genre and executed it amazingly well. But if it doesn't catch on, that's it. Galleries and dealers are all looking for the same thing, the next Ai Weiwei or Anish Kapoor. But they also want to limit supply to keep values high. The result is a very small number of rocket-fuelled artists that no one can get enough of, and everyone else is left in the cold."

"That might make someone pretty angry," said Rose. "You said he's rumoured to be an activist. Maybe the heist was to raise money for some kind of direct action or anti-state terrorism."

"Mighty funny way of funding a terrorist operation. There are plenty of more viable alternatives. It's got to be about the art itself in some way. Maybe he saw the heist as a kind of direct action."

"Wouldn't we know about it already? If it's meant to be a message to the world, they'd be on social media by now."

"Could still happen."

"And wouldn't you just go in there with a can of spray paint or something, instead of making off with the most valuable painting in the world? There have got to be easier ways."

Rose lay down on the floor next to the bed. "Speaking of which, I don't see any sign of their loot here."

On the floor was a worn copy of Vincent Van Gogh's letters. Rose moved it aside, stretched an arm out and felt around under the bed, her fingers reaching right over to the wall.

"You think he's going to stash a five hundred million dollar canvas underneath his own bed?" Fairchild said.

Rose emerged empty-handed. "I guess not. But worth checking for loose floorboards."

They did, and found none.

"Well, what now?" said Rose, standing in the middle of the room.

Fairchild nodded towards the painting.

"Marseille."

"Seriously? On the grounds that there's a painting of Marseille on the wall of his room?"

"Well, there's nothing else to go on, is there? It's the only thing here. Besides, Marseille is France's second biggest city. It's the next best place after Paris to find buyers. And if they'd tried to get to Paris, I think the police would be onto them by now."

He had a point. But the painting wasn't the only thing in the room. Rose picked up the *Letters of Van Gogh*. Something flashed in her head, but went away again. Damn Ollie! He'd really spoiled her concentration.

"We should go," she said.

Yvonne had more luck. She established from Mme Boucher that Fournier had shown up a couple of days earlier in an excitable state and Pippin had gone out with him and not returned since. The robbers had moved on, leaving little behind. Fairchild surely knew more than he was saying, keen as he was to get to the gang first. And whatever was troubling her about Pippin was buried too deep in her mind to fathom.

Chapter 33

Fairchild left and the other three took separate routes back to the Nice apartment. As soon as they arrived, Rose sat them all down at the table.

"What did you see, Ollie? Why the phone call?"

"Honestly, it was nothing."

"It wasn't nothing. It was enough for you to make the call. What was it?"

He sighed. "A guy came past me. Then I thought I saw the same guy again, but wearing a jacket."

"The same person with different clothes? That's an absolute giveaway, Ollie."

"But it wasn't the same person. It was another guy with cheekbones and stubble, like they all have round here."

"What makes you say that?"

"Because his friends showed up. He was hanging around for a while, then two or three people came along, *bonjour*, kiss kiss, and they all disappeared into a restaurant. That happened when I was on the phone to you. He was just a bloke, as it turned out. It was my mistake."

Rose was mentally reviewing her incident with the moped rider. "Did he look at you?"

"Not in particular. He looked around while he was waiting."

"Did he look in your direction?"

"Well, he looked all around, so yeah."

"So he'd have seen if you were on the phone or not."

"I guess."

"And what about the first time you saw him?"

"That was the first time. The other guy was someone else."

"So you say now. But you didn't think that at the time, did you?"

"I was wrong."

"Or you're wrong now. Your Ego has defeated your Id. But your Id could have been right. Tell me about the first guy."

Ollie's eyes went up to the ceiling as he recalled. "Like I said, cheekbones, stubble. Red checked shirt. He walked past. That's all."

"Quickly? Slowly?"

"Pretty slowly."

"And then?"

"That was it. He walked past."

"And the second guy? What was he wearing?"

"A linen jacket. *Our Man in Havana* type thing."

"Shirt?"

"Dark."

"And you recognised him?"

"At first I thought I did. But I must have been mistaken."

"And you phoned me. And then a load of friends showed up and he disappeared."

"Yes."

Rose turned to Yvonne. "Did you see anything?"

She shook her head.

"Have you seen anything at all, the whole time you've been here? Any hint at all that we might not be alone?"

"No, nothing."

"Does that mean you have, Rose?" Ollie asked.

"The day I used the moped to go to the Negresco." She related what happened. "Just like you, Ollie, I wrote it off. I convinced myself it was nothing. That's why I didn't say anything. But my instinct back then said something else. Still does, actually."

There was a long silence.

"If someone is onto us," said Ollie, "then who? And how?"

"And why?" asked Yvonne.

"Those are all very good questions," said Rose. "We need to tighten up even more. Move out of here, probably. Find a new base."

"Report it?" said Ollie.

Rose hesitated. Yes, was the right answer. But if it got up to Salisbury, it would mean the end of the op. "Let's keep that in mind."

Another silence. Yvonne checked her phone.

"Shit," she said.

"What now?" asked Rose.

"More news. It's not great."

She told them what it was.

Chapter 34

After a hurried brainstorm between the three of them, Rose got onto a video call with Walter.

"Just as you think a painting couldn't possibly get any more notorious, now this," she said. "We've just heard that the Kremlin has claimed possession of *Portrait of Theo*. They're saying it was stolen by Mikhail Khovansky from the Russian people, and they want it back. They're appealing to Interpol to issue an international arrest warrant."

"What does this mean for us, my dear? This brings Russia much closer, does it not?" Walter looked tired, but then he always did on screen.

"They must have found Grom's Monaco identity. They've caught up with us, basically. They now have sight of his holding companies to see how the money was channelled to make the purchase. And if they know that they'll know about all his assets, his swanky penthouse apartment, his even swankier yacht."

"Ah, so FININT have done some more analysis for you, have they?"

"They certainly have. They've taken his finances apart with a fine toothcomb. As well as one of these super-yachts that's the size of a small island, he also owns a luxury villa on the coast road, up in the hills. But something else as well, better. It turns out that after buying *Portrait of Theo*, he took out a loan against it from the auction house. That's quite common, apparently. It's a well-established way of unlocking the value in these works of art. Particularly for people who are using fine art to move money around rather than for the love of it."

"Well that rather ups the ante, doesn't it, for our man?" said Walter. "It's not just that the painting was rapidly becoming one of the few significant assets he had left. If he loses it, he's lost the collateral on which his loan was based, if my understanding is correct."

"Well, usually the insurance will pay out. But the actual value of this one is very subjective. Who knows what it's insured for? And the insurance company will be looking closely at the circumstances, let's say."

"Trying to find a reason not to pay? I'm sure. Particularly now the Russians have described the owner as a crook and an embezzler. They'll see it as mighty suspicious that this portrait does a disappearing act like this. But if they don't pay out, what happens to the loan?"

"Worst-case scenario for Grom is that instead of a healthy cashable asset, he ends up with a significant liability. It makes it unlikely that Grom himself had anything to do with the heist. But this theft could mean a lot more to him than we thought. It could make all the difference between surviving his exile from Russia with some resources to fall back on, and actually owing money."

"These intrepid burglars may have unknowingly performed a useful service for the security of the UK and its protectors."

"Well, if we manage to track them down, I'll be sure to thank them."

"How is that going?"

"We have a lead." She told him about Pippin and Gustave Fournier. "So Fairchild is convinced we need to focus on Marseille. I think he's on pretty thin ground, myself. It makes me wonder what he knows that he's not telling us."

"Now, Rose. Just because Fairchild has his own reasons doesn't mean he's exclusively self-interested."

"He's doing stuff without sharing. When we got into Pippin's room, it turned out he'd already been there, but he wasn't going to say anything."

"Well, yes, he can be cagey sometimes. But has he asked for any kind of payment for this work?"

"Well, no," Rose admitted. And it might have been a problem. Fairchild's fees often were, particularly to cash-starved government departments that had to battle to be funded in the first place. "But I still expect him to put his own interests first. Do you know anything about this Japanese print of his, that his parents left him?"

"I'm afraid not."

"Odd that Grom has one just like it."

"They're not uncommon, my dear. They were intended to be mass-produced, after all. Fairchild has contacts in Marseille, I presume?"

"Yes, he's checking them out. But I'm keeping an open mind."

"Well, fair enough, but do bear in mind that this has all become more risky for us. Operatives for the Russian government are going to be on the ground now in Monaco and around. You need to tighten up and take precautions. You are no longer amongst friends."

"Understood." Rose wasn't sure they were amongst friends before, but didn't mention this.

"The Russian government has shone a gigantic flashlight on our man," said Walter. "Everyone knows his name, or one of them anyway. Everyone's interested in the owner of that painting. This is now very much a public event that the world media is going to relish. You don't need me to tell you that MI6 doesn't enjoy the glare of publicity. It would be a disaster for us if our interest in this man became known, and in particular the reasons for our interest."

The reasons of course were highly embarrassing. A British intelligence officer is discovered selling secrets to the Soviets, then escapes justice to become a major force within the KGB. Not exactly what the Service needed.

"I'll bear that in mind," said Rose. "Maximum discretion from now on."

Walter hesitated.

"What?" Rose didn't like his body language.

"Salisbury might think this is enough of a reason to recall you," he said. "Not worth the risk to the Service."

"Well, he never liked the idea in the first place. I wouldn't be surprised if he latched onto this."

"To be fair, Rose, he thinks like a politician, which he needs to do, since our operations and budgets are ultimately controlled by politicians. The risk of the public becoming aware of Sutherland's past is, to some minds, not worth taking, given that the threat Sutherland poses is not necessarily immediate. It's a point of view, Rose."

"Well, I hope you're not telling me you're pulling the plug," said Rose. "We're within a whisker of doing the very thing we set out to do six months ago. We can wipe him out. We can end any possibility of Grom being a threat to MI6. We now have the inside track on everything he's holding in the area. If we play it right with this portrait, he could have nothing left. Less than nothing. If we stop now, everything we've put in over the last six months will be wasted. We'll be discreet, Walter. We know how, for goodness' sake."

"I'm just alerting you to that possibility, Rose. It certainly wouldn't be what I want. It's why we need a subtle approach. Subtle, but effective."

"Is that not what we've been doing, Walter?"

"Of course, but it will be more difficult from now on. I have to consider that, and so do you. The stakes have risen for everybody here."

Walter was right. Everyone had more to lose now. Desperate, determined people were lining up on all sides. Would they kill to get what they wanted? Most of them, yes.

Chapter 35

As Zoe left work that evening, in her mind she was still standing on the sun deck of that yacht. She liked how the day had gone, how her little deception had made her feel. What else could she do? What more? She wanted that buzz of excitement again. That was the thought going through her mind when she turned a corner and a hand closed over her mouth.

Someone gripped both her arms and wrenched them back. The pain made her cry out. The hand on her mouth tightened.

"You come with us," said a voice in her ear, in heavily accented English.

There were two of them. They lifted and pulled her through a door into the bottom of a stairwell. A tattooed arm thick as a drainpipe pinned her against the concrete. In front of her loomed a wall of flesh, two beefy figures looking down on her, angry eyes in shaven heads. A hand was still clamped over her mouth and she struggled to breathe.

"Where is Yunayev?"

His accent was so strong she could barely make out the words. The other guy, the one covering her mouth, shoved her head back. Her skull hit the wall so hard it made her dizzy.

"Igor Yunayev," the first man breathed into her face. "Where is he?"

"Who?" She said it without thinking. The tattooed man shoved her head into the wall again. She felt sick. Fingers tightened on her jaw. He pulled her face forward and stared into it, a cold look.

"You think we are stupid?" said the first man, who was a foot taller than his stocky partner. "We see you at Yunayev apartment. Then we see you at Yunayev boat. Walk up, go in, look round. We watch. We not stupid!"

The tattooed man put his other hand on Zoe's neck and squeezed. She tried to breathe in but couldn't. Her heart pounded. The hand smelled of sweat.

"After you go, we talk to man on boat. He say you secretary. Yunayev secretary!" The tall man sounded outraged at the idea. His eyes flashed. "So you don't mess with us. Yunayev bad man. We look for him. We find him. You help us."

His eyes fixed on her. She could smell stale tobacco on his breath. She swallowed to speak.

"I don't know where he is."

A crack as her head hit the wall, harder this time. Everything went black. A wave of nausea. Throbbing pain behind the eyes.

"Man on boat say Yunayev coming tomorrow. You say that! *You* say it!"

As he said *you*, the tall guy jabbed her hard in the ribs.

"*You* know his plan! *You* know he come here! When? Where? *You* tell me where to find him."

Four eyes bored into her. Thick sausages of fingers pressed on her windpipe again. She tried to swallow. How could she not have thought of this? Yunayev was a criminal. Not a nice man. Of course he had enemies. And now she did, too.

Think, Zoe, think. Get yourself out of this. But how?

"It's not as simple as that," she said.

The tall guy frowned. "Not simple? He come tomorrow. Sound simple to me. When he arrive? Where?"

The grip tightened on her neck even more. She tried to suck in air but couldn't. She closed her eyes, dizzy. The voice came closer, quiet and grainy.

"We don't like games," it said. "We serious people. We have business with Yunayev. Yunayev thief. Traitor. We don't like. You help us. Where he come tomorrow?"

She opened her eyes. "I don't know."

The tattooed guy punched her in the stomach. She thought she was going to puke. Her legs gave way. If she weren't being held up she'd have fallen to the floor.

"How you not know? You don't mess with us." The voice was louder, harder. "We know about you. Where you work. Where you live. We have information. About everybody. You think you have secret, you think you can run away, we find you. We find your friends, your family. If we want, we kill them. We kill you. If we want. Understand?"

His voice echoed up the stairwell. Where was everybody? Couldn't anyone help her? Okay then, she was on her own. She had to say something and the truth wasn't going to satisfy them. What would Anna do?

"All right, he's coming here," she said. "But not tomorrow. His plans changed. It's the day after tomorrow."

The grip hardened on her chin, forcing her to look straight into the tall man's eyes.

"After tomorrow when? Where?"

"At the heliport. Coming from Nice airport."

"What time?"

No hesitation, Zoe. Just keep it rolling. "Late morning. Eleven, twelve, something like that. I've got it written down."

A pause, then: "Where he flying from?"

"Cayman Islands." The first shady-sounding place to come into her head. "Via Paris." There were loads of flights every day from Paris to Nice. The two men conferred briefly in Russian, then turned back to her. The tall man came in close and raised his knee. He pressed it against her groin, hard. She squirmed but could go nowhere.

"Yunayev not there, heliport, day after tomorrow," he said, "we kill you. We kill friends. We kill family."

He stepped back. The tattooed guy let go and she sank to her knees. They gave her one last baleful glare before leaving her crumpled in the stairwell.

The only sound was her own breathing, great heaving gasps of air. She was trembling all over. Christ, what kind of a mess was she in? Never in her life before had she been threatened like that. It didn't even sound like a big deal to them. She thought she was so clever, mooching around playing at being a millionaire, but she had no idea the circles these people moved in, who they really were. And she had no excuse for that. Anna said as much at their very first meeting. So did John Fairchild. But it was too late now. She was trapped.

Her phone rang. She shuffled in her bag, hands still trembling. It was Stella.

"Hey," she said.

"Hi babe, you okay?"

"Sure." Zoe managed to sound casual.

"Listen, right, this may be nothing, but a guy just came to the door looking for you. Big guy, leather jacket, short hair. An accent, Russian or something. Anyway, I said you were on your way back from work but he didn't seem very happy. Just hung about outside. Have you pissed someone off or something?"

Shit. Shit, shit, shit. "Is he there now?" Still trying to sound light.

"Yeah, he's still there. I can see him. He keeps looking up at the window. I don't like it, Zo. Do you know what's going on?"

Zoe didn't answer. A swell of dread was washing over her. *We kill your friends. We kill your family.* Noah!

Stella was still talking. "Zoe? You still there? Listen, is there something wrong? I've barely seen you lately, you just seem to be out all the time. What's up?"

But Zoe's mind was elsewhere.

"I've got to go, Stella."

"What?"

"I'll call you straight back, Stell, promise. It's just – I've got to make another call."

"You sure you're all right?"

"Yes, sure! I'll call you back."

Zoe hung up. She found Noah's number but hesitated. She didn't trust herself not to alarm her little brother. But she needed to know if they were onto him as well.

She sent a text. *Hey, bro! Everything okay with you?*

He usually replied pretty quickly. He might wonder what it was about, but it wasn't too alarming. And now for the call she really didn't want to make. Now she realised what an idiot she'd been, this wasn't going to be fun at all.

She called Anna.

Chapter 36

Rose sat on the balcony trying to clear her head. The low afternoon sun was glaring in her face. She just couldn't grasp what had bothered her in Pippin's room. Yvonne and Ollie were inside, checking out options for a new HQ. This apartment had come through Paris Station, but they needed to sort out a new place themselves. It was the only way to be sure they were clean. Where to go? Being closer to Monaco made sense, but if there were anything in Fairchild's theory, they would be even further from Marseille. There were too many unknowns, and one of them was lurking in the depths of her own mind.

She called Fairchild. He picked up straight away.

"Where are you?" she asked.

"In Marseille, like I said." The background chatter sounded like a bar.

"What do you recall about Pippin's ID card?" She never got a good look at it.

"I have a photo of it."

"Oh." Something she should have done.

"Shall I send it to you?"

"Please."

"Any chance of any of you joining me here? Some help might speed things up."

"It's still a very tentative lead, Fairchild. If you turn up something concrete, let me know and we can take it from there."

"Okay, then. You've seen the news, I take it."

"Yes, the Kremlin announcement. Puts us under extra time pressure."

"Indeed."

A stilted conversation full of unasked questions. Fairchild would have liked to know what her team was working on right now. But she wasn't going to tell him about moped riders and people in red shirts. As she said to the others, she didn't know who to trust.

Her phone pinged. The photo had arrived. Rose noted with irritation that it dated from the previous evening, Fairchild's preview visit to Pippin's room. It was under-exposed and a little blurred. She read all the details on the ID card and enlarged Pippin's mugshot. And then she saw it.

She ran through it all again in her head: the wine, the Van Gogh letters, the neatness of everything. My God. How could she have missed that?

Her phone rang, her other phone, the one she used for her informants that she answered as Anna. It was Zoe.

"What's up?"

"Hi Anna. Listen. Something just happened. You're going to be angry, I know you are."

Rose didn't like the sound of this at all.

"Go on."

"Just now, I was coming out of work and two great big Russian guys grabbed me and pulled me off the street."

"Christ, Zoe. Did they hurt you?"

"Yeah, a bit, but I'm okay."

"What did they want?"

"They wanted to know about the guy. Yunayev. Where is he, when is he coming?"

This was mystifying. "Why do they think he's coming here? And how did they associate you with him?"

Alarm bells were ringing. Did the Russians know about their operation? What else did they know, if they knew about Zoe?

"The thing is…" Zoe hesitated.

"What is it, Zoe?"

"I've been foolish. I realise now, but it's too late!" She was close to tears.

"Tell me, Zoe. I'm sure I can help."

"They've been following me. I didn't realise. They must have been watching me."

"But how did they know to watch you, Zoe? How did they you know you had anything to do with it?"

"I went to his flat."

Rose wasn't sure she'd heard properly. "Whose flat? Yunayev's?"

"Yes."

"What the hell for?"

"I wanted to see it. I wanted to see how these people live. I was curious."

"But how did you get in?"

"I said I needed to measure up for some new curtains and upholstery that he'd ordered."

"You said that?"

"Yeah. To the concierge."

"And they just let you in?"

"Kind of."

Through the shock Rose couldn't help but be impressed. The woman was obviously a natural blagger.

"It was really the guy who was already there," Zoe added. "He said it was his place."

Rose frowned. "What guy?"

"The guy John. He was claiming that he was Yunayev, to start with."

"John Fairchild?" How could Fairchild not have mentioned this? It sounded like he'd been encouraging the woman, with terrible consequences.

"Did he put you up to this, Zoe?"

"No, no! He was just nice, that's all. I couldn't see the harm, Anna! You said yourself, these people hardly ever show up in person."

"No, Zoe, but other people could. We're not the only ones after Yunayev. I could have told you that but I thought you were out of it. A one-off, we said!"

"I know, but I got thinking about it all, these people who are criminals, how they make their money. And I went and looked at how much money they have. It's insane, Anna! Millions of Euros! Billions! It's madness!"

"Yes, it is, but it's also dangerous, Zoe. Wait." Rose was thinking. "If they saw you go into Yunayev's apartment building, how did they know which apartment you were going to?"

"I went to his yacht as well. His super-yacht. Oh, you should see it, Anna! The size of it!"

Rose's heart sank. "And they were watching the yacht, weren't they? How did you talk yourself onto that one, if I might ask?"

"I told them I was his secretary and that he was coming tomorrow and he wanted me to check that everything was okay."

"And they know this? The Russians? That you claimed to be his secretary?"

Rose could hear Zoe crying. It answered her question.

"Zoe, listen. I'll bring you in. We'll arrange to meet and I'll take you to a safe place, okay? But first, just tell me what you said to them. These guys. What did you tell them?"

She was tearful but somehow pulled herself together. "I said it was the day after tomorrow."

"The day after tomorrow? What was?"

"That Yunayev is coming to Monaco. They wouldn't have believed the truth. So I said something that would buy a bit more time."

Good girl. She was a natural. What a way to discover it, though.

"What exactly did you tell them?"

"That he'd be arriving at the heliport in the morning, from Nice airport. Off a flight from Paris."

"Okay. Okay." That wasn't so bad. Quite useful, in fact. They could pinpoint exactly where these Russians would be at a specific time. Her team might be able to tail them.

"And they let you go then?"

"Yes. But – they said if he isn't there they'll kill me!"

"Well, they won't, because you'll have disappeared by then. You'll be gone."

Rose was thinking furiously. They must be watching Zoe all the time. Bringing her in would be tricky.

"And then they said they'd kill my friends and family!" Now Zoe's voice was rising. "And then Stella phoned and said there's someone outside our flat! And I've texted Noah but he hasn't texted back! Oh, God, Anna! What have I done?"

Her voice dissolved into sobs. This was serious.

"We can fix this, Zoe," she said. "Listen to me. I'm going to send you some instructions. You follow them exactly. They're to make sure you're not being followed. I will come and meet you and I will take you somewhere safe. We'll look out for Noah. Don't go home. Tell Stella to stay indoors. If she keeps out of their way she should be fine. Follow the instructions, Zoe. Just do that."

Zoe's voice sounded tight. "But why hasn't he texted? He always replies straight away."

"Did these Russians mention him by name?"

A pause. "No."

"Or say something specifically about your brother?"

"No, I guess not."

"So they might not even know about him. Maybe Noah just forgot his phone or ran out of battery or something. My people will go over there to check up on him. You need to do what's necessary to get yourself to safety. You hear me?"

Silence.

"Zoe?"

Silence, then: "Yeah, I hear you."

"Okay, then. Look out for my text."

Rose updated Ollie and Yvonne then hastily compiled a crash meet plan for Zoe, who was now their top priority. What had come over her? People had no idea who they were dealing with. What troubled her the most was Fairchild's involvement. Zoe was naïve and too bright for her own good, stuck in a job she could do with her eyes closed. She had an excuse for getting curious, and maybe some of the things Rose said tempted her too much. That was a risk of the job – open someone's eyes to the world of secrecy and they could get caught up in the possibilities it offered. But Fairchild? If he'd encouraged this young woman to make a target of herself, with people like Grom and the muscle men of the Kremlin hanging around, there was no forgiving that at all.

Chapter 37

Zoe was following the instructions. She was sitting in a coffee shop waiting. Anna's text was clear and detailed: stay in Monaco, don't go home. Zoe rarely stayed in Monaco into the evening. It was still light but it all seemed unfamiliar to her. At a certain time, about half an hour from now, she should go for a walk. The route, in and out of various places, took her into the Japanese Garden. Zoe should see Anna at some point there but she shouldn't react. Look at what Anna's doing. If she has her phone up to her right ear, carry on to the meet point, a bar near the casino, and arrive fifteen minutes later. If no phone, go back to the coffee shop and await further instructions. Easy. But she had to wait. Anna had to get here, see, from whatever place she was in. So Zoe had time to kill. She'd ordered a tea; it took longer to drink than coffee. She thought about something stronger but decided against it.

She needed to think. Written instructions were fine, but what did it all mean? This Yunayev was wanted by the Russian government. They were prepared to kill to get to him. The way those men handled her in that stairwell, they were more than capable. They were goons, those guys, street mafia, like Epée and his gang but way more serious. And they were acting for the Russian government, so they said. Yunayev was a thief and a traitor. That was no surprise, though the people who were after him seemed just as ruthless.

Russia was an influential country, right? They have mafia across the world. They have money, lots of it. Now Zoe started to comprehend what she'd done. She'd associated herself closely with a Russian undesirable. She'd claimed to be his secretary. As long as the Russians wanted Yunayev, they'd be on her back. And she had no real idea who Yunayev was, where he was, what he was going to do. He could be on the run from these people for years, for all she knew. And they'd be onto Stella and Noah, everyone in her life. What would happen to them? Fool, Zoe! If your little game only affected you, it would serve you right. But she'd endangered other people too.

At least Noah had texted her back now. He sounded fine as far as she could tell. He was at training as usual. She'd phoned Stella back earlier, just after speaking to Anna, but now she called her again.

"Is the guy still there?"

"Yeah, right outside."

"Listen, I'm not coming home tonight, Stell."

"So where are you going?"

"Not sure yet. But not home."

"What's going on, Zoe? What's up with you?"

"Listen, I don't know yet. There's stuff happening, but it'll be fine. That guy, he hasn't come to the door again, has he?"

"No, he's just out there, hanging around. He looks like a bouncer, Zoe. Massive. What should I do?"

"Nothing. Don't do anything. Just stay in, make sure everything's locked. If he comes to the door or does anything weird, call the police. But he probably won't. It's me they're after. That's why they're out there."

"Who's *they*, Zoe? Why is anyone after you?"

"Hon, I can't explain now. But I'll be okay. Just keep an eye on him and stay tight. I'll explain when I next see you."

But the thought in her head as she hung up was, *But I might never see you again.*

She looked at the phone in her hand. Russians were hackers, weren't they? Could they be listening to her calls? What did they know about her? The two heavies had just followed her, hadn't they? They saw her at the apartment building and then again at the yacht. It sounded like they'd spoken to Freddy. She hoped he was okay. But somehow they had her home address. How would they know that? This was a whole world Zoe knew nothing about. Anna knew this world. Anna had texted instructions to this phone. If Anna thought the phone was okay, maybe it was.

Zoe let her gaze move around the coffee shop. Someone here was probably watching her. That was why Anna sent instructions – to throw them off before Zoe and Anna actually met. Most people were chatting away or tapping on a device or something. Apart from two guys in leather jackets sitting opposite each other at a corner table. A backpack was on the table between them. They both had coffees but nothing much to say to each other. Maybe it was them. But what did she know? What was in the bag? A listening device? Or was that paranoia? Come on, Zoe, everything you know about this stuff is from films. You're out of your depth, girl. You've lost control here.

She checked the time. She should start walking in fifteen minutes. Those guys could follow her. How was she going to prevent it?

Shit. She texted Noah again, asking him to call her before he left the club that night to go home. *Got something to tell you, bro.* She left it at that. He'd do it. Then she called Anna.

"Where are you?" Anna sounded breathless. She was walking.

"I'm in a cafe." Zoe stood and turned to look out of the window, facing away from the guys with their backpack.

"You got the text?" asked Anna.

"Yeah, I got the text."

"Well, stay put for a few more minutes then set off, okay? I'll be there."

"I think they're here, Anna. I think they're watching."

"Maybe. But we'll sort that out."

"How? They're going to follow me."

"You don't have to worry about that. I've done this before, Zoe. I know what to do. You just do as I say and it'll be fine. Just do as I say."

Now Anna had the knowledge and power and Zoe had nothing. She was in the woman's hands. A woman she knew nothing about.

"And what then, Anna? What about after that?"

"We'll talk about that later. Let's just deal with this now. Once you're safe we can discuss everything else. Okay?"

Okay? She was being reassuring, like she was talking to a child.

"How do they know where I live, Anna? How did they find out?"

"We'll figure that out. One thing at a time, Zoe."

"What does it mean, disappeared?"

"Sorry?"

"You said disappeared. That I'll have disappeared by tomorrow. What does that mean?"

"I'll explain it all later, Zoe."

"Is it over?"

Pause. "Is what over?"

"Everything. My life here. Friends, family. It's over, isn't it?"

"It's too early to discuss all that, Zoe. We need to get you in and then assess things."

"But this guy, if they're still after him, they'll still be after me, won't they? I mean, when does this end?"

"Zoe, we can't be thinking like that right now." There was tension in her voice though she was trying to hide it. "We'll talk about it. We'll make a plan. We'll figure it out, but first we need to get you safe. So let's just do that, okay?"

Okay? How many times had Anna done this before? How long had she been doing this? Was Anna even her real name?

"I've really messed up, haven't I?" said Zoe. "I'm sorry. I made all this happen."

"Don't worry about that now. Just focus." A neutral response but Zoe didn't need to be told. She already knew she'd fucked up.

"Did Noah text?" Anna asked.

"Yes. He's okay, I think."

"Where is he?"

"At home."

"Okay."

"I spoke to Stella. The guy's still outside our place."

"Well, he can just stay there for now, as you're not going home. It's time to get moving, Zoe."

"Yeah, sure."

They hung up.

Why did she do that? Anna was trying to help her, but Zoe just lied about where Noah was. Her head was telling her, do what Anna says. Do exactly what she says and don't hide anything. Leave all this to the professionals, the people who've done it before. But something deep inside her was saying something else.

They'd always got by, her and Noah, since Mum and Dad passed on. She'd always sorted things for the two of them. She'd always found a way.

The phone lit up. It was Noah.

"Hey, Noah! You all right?"

"Sure, sis. What's up?"

"Everything okay with you? No trouble from Epée or – anyone else?"

"No, I told you that's all cool. You all right?"

"Yeah, sure, you know me, I just worry. You going home now?"

"I guess."

"Is Raoul still there?" Raoul was Noah's best friend at the academy, a promising striker.

"Sure. We're just packing up."

"Will you do me a favour, bro? Will you go home with Raoul tonight? Tell aunt Lily you're staying over?"

"What for?"

"I can't tell you yet, but I'll tell you tomorrow."

"What?"

"Sorry, Noah. But for me, can you just do that? Tell him something's come up. His folks pick him up in a car, don't they? Just ask, say it's an emergency."

"What's going on, Zo? What emergency?"

"It's nothing much. I'll tell you tomorrow. Listen, you remember where we used to go skateboarding on a Saturday morning?"

A pause. "That was a long time ago, sis."

"You remember where it was, though?"

"Sure, it's—"

"Don't say! Don't say it out loud. As long as you know. Let's meet there tomorrow morning. Ten o'clock. Okay?"

Okay? Now she was doing it.

"Christ, Zoe, I'm going to have to skip training. You hate it when I miss a session."

"Yeah, I know. But this is really important. It's – I've got a surprise for you. Just don't tell anyone else, all right? It's a secret. Go straight there from Raoul's. I'll explain it all then.

You trust me, don't you? We've always looked out for each other."

Pause. "Yeah. I guess. Well, I've got to catch up with Raoul."

"You go, you go. Text me when you're at his."

"If you want."

Noah was surprised but she knew he'd do what she said. Zoe should go now to do the walk as instructed, in and out, round and about, through the Japanese Garden. It was getting on for sunset but still light. She gathered her things and walked out. At the door she glanced back. One of the men in leather jackets was looking at her. Instead of turning towards the garden, she crossed the road and went into the shopping mall.

She'd been here many times before – it was one of her lunchbreak hangouts – but she never bought anything. She loved the palatial feel of the place – only Monaco would have chandeliers in shopping malls – and wondered what was wrong with people that they would spend this much on clothes and electronics when you could buy the same thing in France or Italy, or online, for so much less. She knew where she was going: an elegant lingerie shop on the upper floor. She'd been past it many times but today was the first time she went in.

Near the entrance, she browsed the bras and panties section, holding up delicate lacy knickers and checking sizes. An assistant came over. Zoe wanted something special to impress someone, she said. The assistant had plenty of ideas. Zoe got a brief glimpse of one of the men from the cafe hanging around outside. She was right! They had been watching her. But they weren't going to follow her into a lingerie shop. She moved further into the store. She found an excuse to abandon the underwear search and instead went to the accessories section and picked out a bright orange scarf and some hair ties. She paid with a card, forcing herself not to look at how much they cost, and went down to the lower floor of the shop where she spent some time in front of a mirror pulling her hair back and tying the scarf over her head. She had some shades in her bag as well. Was that too much? Never mind. The whole effect was a little bit Grace Jones, but that wasn't a bad thing.

Satisfied, she left the store by the downstairs door that led directly onto the street. Just as she'd hoped, the men hadn't realised it was there, so when she turned and made her way back into the centre of Monte Carlo, she was alone. And she was still alone when she ducked into an underground car park through an unmarked vehicle-only exit, walked through to the other side, and took the internal stairs up into the bank.

Chapter 38

Gustave was crazy. Of course Pippin already knew that, but Gustave had been on a new plane of craziness, a strange light in his eyes when he'd marched Pippin from his room with the gun in his jacket poking Pippin in the back. A tram and then a bus, Pippin doing what he was told. Could he have run for it? Would Gustave have the nerve to draw a gun and shoot someone in plain view in a crowded street? Pippin wouldn't put it past him.

They ended up inland from the coast, in a village. Clem was waiting in a car as the bus pulled in. He stared at Pippin but didn't say a word. He drove them to a run-down farm building. No one was there to see them.

Since then Pippin had been locked in a dark room. They brought him food every now and then. No furniture, just bare floor. Pippin tried to sleep, but he would wake again, cold and stiff, with no idea if it was day or night. Occasionally, he heard the two of them talking but couldn't make out what they were saying. It always sounded as though they were arguing. Then they both came for him and pulled him to his feet.

It was light outside as they got in the car. They ended up at another deserted lock-up. The van was different but the goods were all in the back. Well – almost all. Gustave and Clem worked together to tape Pippin's hands behind his back and shove him in. The doors slammed and they set off.

It was a long journey on a fast road, that was all Pippin could tell. The engine droned. The floor of the van vibrated. The smell of exhaust fumes drifted in. Pippin rolled around and dozed amongst the packaged artwork. Then they slowed, turned, manoeuvred and came to a halt. A door slammed and footsteps walked away.

Silence. Then another slam, more footsteps, and the back doors of the van opened. Clem was standing there, his huge form filling the space. He stepped forward and cut the tape from Pippin's hands with a knife. He stood aside, a silent invitation. Pippin took him up on it, jumping to the ground and stretching his legs. They were parked at an out-of-town shopping mall. The stores, some distance away on the other side of the car park, were lit up, still open. It was mid-evening, maybe. Clem passed him the remains of a half-eaten ham baguette. Pippin accepted.

They stood in silence while Pippin ate. Then he said:

"Gustave?"

Clem pointed to a DIY store but didn't elaborate. He stared into the distance. Pippin was aware of the power of the man, a still force. Clem must have organised the hideout, the change of vehicle. Such practical considerations passed Gustave by. Eventually Pippin asked him:

"Why didn't you just take the stash on the first night? You had the keys. You could have driven off in the van and disappeared."

Clem turned to him slowly. "He said he had contacts. Plans for the paintings."

"Do you believe him?"

The suggestion of a shrug. "I didn't want to get fingered for murder. If the loot was with me, they'd put the body on me too. I won't take the rap for him."

"Where are we going?"

"West." Clem nodded towards the autoroute, lit up behind them. "Marseille, like he said."

"You know people, Clem. You shifted that Swedish Impressionist piece. What's stopping you taking off right now?"

A hint of a smile. "Gustave took the keys to the van. Gustave has a gun."

"You have a gun. You had both guns. You must have given one back to him."

It didn't make sense. But Clem had a question of his own.

"So it's true? You took the portrait?"

A long pause.

"Yes, it's true," said Pippin. "It was Henri that planned it. I didn't know what he was doing until we were inside the place. He was going to take his fee and the painting."

"But he told you about it."

"He needed someone else to help get it into the van, and sell it on later. He wanted us to split it fifty-fifty, whatever I could get for it."

"But then you decided to take the lot."

"Well, once Gustave had murdered him, he wasn't going to want it. What can I say? I'm a thief."

"It's a bad idea to steal from other thieves."

"You expected me to hand it over to Gustave? The man's crazy."

"So where is it?"

"It's safe." Pause. "You think you can shift it?"

Clem's eyes bored into him. "Yes, I can do that."

"Well, then. Same offer as Henri made me. We go halves. I won't share with Gustave, though. The guy tried to kill me. He's a lunatic."

Clem was still staring at him. "You could have got away," he said. "You could have disappeared when you swiped the painting. But you went back somewhere Gustave could find you."

"I didn't think the Freeport would release the list. I didn't think you'd find out it was gone. I thought you and he would just take the loot between you. Or just you."

A turn of the head indicated that Gustave was returning, pacing towards them grim-faced with heavy bags in both hands. He clocked that Pippin's hands were untied.

"This is all very friendly," he said.

Clem reached for the tape and retied Pippin's hands without saying a word. Gustave stared at Pippin with contempt and loaded the bags into the back. Clem manhandled Pippin up into the back and slammed one door. But then he turned to Gustave.

"What's the plan, Gustave? In Marseille. Time to tell me. You have buyers lined up, or a safe hiding place for this?"

"What's your problem, Clem? I said I did, didn't I? What's this little weasel been saying to you? You think you can trust anything from him?" He glanced again at Pippin. "You should do his ankles as well."

He walked round to the front, leaving Clem to climb in and tie Pippin's ankles together. Clem slammed the door shut. Footsteps round to the front. After a pause the engine turned and they were off again.

More fast-moving road. The sound changed. A bridge or a tunnel. Then they slowed. Stop, start, stop. They were in the city. Slow turns, hesitations. He could hear people talking – they were in an area with pedestrians, busy streets. At one point they jerked to a halt and Pippin heard shouted conversation with someone outside. Then they started again and made a series of sharp turns. They were going up a hill, steep enough to make the packages slide to the back. One of Gustave's bags fell open and the contents rolled out. Pippin felt around. A heavy-duty plastic container full of liquid. It was too dark to see what it was.

They stopped. A door slammed. Footsteps, and the van door was unlocked. Both doors were thrown open. Gustave was standing there, his arms wide like Christ on the cross. Some breeze was blowing, making his hair rise. Behind him was nothing, distant lights below and an expanse of darkness, obsidian black.

"This is it, Pippin! This is where we tell people what it's all about! This was meant to be! Can't you feel it? Come on, I know you're more than some sneaking thief. I always knew that."

He shoved his DIY purchases back into the bags and walked off with them. Pippin shuffled forward and managed to stand, leaning on the door of the van. Some eerie background light was coming from somewhere. In front of them was a promontory, a patch of grassy open space that dropped down dramatically on three sides. Pippin looked round the door of the van and took a breath. Rising high above his head was a huge church, its arches and brickwork brilliantly floodlit, its immense tower topped by a golden statue of the Virgin. It was the church in Gustave's painting.

Pippin looked round wildly. The whole scene was Gustave's painting: the hill, the city below, the ocean beyond, the promontory. The only things missing were the crowds of people and – no. Pippin went cold. Surely not that. Not even Gustave would do that. He was an artist himself, for God's sake. But Gustave was moving with demonic energy, unpacking his bags in the middle of the open space.

Clem was standing back, watching.

"Clem, you know what he's going to do!" shouted Pippin. "You know what he's got there! He's going to burn it! He's going to burn everything! He's mad!"

Gustave turned. "The world is mad, Pippin! This will show people how! We're waking them up now! Feel that sea air! Come on!"

Gustave stepped into the van and pulled out one of the large framed packages. He handled it as if it were rubbish to be hauled into a skip. Pippin worked his wrists but they were fastened tight.

"Clem! Stop him!"

Finally Clem woke up and strode over as Gustave manhandled the frame.

"Gustave. Stop. This isn't the plan, you know it."

Clem had his hands up, blocking Gustave's route. Clem was broader, stronger than Gustave. He could knock the guy down. But Gustave seemed high on something. When Clem stopped in front of him, he threw the frame onto the ground. It landed on its corner and twisted, making a cracking noise. Pippin felt sick. Clem had his hand on Gustave's shoulder – but then something inexplicable happened.

Gustave's hand came out of his pocket holding something small wrapped in plastic. He pulled at it and grabbed at Clem's face. He reached for the back of Clem's head and pushed it forward into his other hand. Clem was stronger but Gustave was quick, taking him by surprise. With horror Pippin recognised the manoeuvre; he'd done something similar in the Freeport.

Clem sagged. All you needed was one deep breath of the stuff to go dizzy. Then you could be controlled into taking another one and it was over. It was almost comical, the big muscle man being lowered to the ground by skinny arty Gustave. With Clem lying prone between them, Gustave turned to Pippin.

"You want some too? This is good stuff! You know that. You showed me how to use it. Not hard to find it if you know where to look. That was the easy part."

He came up to Pippin and stood over him with the handkerchief. The fumes were escaping into the air. Pippin got a whiff; that alone made his head buzz. He shook his head.

"So you'll be a witness, then," said Gustave. "Good. We need those."

He gave Pippin a long look before stepping up and getting another canvas out of the van. Pippin had no choice. Trussed up like this he wasn't going anywhere. He sank down and watched Gustave heave on the mighty frame, pulling it down and dragging it bumping over the rough ground.

Gustave flung the piece down on top of the first one and came back for more. Pippin watched. Back and forth went Gustave, building his bonfire, finding some source of energy in his madness, years of anger funnelled into this futile act of destruction.

"You know, you could help," he said one time, stepping up past Pippin to grab more of the loot. "Don't tell me it doesn't excite you."

Pippin shook his head. "This isn't where I'm coming from. This is mad. All art is precious. Yes, it's valued all wrong but that doesn't change its real worth. It's society that's wrong, not the art itself."

But Gustave was already walking away with another armful of artwork.

Pippin tried again on his return. "Where's the audience, Gustave? In your painting people are watching. People are taking part. But it's just you. There's no one here to see this. It's pointless."

"You're seeing it," said Gustave. "You can tell the story."

"I don't want to tell the story. There is no story."

Gustave slapped him hard. His head hit the metal side of the van.

"You know better than that. It'll be out there, believe me. Everyone will see it."

Pippin leaned his throbbing head against the van, closing his eyes. These days you always had an audience. All Gustave needed was a phone and he could broadcast the whole thing to the world.

Back and forth, back and forth. It was cold, on this hill. Pippin sat and shivered. Gustave emptied the van, striding up and down, powered by zeal. Clem lay unmoving, a dark mass on the ground. How long had Gustave been planning this? Was this his aim right from the start? Or was it some kind of elaborate cover-up to draw attention from what had gone wrong, or from the damned Van Gogh that had distorted everything?

Henri was always blunt about his motivations, if not the scale of his intentions. Why was Clem involved? If theft were Clem's game, there were a hundred easier things to steal. As for Pippin himself, Pippin would have long gone. Pippin saw the futility of this from far off. And yet here he was, trapped, a reluctant witness to an abhorrent act of vandalism.

The van emptied. Pippin's heart raced. Gustave picked up the plastic container, unscrewed the lid, turned towards Pippin and smiled. Pippin wanted to turn away but had to watch. Gustave took his time, shaking the canister and pouring fluid all over the pyre.

What was in there? Beautifully crafted works, hundreds of years old. Sketches, seascapes, nudes, dramatic stories enacted in shapes and colour, the faces of people long dead, scenes of everyday life injected with joy and flow and meaning. The best of the human spirit, canvas and oil and bronze and wood made into so much more than that. The essence of existence captured in a shape, a combination of colours. The world presented in a way nobody had seen before. All of this would soon be nothing more than charred remnants and ash. Pippin felt tears on his cheeks.

Gustave struck a match.

Chapter 39

Fairchild was running uphill, the cold air making his lungs ache. He'd got a taxi halfway up but came on foot after that to approach quietly. But he needed to be quick, too. He had a bad feeling about this.

He'd just taken a call from an old contact. Two guys in a van just stopped in the Old Port area of Marseille and asked for directions up to the Notre Dame de la Garde church. They did this near a restaurant on the harbour front, run by his friend, who was outside at the time keeping an eye on things. A beat-up old van, two serious-looking men, nine o'clock at night – odd. To top that, Fairchild's friend, who had the kind of history to know about these things, thought there was something very off about the number plate on the van. It was a strong enough lead to take seriously.

Legs burning, he pushed himself onward. Where was Rose and her crew? He'd texted her from the taxi. Her emphasis on teamwork didn't seem to apply the other way. He turned a corner and slowed. In front of him was a van with the doors open, a small hunched up figure sitting on the back, and a body lying on the ground. Behind the body a tall man – Fournier – was looking up, his face illuminated by the giant orange flames of a bonfire. Smoke billowed off, and Fairchild could feel the heat even from a distance. Above all of it the immense floodlit church looked down, making a recognisable pageant.

Fairchild crept closer, the van on one side, the bonfire on the other. The small guy sat still, his eyes round as he watched. His arms and feet were bound up. Behind him, the van was empty.

The fire crackled. The flames grew. Something broke and collapsed in the pyre, sending sparks into the sky. Gustave was smiling as he stared up.

That bastard Gustave. Now Fairchild realised what the madman had done.

Chapter 40

The first of Gustave's matches had blown out in the wind. And the second, and the third, as if some divine force were intervening to save something of itself. But the fourth match took, and Gustave dropped it on the pile. Flames leaped up and licked the angular shapes. Gustave lit more matches, moving round the fire, a whirling dervish. The smell of the fuel reached Pippin, then a wave of heat as the flames rose and bent in the wind. The cardboard corner of one of the huge frames burned away. Inside Pippin could see paint on canvas bubbling and running. Tears rolled down his cheeks.

A shadow passed in front of him. No, not a shadow: the shape of a man, his silhouette against the orange flames. Where had he come from? The silhouette went straight for Gustave, who turned and backed off. But whoever this was, Gustave was no match for him. A series of tidy punches, a couple of kicks and Gustave was on the ground as motionless as Clem. Then the guy turned to the pyre.

Moving upwind, he grabbed a length of wood that was once part of a frame, and pulled it out of the fire. He stepped in close, so close he had to jump back when a gust hit the flames. He swung the wood through the heart of the fire, forwards and back, pushing and jabbing, leaping back like a fencer from flames and sparks. The burning contents toppled and scattered over the ground. The pieces lay flat, some in flames, some not. Now the man moved among them. He took off his jacket and wrapped it around his arm and hand. He picked up each piece in turn, lifting it by its edges, peering at it in the dim light. Was he looking for the portrait? If so, he'd risked a lot for nothing.

He stopped suddenly, staring at something. He picked it up. It was flimsy, made of paper, small. He held it up and looked at both sides. Ignoring the other objects, lying like soldiers fallen in a battlefield, he rolled it up and stepped away. Only then did he look around at the two prone bodies and at Pippin, watching from the van.

Please, come over. Please, release me. Take me with you. I don't want to be here any more.

The two figures on the ground were stirring. Clem had his head up already. In the distance a siren wailed.

The man paused, listening, then tucked the roll close to his chest and strode away.

Chapter 41

Fairchild tasted the smoke in his mouth, and his clothes stank of the stuff. He clenched his fists as he walked off. That madman Fournier! What was the purpose of it? Fairchild only just arrived in time, but even so the print was sure to have suffered some damage. If he'd got there to find nothing but charred remains, he'd have killed the guy for sure. If sheer protest stupidity got in the way of Fairchild fully understanding the significance of this print and why it was so important to his parents, someone would pay a price.

How had Gustave managed it? The other two clearly weren't willing participants. The guy on the ground was a big bloke. He must have been the driver for the heist. Pippin, the diminutive thief, was the guy tied up at the van. Gustave must have had some tricks up his sleeve to carry that off.

Fairchild had been right about Marseille, right about the painting too, that it meant something. He'd been caught out before seeing links where there weren't any, adding two and two to make five. It was only a gut feel, but he'd been right. It had crossed his mind as well that Pippin had left that painting there deliberately, as a kind of message. But he couldn't be sure. He wasn't sure about anything when it came to Pippin.

All he'd got back from his text to Rose was a perfunctory reply. The sirens meant someone had called the police, but it certainly wasn't him. He didn't want to explain himself to local law enforcement any more than Rose's lot would have done. No one else was up on this hill apart from the gang and himself. When he'd heard the sirens he'd paused, the print rolled up in his hand, the two on the ground stirring, Pippin at the van, pale and silent, no sign of anyone else.

He'd done what he promised to do. More people would have meant more options, but he was alone. So he turned and left the three of them up there, getting himself and his print out of harm's way while he still had the chance.

Chapter 42

Pippin watched the man disappear. He wasn't going to be rescued. He was left here alone with the two of them. However much he wanted to, it wasn't his time yet to leave.

Clem was up first. Pippin watched the back of the big guy's head as he sat up slowly and surveyed the chaos in front of him. Gustave was stirring too, groaning. That guy couldn't do anything quietly. Clem climbed to his feet and stepped amongst the damaged artwork, walking around, lifting corners of frames with his foot. He looked up and met Pippin's eye. Gustave was sitting up now, coughing thickly. There was blood involved, a broken rib maybe.

A flash of blue lit the scene for a split second. This galvanised Clem. He stepped towards Gustave, reached into the guy's jacket and pulled out his gun. He took a step back and aimed. A babble of words from Gustave. Was it coherent? Pippin couldn't tell.

Clem shot him in the head, a spray of blood and brains. Gustave fell back, truly silent now.

Three strides and Clem was towering over Pippin.

"Get in," he said.

Pippin scrambled but couldn't get his feet up. Clem lifted his legs and shoved him. He slammed the doors shut. Moments later they were on the move, accelerating and twisting. Pippin rolled about in the empty van, thrown against the sides. The sirens were close now, wailing all around. Someone shouted through a megaphone. But the van didn't stop.

Gunshots, three or four, then a lurch and a burst of speed. Loud bangs on the sides of the van. They were being fired at. But they carried on without slowing, crazy driving, twisting and braking, skidding on every turn.

The sirens faded. Their pace didn't diminish. Pippin buried his head under his arms and wished he were somewhere else.

Someone else.

Chapter 43

Zoe and Noah used to go skateboarding in the *Place des Marseillais*, below the steps up to the *Gare St Charles* in central Marseille. It wasn't allowed, but a few of them met up and did it anyway until they were moved on. Those carefree weekends were all about harmless playing, enjoying movement for its own sake, back when everything was okay, when Mum and Dad were still around. Zoe tried to remember how good it felt just to be moving, the uncomplicated companionship they all shared for an hour or two. She'd been proud of being a big sis to her little brother back then. She still was.

She stood by the iron railings and looked down at the Place from above. Tears filled her eyes as she watched Noah saunter up and look around for her. So grown up and yet still so vulnerable. It was a lot, what she was going to pass to him now. She'd spent all night working it out and had a plan, but this part of it, Noah, was her biggest regret. Unbelievable how much everything had changed within the space of a day.

Noah sat on a bench and stretched out, playing around with his mobile. Her phone beeped. He'd texted her: *You here, sis?* But she wasn't ready for him yet. She wanted to stay up above, standing and looking down. Noah didn't look this way, and if he did he probably wouldn't recognise her. Zoe was doing what Anna was going to do to her at the Japanese Garden. She was watching for watchers.

She scanned the crowds, looking for anyone who arrived the same time as Noah and was still there. A guy smoking, a woman standing looking at her watch, a group of three talking and laughing as they crossed the square, they all melted away. How long would Anna give it?

She texted: *Be there in 20* and a smiley face.

FFS came the answer. Yeah, well, he'd have to be patient.

She ticked the people off in her head. All accounted for: those who had arrived had moved on. This wasn't perfect – all you needed to do was change a hat or a coat or a scarf and the job was much more difficult. She was relying on that herself. At least she was sure no one was on her tail.

She'd been at the bank all night, putting things in place, things that before were only ideas. But when she realised how much she'd changed things without even knowing, what she'd lost already, she went back to them and thought again.

After twenty minutes she came down the steps and sat on the bench next to Noah. She was glad she'd chosen somewhere so busy, where they could just blend in. Noah didn't register her at first. She still had the scarf, and her tied-back hair thinned her face. She'd also splashed out earlier on a hip-length close-fitting buttoned jacket to try and change her shape and style. Eventually she turned to Noah.

"Hey, bro," she said softly.

Noah turned and his eyes widened.

"Zoe! Oh my God! You look fantastic!"

"Don't over-react! I'm just trying a new look. What do you think?" She grinned.

"Wow! Great! I mean – older, I guess. But in a good way."

"Like Grace Jones?"

He shrugged, too young for that.

"So what's going on with you? You're being weird, Zoe."

"Did you come straight from Raoul's this morning?"

"Yeah, like you said."

"And you spoke to Lily? Told her everything was okay?"

"Yeah, she's cool. You're not, though, are you?"

Zoe took a breath. "Noah, some things are going to change. I have to go away for a while."

"Away? Where? How long?"

"I'm not sure. It's just – some people are after me."

His eyes widened.

"It's okay, Noah. They're not going to find me. I didn't do anything wrong. I was just in the wrong place at the wrong time, that's all."

He seemed to accept that. It had happened to him, after all.

"But I've got to get clear of them," she continued. "Stay out of their way."

"For how long?"

"I don't know."

"Where will you go?"

"I don't know. And even if I did, Noah, I wouldn't tell you. You know why? Because they may come and ask you that. And you need to be able to say to them honestly that you don't know where I am and have no way of getting in touch with me."

"Seriously? I won't be able to call you? Not even a text?"

"Nothing, no texts, no messages. If you send me a text, I won't get it. When it's safe again I'll contact you."

He looked troubled. "And what if I don't hear from you?"

"You will. You will, I promise."

Zoe gave him her best reassuring big-sis squeeze of the shoulder.

"Now listen. Watch yourself for a little while. Careful where you go. Look around, see if anyone's following you. Stay tight with your mates. Keep to places where there's other people about, public places. Get taxis if you need to instead of walking. I'm gonna give you some money."

Now he looked suspicious. "Where are you getting this money from, Zo? Is that why they're after you?"

"No. Well – not exactly. No, that isn't it. They think I'm involved in something I'm not. They're Russians, Noah. You see or hear of any Russians hanging around, just avoid them. Be careful for a while. When they realise I'm not coming here and you don't know anything, they should disappear. The most important thing is that you keep up with everything. Studying, the academy, the practices. 'Cos this is what you want, isn't it, this chance?"

He shrugged, casual as ever.

"I don't want some silly mistake of mine to mess things up for you."

She felt tearful again. Hold it back, Zoe. Now isn't the time for that. You have to be strong.

"How are things with Epée these days?" she asked.

"Cool. His crew are still around but they don't come near me."

"Well, tell you what. Any trouble from any Russians, any Russians showing their faces near you, you tell Epée they're trying to take over his turf. Tell him he should scare them off. That he should do something big to show them who's boss. You up for that?"

"I thought you didn't want me getting involved with them."

"I don't. This isn't getting involved. Don't start doing things they ask you to do. But since Epée and his people are looking out for you, maybe we can use that."

He grinned, a flash of joy. "You were always the clever one. You got it all worked out, haven't you?"

She messed his hair, feeling all churned up inside.

"Yeah, I got it all worked out. You think you can do this, bro? Trust your big sister and carry on?"

He gave a curious half-smile. "Yeah, I guess. You're a sister of mystery now, but I'm cool with that. Just get in touch when you can."

They hugged briefly. Zoe wanted to drown him in a massive bear hug, but had to keep it in check. She watched him lumbering away across the square, letting a drop or two fall from her eyes. She had no idea when – or if – she'd see her little brother again. It could be never, and that thought tore her apart. But as long as he was okay here, doing what he wanted to do, that was enough.

She stayed for a while, scanning the crowds again for any changes in direction, anyone going Noah's way, before leaving for the train back to Monaco. Family came first and she'd done her best by her brother. Now that was out of the way, she had to sort things out for herself.

Chapter 44

Rose stayed prowling around the Japanese Garden until well after dark and repeatedly tried Zoe's phone, but no luck. Next morning she got on a train to Marseille. Yvonne, who had gone the previous night, hadn't set eyes on Noah at all. That worried Rose, particularly on top of Zoe's no-show in Monaco.

The second conversation she'd had with Zoe was troubling her. It was understandable that Zoe didn't want to put herself in Rose's hands. But it felt as though she were slipping away. Zoe was a clever woman, frustrated at not having the chance to use her talents. But it was dangerous if she felt empowered to do things that she had neither the knowledge nor the support to do. Rose's time as an agent runner in Moscow was still vivid in her mind. It didn't matter how bright you were; if you were going to take on the might of the Russian government, you needed knowhow and you needed backup. Without either, Zoe had no chance. And things may get dangerous for those close to her as well, which was why Rose was coming to Marseille. Aside from checking if Noah was safe, he may have some idea what his sister was up to.

After Monaco, very late last night, Rose had passed by Zoe's flat in Nice. No sign of any Russian heavies hanging around. Hopefully that meant that Zoe didn't return there and the Russians had withdrawn. They still had a day in hand; Zoe told the Russian goons Yunayev was arriving in Monaco tomorrow. It was then, when he didn't appear, that things would really start to get ugly.

So where was the woman? She could be anywhere. Most people, though, would not be able to stop themselves making contact with people in their lives and going to familiar places. That would make it easy for the Russians to find her. If they got to Zoe before Rose could, it didn't bear thinking about. But Rose was running short of people. Ollie she'd sent back to Monaco, to the bank. That would be tough for one person, as they'd already discovered that the bank had multiple ways in and out. He'd have to do his best; she needed Yvonne in Marseille. Zoe's apartment wasn't being watched. Rose had to trust that Zoe was smart enough not to go home. As for finding a new base, that was on hold; all efforts had to be on Zoe for now.

Even though Fairchild was in Marseille, no way was Rose going to appeal to him for help on this. From what Zoe had said, he bore at least some of the blame. On top of everything, Fairchild had texted late last night claiming a possible sighting of the Freeport heist gang. Well, that would just have to wait for now.

Noah finally appeared mid-afternoon. Yvonne was watching the flat while Rose staked out the Metro. Rose caught sight of him coming out of the station and followed him to the square below the flat where Noah went into a shop. He emerged eating something packaged and unhealthy, and stood around chatting with a couple of other young men. Rose and Yvonne kept away from each other, but Noah seemed very aware of his surroundings, looking around frequently. He noticed Yvonne, standing well back smoking a cigarette. He gazed curiously. Rose walked towards Yvonne and let him catch her eye. Then he stared at her. It was as if he were expecting them.

He finished eating whatever it was and set off towards Rose, though that wasn't the way up to the flat. He didn't go straight to her, but glanced as he walked past. They both followed him, Rose moving ahead of Yvonne. Noah carried on out of sight of the square, then slowed to a halt and turned round, folding his arms. He'd picked a good spot, next to a busy road, plenty of people. They stared at each other.

"Whatever you want, I can't help," he said finally.

"But you knew someone would come here asking," said Rose.

His eyes widened. "You're not Russian."

"Lucky for you, no. But they'll be here."

Yvonne came up behind them, hanging back slightly. He looked from one to the other.

"Holy shit! Are you the babes from Paris, that had Epée on his knees? You know he'll never get over that."

Rose acted cool. "Well it's good to know word's got round on the estate. Positive female role models are no bad thing. You've spoken to your sister, haven't you?"

He didn't try to deny it.

"What's she doing? Where is she?"

"I dunno. She said she didn't know either."

"Can you get in touch with her?"

"No. No messages."

"What about her phone?"

"She said she wouldn't be answering it."

He didn't seem overly concerned. But he should be.

"Listen, Noah. Zoe's in a lot of trouble. Maybe she made light of it, but she is. Not because of something she's done, exactly, but —"

"Yeah, I know. Wrong place, wrong time. She saw something, didn't she? A witness."

Not quite, but there was no benefit to Noah having the full story.

"We can help her, Noah. We know how to keep her safe. And you as well. But we need you both to trust us. Can you do that?"

"Hey, I don't even know who you are."

"Zoe knows who we are."

"Well, she didn't say anything about that to me. I trust my sister. I do what she says. She's always looked out for me."

"The thing is, Noah, I'm partly responsible for all this. That's why I want to fix it. Zoe may think she has it sorted, but she's out of her depth. She doesn't even realise how much." Rose saw a shadow of doubt cross Noah's face. "Of course she's doing her best by you, but you both need help and we can provide it."

A pause. Noah looked at his feet.

Rose continued. "Zoe told you to look out for Russians. Did she tell you they jumped her after work?"

He looked up, alarmed.

"She didn't tell you, did she?"

He frowned. "She's okay, though."

"So you've seen her in person? She came here? When was that?" Silence. "Is she still here now?"

"No, she's gone. But I don't know where, like I said."

"How did she look, Noah? How did she seem?"

"Good!"

"Really?" Rose couldn't keep the surprise out of her voice.

"Yeah. Different. Older, thinner. Had a scarf on. Her hair was – different."

So she'd changed her appearance. A positive sign but unlikely to be enough given who was after her.

"Okay. And what did she say exactly?"

He was still holding out. "Like I told you. She's going away for a while, doesn't know where or for how long. And

I can't contact her. And," – a shadow of a grin – "if any Russians show up, I tell Epée they're after his turf."

"Epée?"

"Yeah. So he'll chase them off. Make them feel unwelcome."

That sounded like a bold move.

"Epée is a friend these days, is he?"

"Nah. He keeps his distance. So do his people. He seems almost – scared of me." Noah frowned. "Was it you that did that? What did you say to him?"

No way was Rose going to tell him that.

"You think he'd go for it? Face off the Russian mafia if they show up?"

"I reckon he'd try."

It was a clever idea of Zoe's and might just work. Alternatively, it could pull a lot of people into an ugly confrontation and get Noah involved with the *Pirats* again. Worst-case scenario.

"Well, if that happens, let them know you had a visit from the babes from Paris. Tell them we don't like the Russians either and we hope he'll sort them out. Otherwise we may have to get involved as well."

"Sure."

He liked that idea. Rose got out a business card and passed it to him.

"Listen. If she gets in touch, will you let me know?"

He took the card but looked uncertain.

"At least tell her I was here. Tell her I want to help. Tell her to call me. Will you do that? That's not breaking a confidence, is it Noah? It's just passing something on."

"I guess not."

"Okay then. But I'd still like to know if she gets in touch."

A pause. "We'll see."

It was the best she was going to get. "Okay. Well, go safely, Noah. Your sister's a pretty impressive person. You're lucky to have her."

"Yeah, I know." Quietly, with meaning. He ambled away.

Rose meant what she said. Somehow Zoe, a complete novice, was a step ahead of her. But with Russia involved, and with Grom's non-appearance tomorrow, that couldn't possibly last. Which made it all the more frustrating – and probably tragic in the end – that Zoe now seemed out of reach.

Yvonne checked her phone on the way back to the car.

"Oh, great. You're not going to like this."

"What?"

"Gustave Fournier's dead. He was shot last night in Marseille."

Chapter 45

The sun was setting, turning Marseille's *Fort St Jean* and the spidery walls of the MuCEM complex across the harbour a delicate pinky orange. Fairchild had suggested a small bar a few streets up from the Old Port, overlooking the harbour mouth. Pleasure boats filled the long rectangular port, their masts criss-crossing as the yachts gently bobbed. Most of the bar's few pavement tables were occupied, the ambient noise was congenial, and the whole scene looked restful and idyllic. However, from the tone of Rose's message demanding a meet, Fairchild suspected this encounter would not be idyllic at all.

Rose was already there, sitting with her back to him, looking out over the harbour, two drinks in front of her. He slid into the empty chair.

"I got you a gin and tonic. The ice has melted," she said.

"Thanks."

Fairchild took a sip. He waited.

"So you got what you wanted, then," she said. "Last night?"

"You mean the print? Yes, I did. But I also located the crew, and told you where they were."

He leaned back, giving an appearance of nonchalance that didn't match his mood. Her eyes were cold.

"Care to talk me through it?" she said.

He gave her a quick summary of what happened on the hill. Her expression didn't change as she listened. He downed his gin; he was going to need it.

"Let me get this straight," she said. "One of them was tied up, and the other two were passed out on the ground. And the only thing you could manage to do was grab what you wanted and get out of there? You've heard the news. Now Fournier's dead and the others are in the wind. How did that happen, Fairchild? Could you not have incapacitated them, or stayed on their tail?"

She was pale and furious. There was more to this than the job in hand. Something else was troubling her. But she was still out of line.

"I led you to them. I located them for you. That was the deal. Where was your team, Rose? There was nobody else up there. The police were on their way. What did you expect me to do? I can't explain myself to the police any better than you could have done. I said you should have had people in Marseille already. What were you all doing that was more important than this?"

She ignored the question. "What the hell even happened up there? How did Fournier manage to overpower both the others and start a bonfire?"

"I don't know. He was manic. Somehow he kept the others with him so that he could pull this stunt, but they can't have known what he had in mind. The big guy, the getaway driver, was out for the count. Pippin, the thief, was tied up at the back of the van. He was just watching."

There was something in her face when he mentioned Pippin, something unreadable.

"And you made sure to retrieve what was yours."

"Yes, actually. Like I said I would. Then I heard the police sirens. I don't know who called them. Maybe someone saw the fire."

"Couldn't you have tied them all up so they were there when the police arrived?"

"There wasn't time."

"You could have untied Pippin. There was time for that."

"Why would I do that?"

"Well, clearly he wasn't a willing participant."

"In the fire, no, but in the theft he was, wasn't he? What's this really about, Rose? Why wasn't your team there? You haven't answered that."

"All right, I'll tell you what this is about. My team wasn't there because they were on a crash mission to bring in an informant who's now disappeared. Her name's Zoe. I believe you've met."

If Rose's look was cold before, it was freezing now.

"In Grom's penthouse apartment?" she continued. "She decided to see if she could talk her way in, and you were already there. Offered her a drink, judging from those two glasses. What did you tell her, Fairchild? That messing around with people like Grom was easy? That anyone could do it? That she should carry on playing her little games?"

"What do you mean, disappeared?" A heaviness settled in the pit of his stomach. He'd worried about Zoe right from the start.

"Exactly that, Fairchild. Gone. She's been having a good old laugh, by the sound of it. Getting a tour of Grom's super-yacht by posing as his secretary. His secretary, Fairchild! The Russians spotted her. They found out where she lives. They cornered her coming out of work. She said Grom was due in Monaco. The Russians took all this literally. They're expecting Grom to arrive tomorrow. What do you think they'll do to her when he doesn't show up?"

Fairchild didn't want to think about that.

"When did you last see her?" he asked.

"I spoke to her yesterday. She phoned me just after it happened."

"Was she hurt?"

"Not seriously. Very shaken up, though. I sent her instructions to bring her in, but she didn't show."

"Where was this?"

"Monte Carlo. They were waiting for her outside the bank. They also sent someone to her flat in Nice. They associate her with Grom now. Think what that means. Did you put her up to it?"

Was that what she thought of him? "No, for Christ's sake! I had no idea who she was when she showed up at the flat. Then I realised she must be your informant at the bank. I warned her off, Rose. Told her not to mess with people like Grom."

"Well, clearly, whatever you said didn't have a great deal of impact. I can't get in touch and I have no idea where she is. This time tomorrow she'll probably be dead."

Her tone was too accusing for him to ignore.

"You're blaming me? She was your informant, Rose. You're the one who approached her and got her involved in this. Before that, she'd never have considered it. What did you say to her, to get her to start spying for you? What kind of warped justification did you give her? Did you tell her it was important for the defence of the realm? Did you promise her you'd keep her safe?"

He was spouting bile and it wasn't meant for Rose. It was the organisation she represented, the high-minded ease with which officers justified putting others in harm's way, their making light with human lives, their balancing of means versus ends, that could be used to explain away anything they wanted. How many people like Zoe had done what they were asked for good reasons, only to find their lives altered beyond all recognition and their fates written off, while the people they'd risked everything to help shrugged their shoulders and carried on?

"In case you'd forgotten," said Rose, "this whole operation is designed to disempower the man who killed your parents and came very close to killing you. You're just as much against Grom as we are. You may dislike any whiff of loyalty to queen and country, but about this we're on the same side, or so I thought. Zoe's role was already finished. She looked up a name, that's all. A name and an address. It was made very clear that was the end of the arrangement. And she was paid pretty generously for her trouble. Whatever she did later was her going completely off-piste. It wasn't in any way sanctioned by me and if I'd known about it I would have put a stop to it pretty sharply. Aside from the risks to herself, she's put the whole mission in jeopardy."

"Oh, I see." Fairchild couldn't stop himself. "You're concerned about her, but also the mission. Of course."

"Well yes, as a matter of fact. I'm not going to apologise to you because I believe in what I do. We make a difference, Fairchild. We save lives, though we're not perfect. The way you go about things, you don't seem too worried about that."

"You're accusing me of what, exactly?"

"Indifference. You're so caught up in your own crusade you're not looking out for anyone else. Your talents, Fairchild! Your skills! What could you do with those if you chose to? But instead you're intent on pursuing some personal crusade, even now, even though you've got the answers you were looking for. But it's not enough. It'll never be enough because you're locked in now to everything being about you and your parents and how you were betrayed and how unfair it all is. You recruit all these people to your cause but do they mean anything to you? Zoe may have worked for me, but if you said anything to encourage her in this, her blood is on your hands."

Fairchild couldn't trust himself to say much.

"I didn't."

"But you didn't tell me about it, did you? You managed to figure out she was involved, but you didn't say a word to me about what she was up to. What else have you messed with? Are you ever going to figure out whose side you're on? Or will you forever be happy in self-satisfied isolation, congratulating yourself on never getting your hands dirty with any cause except your own?"

A long pause. Fairchild felt the soft breeze, heard the buzz of conversation around him. It was as if she were writing the words with a knife on his skin. Did she know the impact she was having on him? He'd never told her how he felt about her, and he probably never would. It was his misfortune to be in love with someone who stood for everything he hated the most.

Her phone rang. She answered and her expression changed.

"When? Okay. Yes, send it."

She hung up and waited, looking at her screen. Something popped up. She stared at it, then looked up at him. He recognised what was etched into her face: fear.

"Well, I guess we were both wrong. Yvonne got a tip-off via Paris Station that some Russian claiming to represent Yunayev showed up at the office of the Monaco clearing agent this afternoon. Angry, shouting, accusing everyone of being in on a conspiracy. Threatened to break the receptionist's fingers, apparently. The police were called. Ollie just managed to talk his way in and view the CCTV footage."

She held up her phone. There on the screen was a photo of an old man with white hair, solidly built, less sure of himself than when Fairchild last saw him, his face angry, accusing.

"Not someone representing Yunayev," she said. "That is Yunayev. And Grom. And Khovansky. And Sutherland. He's broken all the rules and come here himself. He's desperate, Fairchild. And we know what desperate people do."

Fairchild didn't answer. He was thinking about the penthouse, sitting on the terrace with Zoe drinking the man's gin. A bright girl, a super-yacht, an informant in the wind. And now the worst possible news: the man had shown up, exactly where he was least expected.

"What do you want me to do?" he asked.

"Nothing," said Rose. "Go. Leave. You've done enough damage already. I knew it was a mistake asking for your help. Seriously, Fairchild, you could do anything, be anywhere. Go do something else. You're not wanted here."

Simple words, clearly spoken. But the feelings they prompted were harsh, turbulent, too painful to explore, too complex to express.

Without saying a word, he got up and left.

Chapter 46

It started as an idea, just a *what-if?*. Then it became a possibility, a *why-not?*. Now it was a certainty and it was happening today, had to happen today. Zoe couldn't quite believe it. She was watching herself doing these things, like it was someone else. She didn't do stuff like this. It was dangerous. Against the law. Maybe that made her a criminal. But that didn't seem to matter now. She'd gone so far and had to keep going. She couldn't return. It wasn't safe any more. Her old life, the old Zoe, was gone.

She'd stayed in a hotel last night. Quite a nice one. Why not? She had the money, or soon would. The hotel was in France half way between Nice and Monaco. They took a note of her ID card, but on paper, unlikely anyone would take much notice of it. She paid cash. They were surprised but didn't say anything. Zoe acted like it was the most natural thing in the world to produce a purse full of notes to pay for a hotel room. Some of these people must do it all the time. And starting from now, she'd become one of these people.

And today she came to work. Oh, they'd be watching, she knew that. Anna too, probably, and her people. But there were other ways in through the underground car park. She used a fire exit that should have been locked but never was. Waited to check whether anyone was loitering. Went up to the top then back down the stairs, the most round-about way to get in. From there she held her head up and walked in as if it were a perfectly normal day. If it turned out that it wasn't – if M. Bernard appeared, hovering, and invited her into his office – she'd just have to deal with whatever was coming. But M. Bernard didn't hover or summon her in. Everyone was perfectly, unsettlingly normal.

Zoe got to work. It would be her last day here and she had a lot to do.

Signore Moriotto had just instructed the bank to set up a new company in Monaco. With nominees as director and secretary. Zoe was the secretary and M. Bernard, unknowingly, the director. Signore Moriotto had an address in Monaco, and Monaco residency with all the correct identification as confirmed by the secretary. Signore Moriotto had big plans. He wanted a company set up in the Seychelles where he was expecting to deposit large sums of money. But Signore Moriotto was very shy. So his name didn't appear in any of the official paperwork for the company or its associated bank account. The nominees were dealing with all that – under his instruction, of course. In fact, the only named shareholder of the Seychelles company was Zoe herself.

Zoe had compiled a list of companies. To be on this list you needed to fulfil certain criteria. You needed the right nominees: Zoe as secretary and M. Bernard as director. There were many of these. You also needed large sums of money in the bank accounts of offshore companies accessible through a Monaco management company. Sums so large you wouldn't miss a little. And even if you did, it wouldn't cause hardship. You also needed to be a criminal. This was something Zoe had thought about a lot.

Who was a criminal and who wasn't? This was a matter of opinion since she would shortly be one herself now. Bad people, was what Zoe meant. Not which side of the law you were. Anna had shown her that. She went back to the research she'd done earlier, the Mexican, the Russian, the Korean, plenty of others. With her nominee powers, Zoe could transfer funds from the accounts of such people to an account like Moriotto's, for example, simply by claiming that she was doing it on request. She could also transfer funds from the Seychelles account into the Monaco account. Useful if Signore Moriotto had a requirement for cash here in Monaco. And it turned out that he did. The bulk of his holding would be in the Seychelles, but you always needed something in hand. Something liquid, acceptable and accessible. They did this kind of thing occasionally for some of their high-value clients – made substantial cash withdrawals and delivered them as requested. Sometimes to the client's local address, sometimes elsewhere. Of course they needed very precise instructions in writing to cover themselves. Zoe had ensured that Signore Moriotto, via his representatives, had been very clear where he wanted this cash to go, and it was all duly documented.

The fact that Signore Moriotto didn't exist was a minor issue. Her fabricated Italian businessman was only as obscure and distant as many of their clients. He was a business mogul, she had decided. Made a lot of money in the fashion world, at least that was the legitimate side of his affairs. She knew what he looked like, too: dark hair flecked with a little grey, older, distinguished, managing to stay trim, excellent taste in clothes. At home on a yacht, in a penthouse, behind the wheel of a Ferrari.

Between keeping on top of her regular administrative tasks, Zoe checked the balance of the various accounts. She had set up the Seychelles company the night she stayed over at work. She'd also authorised a number of transfers into that account. As soon as she had a positive balance, she requested a transfer to the account of the Monaco entity.

All these transactions required authorisation from M. Bernard as well. This was where the blank forms came in. Pre-signed blank pieces of paper with the signatures correctly placed so that the relevant form for that entity in that domain could be printed out, and they'd be signed in the right place. No need to trouble M. Bernard himself; he was a busy man after all. Zoe ensured the paperwork was all correctly filed.

Often a letter would be generated from the offshore entity documenting a withdrawal, redirected to the bank. Zoe kept an eye on the mail when it arrived that morning, and buried anything that looked relevant. Normally, they would put it in an envelope and forward it as instructed, but not these, not today. As for after today, well, everything would be different by then.

How long would it take, she wondered, for these people to notice? Maybe some of them wouldn't. It would depend who they had working for them. How carefully the accounts were scrutinised, how often the totals were checked. The thought made her heart jump in her chest, and interrupted her concentration. She could only bring herself to do this if she didn't think too much about what might happen. She needed to stay with what probably would happen, and when. That was a lot less scary.

She checked the Monaco account. The money had gone through. She had the paperwork ready and went down to the post room to book the security van for later that day. She stayed a while and chatted to the guys before booking the run. Early afternoon, she said. As good a time as any and (a thought she kept to herself) M. Bernard would still be at lunch.

Withdrawing cash needed signatures and cross-checks, so she was good and early for her colleagues in the retail section. It all followed the protocol and pretty soon the modest sum of two million Euros – mere spending money, a drop in the ocean compared with the new net worth of Signore Moriotto – had been packed in cases into the security van. Zoe also had some boxes brought up from the vault. Paperwork the bank had been storing for Signore Moriotto as a favour, she said. He'd now asked for them to be delivered with the cash. She had the documentation to prove it, of course. And where did the Italian gentleman want all this delivered? To his yacht, of course. This was Monaco. This kind of thing happened all the time. The van loaded, Zoe climbed into the front with the guys – always space for a little one – and they set off down to the port.

Chapter 47

Signore Moriotto wasn't, of course, there to sign for the delivery himself. Multi-millionaires had other people to do that kind of thing for them. A named representative of the port was on hand, as agreed in advance. Zoe had the paperwork to prove it, a letter from the man himself. Once everything was stowed away and signatures in place, she sent the security van back to the office. She wasn't going with them, she said; she had a few errands to run before returning to work. As soon as they'd gone, she got a taxi to M. Bernard's usual lunchtime restaurant. It was a wrench to leave the yacht loaded up as it was, but she could think of no other way, and this conversation with her soon-to-be-former boss was critical.

She was shown to his table. He'd finished lunch and was enjoying an espresso. His white tablecloth was unblemished: a proper, respectable man, when eating and in all things. He was of course surprised to see Zoe; she'd never done this before.

"Something's wrong? Some problem?"

Zoe sat down. "There's no problem at the office, if that's what you mean."

His face was a picture of puzzlement. "So, may I ask why you are here?"

Zoe made herself comfortable. She thought about ordering a drink but settled for a glass of water from the pitcher on the table.

"I'm afraid I have to hand in my notice."

He looked gratifyingly shocked. He probably thought she'd stay at the bank forever.

"Well, I'm sorry to hear that. Can I ask what your plans are?"

"Plans? Very open at the moment. Nothing definite. I'll be leaving straight away though. I won't be back at the office."

That puzzled look again. "Well, Zoe, you may be overlooking the fact that your contract includes a notice period which you're obliged to work."

"Yeah, maybe. But you've got bigger things to worry about than that." Zoe managed to sound regretful. "Some of your clients are probably going to get in touch. They may be wondering what's happened to their money. Only a bit of it. Just a little. They may be asking you to look into some recent transactions."

M. Bernard was looking unsettled. "I don't really understand what you mean."

"Do you know how many company accounts I am named on as secretary?"

He shook his head.

"Over three thousand. I mean, wow! I must be such an important person to have all that power! Except I'm not, am I? Because there's always another nominee, and often that's you, as company director. And besides, nominees only have the power to carry out what's specified in the management contract."

M. Bernard looked a little relieved. "What point are you making, Zoe? If this is some way of requesting a salary review, I'm sure —"

"But what if a nominee did something that wasn't in the management contract? An unauthorised transaction? Or maybe quite a lot of them?"

M. Bernard's relief vanished. "Well, that would be – I mean, the bank, as you know Zoe, the business of the bank—"

"Is trust? Yeah, I know that. I've heard you say it often enough. Which is why you have a little bit of a problem now. Because that trust has been breached. Sorry."

She waited for the penny to drop.

"By – you?" He sounded so sceptical.

"Yes. By me." She made her voice sympathetic, a doctor delivering an unwelcome prognosis. "You see, you need clients to trust you. But you trusted your own employees a little too much, Monsieur. All those blank authorisation forms just sitting in a filing cabinet."

His jaw fell. "But – I never expected…"

"No, you didn't. Nobody did. Nobody does. But why not? Other people do. Some people are expected to break confidences, break trust, break the law. Others aren't. Who decided which was which?"

M. Bernard looked angry. "If you've done this, you've betrayed the trust I put in you, Zoe! I gave you a good job, didn't I? Treated you well? How many years have you worked for me?"

"Yes, and that ought to be enough. I should be satisfied with that. Being paid little more than a living wage, commuting in by train because I can't afford to live here, my salary eaten up with living costs, while the people we serve have millions. Billions! Way more than anyone needs. And how do they get these massive sums of money? They break the law. Some of them, anyway. They steal. They extort. They take bribes. So, who says it's okay for them and not for me? That's what I started wondering. I'm still wondering now."

He was shaking his head. "Zoe, I don't know what foolish thing you've done, but you'll never get away with it. We have checks in place, warnings, processes."

"If they worked, you'd know about this already. They could all be bypassed by someone who knows the system. Your clients are going to want to know how that was possible. I could tell you, I guess. But by the time the questions really start, I'll be long gone."

Now he was furious. "You're not going anywhere. I'm calling the police!"

He reached for his jacket. Zoe touched his arm.

"I wouldn't do that. You said your business was trust. Getting the police involved is going to bring that trust to an end quite fast, don't you think?"

Would he listen? Would he bite? If he didn't, Zoe was as good as dead.

He paused. His shoulders slumped. He was listening, at least.

"I'm a bad girl. I accept that. When people start to ask where their money is, you'll want to lay it all on me. And hey, you'd be right. Except for all those security issues that allowed me to do it in the first place. Maybe the business can survive that. I didn't steal from all your clients. Only the ones who deserved it, and had plenty to lose. They're a shy bunch, aren't they? For good reasons. I know what those reasons are. So if there's a public outcry from anyone about what happened to their funds, there'll also be a public exposé about where those funds came from, who exactly the beneficial owners are, and what kind of things they do. I can link it all up, see. Do exactly what these people don't want anyone doing. Connect them with their ill-gotten fortunes. That's not great for you either, is it? People might start to ask why you didn't mind servicing gangsters and drug-runners and murderers."

M. Bernard glanced around as if saying those words out loud were taboo.

"I did due diligence," he protested.

"But it didn't work, did it? If you were serious about it, none of these people would have been on your books at all. It was just a paper exercise. Just for the files."

He shrugged. "Well, if what you say is true, I don't need to do anything. Such people won't tolerate some young woman waltzing off with their money. They will find you themselves. You can't hide forever, not from people like that."

"Not without some help. But you're going to help me, M. Bernard."

Now he started to smile, but it was his cold smile, like they all were.

"I don't think so."

"Well, I do."

Zoe paused to pour herself more water. M. Bernard didn't move. He had to know what she was talking about. He was hooked. She enjoyed the moment. When she was ready, she resumed.

"Bearer shares. They're a bit like gold. That's what you say, don't you? A commodity that can be bought and sold. You don't have to pass them around for them to change hands. They can stay locked in a bank. The share registers show who owns them. So the share certificates themselves aren't needed, as long as they're safely in the bank. Right?"

He looked cautious, trying to figure out where she was going. She continued.

"But who would know if they weren't in the bank? Have any of our clients ever shown up, saying I just want to check that my bearer shares are still stored in your vault?"

M. Bernard was pale. "Zoe, what have you done?"

"Do you know how many bearer shares are in the vault right now?"

He shook his head, eyes wide. "A few thousand, who knows?"

"None. There are no bearer shares at all in the vault."

His hand clenched. "Then where are they?"

"Safely in my custody. And that's where they'll stay. I'm going to take very good care of them. Don't worry about that. As long as I'm okay and in good health, and am enjoying my freedom, those bearer shares will be as safe as anything, just as if they were still in the vault. No one will have any reason to doubt that's where they are."

M. Bernard half stood, then sat again, a distracted look on his face.

"But," continued Zoe, "if anything happens to me, that would change. Say I died suddenly, or disappeared. It would all come out then. Or if I was arrested. Or threatened. I may not be able to look after them so well, see. I may feel the need to confess to what I've done. Which would be the end of the bank, I think. Don't you? I've set it up so that these things will happen if I'm not around any more."

This was a lie, as of now. She hadn't had time to do all this. But with the services of a lawyer she knew she could, pretty easily.

"I can't believe…" His voice was hoarse.

"Take a look when you get back. It was quite easy, I have to tell you. Careful no one gets too curious about what you're doing down there. From the outside everything looks normal. They're just – not there."

"But…anyone could ask. Anyone, at any time, could ask to see them."

"But like I said, how many times has that happened? Not in my time at the bank. And if they could be persuaded that photographic evidence is okay, maybe I could help. Perhaps even if some real stickler wants to count his actual shares, something could be arranged. If you and I stay on good terms. I'll take good care of them. Imagine me as an extension of your vault. Just that to get into it, you have to be nice to me."

A long silence. The implications were sinking in. And also, what M. Bernard would have to do if he had any chance at all of being able to ride this out. Zoe had thrown him a lifeline, a way of saving his livelihood, his reputation. But it also involved saving her.

"So you see," she said, "it's really in your interests that nothing bad happens to me. Think about that when the questions start coming from those clients. Maybe the discrepancies could be written off as – administrative errors."

Of course Bernard would have to stump up the money to rectify these so-called errors. That was his problem. Zoe had always suspected her boss secretly had a pretty high net worth himself. And if it weren't enough he could borrow, couldn't he? He was a banker after all.

The restaurant was almost empty. She should be getting back to the yacht. She stood. He barely registered.

"Well, goodbye, Monsieur," she said politely. "I'll be in touch. Let's both try and stay safe, shall we?"

He sat, still as a statue, as she walked out of the restaurant.

Chapter 48

It was, Rose admitted to herself, not much more than a hunch which caused her to get on a train to Arles. Very similar to the hunch which took Fairchild to Marseille. It turned out he was right, though. She hoped she was too, as to say the team was stretched would be an understatement. Ollie and Yvonne were in Monaco trying to cover the penthouse building, the super-yacht and as much of the bank as they could. As time went by it became less and less likely they'd catch up with Zoe, and they urgently needed to focus more on their prime target. Grom was what this was all about, and that was why Rose was in Arles. But she wasn't ready to give up on Zoe just yet, so she came alone. And besides, this was only a hunch.

Rose was keeping Walter reasonably up to date. He knew about their missing informant, and he knew about Grom's unexpected presence in Monaco. He'd also come back and confirmed what Rose had already realised about the mysterious Pippin. But what to do about it? This started as a search for one man and his wealth. Now they were trying to find three different people: Grom, Pippin and Zoe. And Rose hadn't yet told Walter that she'd ejected Fairchild from the team. She had no regrets, but Walter wouldn't see it her way. In her last briefing she was circumspect about who was where, and avoided the topic of Fairchild completely. Walter also didn't know about the moped rider or the man in the red shirt, a matter which had by necessity been shoved to the bottom of the pile.

So why, if they were so short of people, was Rose in Arles? This had to do with a big unanswered question: where was Grom's painting? Police reports confirmed it wasn't part of the stash on Gustave's bonfire. Somewhere between the Freeport and Marseille it had gone missing. It could only have been taken by one of the thieves. In Gustave's care it would have ended up in flames. The driver could have taken it. Would he have known what to do with it? And then were was Pippin. Pippin, who had the *Letters of Van Gogh* in his room. What if he got his hands on it? Knowing what she knew now, that idea opened a whole new raft of possibilities.

Hiding something valuable didn't necessarily mean locking it up. It could simply mean putting it somewhere no one would think of looking. Except maybe someone who knew you very well. Thinking afresh about motivations and where they might lead, weighing up all the options, that was what had sent Rose to Arles.

She started with the Yellow House, Van Gogh's own name for his home here, which he dreamed of turning into an artist's colony. The Yellow House didn't exist any more, having been bombed accidentally by the Allies during the Second World War. An irony that seemed to sit nicely with the constant misfiring and self-destruction that marked Van Gogh's life. Rose was hoping there'd be something here, a memorial, a token, a wall or building of some kind. But no. It was, disappointingly, just a piece of green space in the middle of a traffic roundabout.

Where else? In her head Rose saw a painting of a cafe with tables outside under a night sky filled with luminous stars. And another of a late-night bar, people sitting alone in a dimly-lit room. But there was also the hospital, with its cloistered garden, a place of recovery for the troubled artist. She went there next. As she'd expected, tourists thronged the yellow arches. The information boards showed Van Gogh's paintings of the garden. You could tell, more or less, where he'd been when he painted them – in an upstairs room. Upstairs was closed to the public. No matter.

Rose made a number of circuits of the garden to check out the most likely-looking doors. Upstairs was some kind of staffing area, the entrances protected by a combination code. She could, if she stayed in the right place, observe someone punching it in, but it was a tiny place and not much traffic came through at all. In the end she got lucky. A staff member breezed out at some pace and let the door close behind them, except that it didn't quite click to, and Rose could saunter up and push it open.

She crept upstairs and found offices and storage rooms, random furniture and objects. What a waste. As she worked her way silently round the upper floor, she didn't encounter anyone. The historic spot where Van Gogh must have been when he painted the garden was marked by desks, boxes and shelves. She started rifling through them.

Voices approached. She ducked down behind a desk and two people chatting walked straight past. She waited until they had gone then continued searching, not really knowing what it would look like but confident she'd recognise it when she found it.

And she did. In the bottom of a deep musty-smelling drawer she caught sight of something older and rougher that didn't belong. Nestled within tubes of paper was a rolled canvas, smaller than she'd expected. She picked it up.

He'd brought it home. He'd brought the thing the closest place to home he could think of. What Rose didn't know was whether he expected someone to find it. Or was he hoping this would be some kind of final resting place?

She wouldn't risk causing damage by unrolling it; this was definitely the portrait. She stowed it in her bag and left. Now back to Grom, back to Zoe. She tried to enjoy the walk through the historic town centre without thinking about what was stashed in her backpack. But she felt her neck prickling. That sophisticated internal warning system was clanging, telling her something was wrong. An instinct so deep she couldn't pinpoint what had set it off.

She quickened her pace through the narrow lanes. Walking fast down a long straight road she made a sudden turn into a smaller side street. She was at a disadvantage; she wasn't expecting this and didn't know the town. She got out her phone and called up a map, but doing this on the fly was difficult. She stopped abruptly next to a tourist trinket shop, glanced in the window and looked back. A guy walking along, hands in his pockets, stopped just after she had. He didn't look at her. He was fumbling in his pockets, as if his phone had just gone off. But then she saw his lips move. She went cold. That guy wasn't alone.

She glanced the other way. Clear so far, from what she could tell. She set off and hung a left, checking she was still heading towards the train station. The street bent round ahead of her. Behind, she knew the guy was there. He wasn't exactly subtle. He had Russian secret service written all over him. They didn't have to be subtle. There wasn't much they needed to be afraid of.

She turned a corner and a man sitting at a table outside a cafe raised his head and looked at her. Her breath caught in her throat. It was the guy on the moped. He turned away, speaking into his phone. Coincidence? No way. It was the same guy, and he'd been looking out for her.

She could go right or left before she reached the cafe. She checked the map again as she walked. Right would take her up to the amphitheatre, left down to the river. Right was better. But at the next right, she glanced up and a woman walking down towards her caught her eye. She then looked past Rose, but it was too late to disguise the recognition. Rose sped up and carried on. A street on the left was clear; she took it.

Out of sight of the watchers she broke into a run and darted left then left again to double back on herself. But somehow the first guy was already there, just standing and watching. She turned back the way she came. Now the woman was approaching, no longer trying to hide her interest. Rose turned again and continued down. She needed to loop back but was running out of space. She tried a right but the street bent round and came out at the cafe where the moped guy was sitting before. He was standing now, waiting for her. And when he saw her, he started out towards her.

Back down, then, towards the river. It was the only route open to her. And that was when she realised she was being pushed in that direction. The lack of subtlety was deliberate. She was being caught in a trap.

She could still outrun them, or out-manoeuvre them. She came out on the road by the river. There was no bridge nearby. Her three pursuers emerged behind her. She broke into a sprint along the embankment. Maybe she could break free of them and shout for help, claim it was a mugging.

A screech of car tyres made her accelerate. Her breath rasped. She was sprinting so hard her legs burned. She was ahead of them all, but they were close enough that she could hear them breathing.

A black car with tinted windows mounted the kerb in front of her. She dodged but it left no space to get past. Two guys got out. They spread, cutting her off. It was no use. She was trapped. The three watchers came up behind her. She couldn't get away from them now.

The back door of the car opened and a man got out. Well dressed, white hair, solidly built, less solid than when she last saw him. More gaunt, more determined. Suddenly Rose had no breath left in her. There was a pause. Everyone waited.

"Hello, Rose," said Grom. "Let's take a ride."

Chapter 49

Fairchild didn't have to work hard to discover which was Grom's super-yacht. From the walkway on the level above, he saw two goons standing, arms folded, staring into one of the shiny white giants while their colleagues moved around on board turning the place over. A port official of some kind was standing nearby, nervously talking into a mobile phone. This wasn't an official search. The Russians were systematically ransacking Grom's possessions, looking for the portrait, yes, but also just grabbing whatever they could. No sign of Rose's posse watching here. No sign of Zoe either. If she showed up she'd be in a lot of trouble.

The proceedings were attracting stares. Fairchild watched briefly, then walked on and called in at the harbourside office of one of Monaco's premier yacht brokers. He could have browsed in the window, but like a genuinely high-net-worth individual he walked straight in and engaged the sales manager with a set of informed questions that a well-heeled resident new to Monaco might have about the ins and outs of owning one of these boats. The sales manager, a boarding-school-English gentleman with blond hair and a blazer, helped him out for some time before Fairchild steered the conversation where he wanted it.

"So, the one out there? There seems to be something going on with it. I hate to be indelicate, but it looks like some kind of repossession to me. Maybe someone's called in the administrators?"

The manager knew what he meant. "There's been some speculation about it today. Not on our books, though, that one."

"Curious," said Fairchild. "If it were up for a quick sale, I might be interested. It would need some work but it's along the lines of what I'm after. I could do with spending the money fast, if you know what I mean."

The two salesmen exchanged glances and the other one picked up the phone. "Let me see what I can find out," he said.

The blazered salesman showed him brochures of sleek modern craft, and explained the merits of buying an existing yacht versus the preferred current trend of having one purpose-built, until the phone calls yielded something.

"Apparently it's changed hands very recently. The owner's picked up a smaller sailboat at *Port de Fontvieille*. He must have sold to a dealer. At quite a low price probably, given it was all done in a hurry. Want me to investigate?"

"What kind of price?" asked Fairchild.

The broker told him. Some staggering amount.

"And what about this other craft, the sailboat?"

Downsizing didn't sound like Grom. Was he planning some kind of daring escape by sea? Or maybe someone else was.

"A classic forty-footer, I'm told. Completely different. Not worth anything like the one out there."

"And it's at Fontvieille?" The neighbouring Monaco port. The conversation moved on to the principality's berthing options and eye-watering fees. Fairchild made his excuses as politely as he could, and left.

He jumped into a bateau-bus to cross the port, then a taxi round to Fontvieille, the other side of Monaco's royal palace. It wouldn't be long before it occurred to the Russians to do a bit of research on top of old-fashioned looting and intimidation. They could have done that already and be there right now, but their focus still seemed to be very much on the dumped super-yacht. At the other port he scanned for traditional forty-foot sailboats. He didn't know what, or who, to expect when he found it. So it was relief he felt when he caught sight of an athletic, dark-skinned figure busy on the deck of a classic wooden yacht named *Ocean Joy*.

He was only just in time. She was coiling the last rope just as he got there.

"So you know your way around a yacht, then?" he called out, trying to sound casual.

Zoe looked up. She was alert, pre-occupied. When she saw Fairchild she glanced around, watchful.

"I know enough."

The sun was behind her. Fairchild had to shield his eyes to look up at her. Why was he so nervous? In this state of mind everything seemed to get to him.

"Where's your crew?"

"You're looking at it."

"You're going single-handed?"

Impressive, or foolhardy, one or the other.

"There's no one I can take. Not on this journey." For the first time he heard some stress in her voice.

"It's quite a journey, too," he said.

"You don't know where I'm going."

"I don't mean where in the world. I mean the path you've chosen. They'll be after you, Zoe. You're ahead of them now. Do you know how to stay ahead?"

She looked at him calmly. She knew the situation she was in, what she was doing. For now.

"You've done well getting this far," he said. "The Russians are on board the other yacht right now, pulling it apart. They'll pull you apart if they find you. Did you know that Yunayev is in Monaco?"

She stared. That was news to her. But she recovered herself.

"Well, I'm not intending to stay."

"Good."

She was doing the right thing, thankfully. Rose had burned a hole in him with her words, shown him a picture of himself that he hated, though recognised. It was over, that much was clear. Whatever was between them, from her side a grudging need, from his a deep unwanted obsession, she had brought a stop to it, and the rising waters of panic, the fear that froze him, feeling the emptiness that would be left after she were gone from his life, that was for him to deal with. Probably a good thing, anyway, he'd told himself a thousand times. It was unhealthy for both of them.

Rose was right; the world was big and there were plenty of places he could go to be away from her. He should have left already but couldn't simply walk out without trying to make things right. He needed to reinvent himself and come to terms with an existence that didn't include Rose. He also had to make sure, as far as he was able, that Zoe was okay. Standing on that jetty it suddenly came to him that he could do both at once.

"Take me with you," he said.

Her eyes widened. He could hear the neediness in his own voice. He tried to skate over it.

"I can help you. I can give you the skills you need to survive. The contacts. If this is really what you choose, this life. And besides, it sounds like you could do with a crew."

Her eyes narrowed. "Why do you want to?"

"Because – I owe it to someone."

"Who? Why?"

Direct questions, but he had no direct answers. Guilt, shame, self-loathing, a need to make amends, get at least one small piece of all this right, even if the rest of it were so grubby and wrong. And then the idea, born in that moment, seeing Zoe standing barefoot on the deck, the sun behind her, the sleek hull below representing escape and cutting through the waves and the wideness of the ocean, that this might be how he could disappear, get away from this crushing angst and be somewhere else.

"I like you," he said. "You've got style. You're good. But you're not good enough, not without help. I don't want to see you a few days from now washed ashore with a bullet in your head. Those people, Zoe, they're not going to give up. You've outsmarted them better than most people could have done. But there are things you need to know. People you need to know. I can help you."

He was repeating himself. She was listening, not just to his words but his tone, what he wasn't saying.

"Why else?" she asked. "Why do this for me? You don't owe me anything."

He could try the truth. It didn't hurt every now and then.

"I need to get away from here. It's gone wrong for me here. I just need to leave. I need to leave now. Will you take me?"

She thought for a few more seconds then nodded him on board.

With a slow motor they edged out of the marina into the open water. She got him to work straight away. She was competent and could have managed alone, but he knew enough about yachts to make himself useful. She set sail as soon as she could, running south east with a solid breeze behind them, the sun sparkling on the surface of the waves.

In a short while, Monaco was visible no more.

Chapter 50

Pippin had nothing left now, no more reserves. Pippin was becoming undone, fraying at the edges, blurring and smudging and cracking. He couldn't stop crying. The heat of the flame, the blistering of paint, the splintering of canvas played in his head over and over again. A silhouette of a stranger walking away. Gustave, falling back, blood spray catching in the firelight.

After they left the sirens behind, Clem kept going, out of the city and further still. A sudden lurch and they were bumping violently like they were driving over rough ground. They stopped. It was quiet. When Clem opened the van door, Pippin could see nothing behind the man's shoulders, no lights or shapes.

Clem untied him long enough to drink from a water bottle, then secured his wrists again and slammed the door shut. The van rocked as Clem climbed into the front, but there was no more movement all night. Pippin shivered in the back and was woken by the heat when the sun came up and warmed the sides of the van. Hour after hour, hotter and hotter. Clem moved about, out of the front seat and in again, talking on the phone. Out again, the door slammed, footsteps led away. Then back again and the van door opened. Clem had a baguette and a bottle of water. He untied Pippin and stood watching as Pippin ate and drank. He let Pippin out for a toilet break. Pippin saw a flat beach, wind-battered flags, rough grassland.

"Come, sit," said Clem when Pippin had finished. He was sitting on the back of the van. Pippin joined him. They stared out at the featureless sea, ivory with a tint of blue under a blanched sky.

"I need that painting," said Clem. "People want it, people from my world. You don't say no to these people. They're serious people. Powerful. Lots of friends around here. You tell me where it is, they take it, we're finished. You go your way, I go mine. Don't lie to me, Pippin. You already told me you know where it is."

A long silence. When would this end, this chasing of money? What did these serious people want with a Van Gogh? Would they appreciate the brushwork, admire the energy, gaze at the colours, reflect on its influence? It was just money to them, nothing else, a prize, a trophy.

Pippin was broken. Pippin had little left to give. Pippin would not be rescued. Pippin had nobody. This should be over already. But he couldn't give it up. Not yet.

"I thought we were doing a deal," he said. "You shift it, we split the prize fifty-fifty. It seems fair to me. We need each other."

Clem shifted his weight. The van creaked.

"You need to understand these friends of mine. They're Russians, you see. To them, the painting is theirs. They want it back. They know you have it. They won't bargain. I can't let you go until you tell me. So it's a new deal now. The painting for your freedom. That's the only offer."

He folded his arms and stared out to sea. He wasn't a man who was afraid of silence.

Pippin persisted.

"You never mentioned these friends before. I thought you were just in it for the money."

"None of us were in it for the money. Except maybe Henri. Gustave wanted to burn all of it. I had my orders from the Russians. They heard about a plan to rob the Freeport and wanted me to be part of it. And you… well, you're not really a thief at all, are you, Pippin?"

Pippin stopped breathing. Clem continued in his low grainy voice.

"I know about that. So do the Russians. They know who you met in Arles, and why."

Pippin could hear no sound except a faint rustling of the wind.

"How do they know?" he asked.

Clem shrugged. "These Russians have many friends. People who tell them things."

"But no one knew about that!"

"Someone must have. In Arles, you didn't tell your contact about the painting, or where it was. And then you returned to Nice, to your room, where Gustave could so easily find you. You make life difficult for yourself, Pippin. Time to make things easier. Tell me where you put it. Then this can come to an end."

Pippin wanted it to end. But still, he wasn't sure he could let it go.

"If all you wanted was the painting," he said, "you should have taken it that first night. You could have driven off in the van with everything. But instead you carried on with Gustave."

"The painting isn't the only thing they want. They want the man who bought it, too. They came looking for the portrait. I brought them to the van. But you'd already taken it by then. Left the empty frame behind. I knew it was you. But robbing the Freeport wasn't your idea. It was Gustave's. Where did that idea come from?"

"They thought Gustave was working with someone? The owner of the painting? Why would he get his own painting stolen?"

"To hide it from Russia," said Clem simply.

"And you? Do you think Gustave was secretly working for someone?"

Clem gave a humourless smile. "Gustave was full of noise. He had no contacts in Marseille, maybe not even in Paris. When I realised that, I shot him." He said it flat, with no emotion. "We should never have bothered with him. We should have come straight to you. Maybe you're working for this guy they call Khovansky. That's what they think now. That you've given the painting to him."

"I haven't given it to anyone," said Pippin. "I've hidden it."

It was enough, now, he thought. He could give it up now, finally walk away.

"Where?" Clem's rasping voice dropped to a new low.

"I took it home."

"Home?"

"Back to where it came from. Where it belongs."

Clem looked blank.

"It's in Arles. In the hospital. Where Van Gogh stayed, after he… in an upstairs room."

"You give me the exact name," said Clem. "The exact location. They will send someone. When they find it – I let you go."

"You promise?" Pippin heard his voice break.

Clem heard it too. He nodded. "I promise."

Pippin told him what he wanted to know. Clem locked Pippin back in the van and made a phone call. Then nothing. More nothing. The sun went down. It got cold. Another long night shivering in that van. What did it mean? Pippin thought he knew what it meant. The painting wasn't there any more.

No more visits from Clem. The next morning the engine started and they set off. Another unbearably long journey. It was always Clem they should have looked out for. Gustave was just noise, wind in the trees, a storm passing overhead. Clem was the tide behind the waves, the bricks that made up the wall, the rock on which they built their mad little scheme. Clem was often silent but always had a plan, had his orders right from the start.

Hours went by of long flat driving. Then a change. Uphill, round bends, winding up and up. Third gear, second gear. A slowing down. The crunch of an unmade road. Then a stop. Voices, Clem and an intercom. A pause, a jerk back into movement but slower. A sweep around, almost a full circle, then they came to a halt. Clem got out and opened the back. He untied Pippin and flung the doors wide, stepping back to get a cigarette out. He lit it and took a drag, looking up at the sky.

Pippin rubbed his wrists and ankles. He shuffled to put his feet on the ground and almost fell as he tried to stand. He took a few steps forward and felt dizzy. He looked around. It was daylight, afternoon maybe. They were on a wide driveway in front of a flight of steps. At the top, a row of white columns and in the middle a heavy wooden door. Green gardens were laid out all around, manicured lawns, topiaried bushes, ornamental trees in terracotta pots. The building stretched away, white and rectangular, large windows framed with climbing plants, their flowers saffron and plum. Behind the house the ground dropped away and the sea rose to an ultramarine horizon.

Clem was still watching him.

"There's no point in running," he said. "The grounds are fully secured and guards are patrolling everywhere. You can't get away."

Pippin nodded. He wasn't sure he could run anyway.

"Your place?" He wanted to see if Clem would smile.

Clem didn't. "Belongs to some friends."

At that moment the door opened. Two men walked out and stood at the top of the steps. Big, well-built men, tattoos on their arms, hair short like Clem's.

"Good friends?" asked Pippin, his mouth dry.

"Russian friends."

They all stared at each other.

"Don't make this messy," said Clem. "The painting isn't where you said it was. They checked."

He looked around. "This place we're in, it belonged to the guy who stole the painting. Khovansky. They got the house back, and now they want the painting, and they want him. It's a very nice house. Very exclusive. Very private. Nobody comes here." He stared at Pippin. "No more lies, Pippin. They will get you to talk. Look after yourself. I give you this advice."

Clem's face was dark as he stepped back. The two Russians came down the steps and took Pippin by the arms.

Chapter 51

They were speeding back towards Marseille. It was a plush car, of course. Leather seats, tinted windows, the works. Rose wouldn't have expected anything else from Grom. The man sitting next to her was ruthless in the pursuit of his own ends. He had a generous sense of his own worth.

"Go on, then," said the man she'd spent the last six months trying to bankrupt. "Ask me how I came to be on your tail. I know you want to know."

Rose wouldn't give him the satisfaction. "You're the kind of person who needs to be congratulated, are you? Told how clever you are?"

"I can smell MI6 a mile off." It sounded like he was going to tell her anyway. "I saw your people in Monaco, hanging around my flat. Had you followed to your place in Nice."

That didn't tally. Ollie and Yvonne were good at what they did. So was she. And it didn't explain why the moped rider was already following her in Nice just after they arrived.

"When I heard you were involved I wasn't surprised," he was saying. "I guessed they might have got you involved. That's how they work. If someone has an 'in', they're persuaded to make best use of it. You have an 'in' with me, they reasoned. Probably that slimy tart Walter. Ergo, I'm your responsibility. You're so blindly ambitious you ignored how warped that really was and took the role anyway."

Rose had multiple reasons to be afraid of this man. But no way was she going to let it show.

"An 'in'? Is that what you call it when someone tries to kill you?"

He feigned surprise. "You mean Georgia? I didn't try to kill you. I put you in a situation where you might easily have died. It was immaterial to me whether you actually did or not. You're unimportant. You know that really. That's why you're so keen to develop your career. It helps you make you think you're somebody. But actually you're nobody. Ordinary. Boring Surrey stock. Middle-class nothing."

"Whereas you are terribly important, I can tell. You've spent your life trying to prove it by messing up other people. As long as you're doing something exceptional it doesn't matter if it's good or bad. The suffering of others, even complete innocents, is irrelevant, if it demonstrates your greatness."

He seemed to find that funny. "It really cut you up, didn't it, your Georgian experience? Crammed into that fortress with the shells raining down day and night. Plenty of innocents suffering there. Of course you blame me for it all."

"You set me up. You tricked me into going there. For some feud that had nothing to do with me. Some baseless grudge against John Fairchild. I was just an instrument."

"You're welcome to blame me if you want. You were stupid enough to go there, and ignore all the obvious signs that it was a trap. And your idiotic boss Craven."

That rankled. Her Moscow boss Peter Craven was a good all-round guy, but he had to return to the UK after being shot by one of Grom's thugs.

"I didn't prompt Russia to invade Georgia," Grom continued. "That was the Kremlin. I don't make people what they are. Greedy, cruel, insecure, bitter. I see all that and I make something of it. You do the same. We were both trained by the same organisation, after all."

"I'm not like you. I do this for a purpose."

"Ah, the ends justify the means! That's important to you, isn't it? National security. Saving lives. It makes you sleep better at night about the things you make people do."

"I don't suppose sleeping at night has ever been a problem for you."

"No, it hasn't."

"So where are we going?"

He ignored the question. "I'd like to see it, please. My painting."

She gave him a blank look.

"Oh, come now, Rose. You came to Arles to pick up the painting. Why else would you come all the way out here when the rest of your unit is off trying to cover fourteen positions at once? You made some arrangement with one of those thieves, you picked it up, and it's in your bag. And I want it."

He held his hand out. Rose hesitated, then got it out and passed it to him. He unrolled it on his lap. A thin piece of paper had been placed on the surface of the paintwork to protect it. Inside was a tube keeping the whole thing rigid. It was, given everything, reasonably well protected although a professional art courier would probably have been horrified.

Grom removed the paper and examined the painting, a thoughtful expression on his face. Rose looked across, curious at this object they'd all been chasing for so long. She'd always only seen great masters framed and on the walls in art galleries. This little piece of canvas seemed inconsequential presented like this. Unbelievable what it was worth.

"Amazing," said Grom, echoing her thoughts. "I mean, it served a purpose. I needed to offload money. Silly, silly money but I shifted it. That's what art is good for, all a big conceit but useful. I can't see much merit in the piece itself. Some nutcase failure of an artist who happens to have caught on in recent years paints a fond portrait of his doting overindulgent brother, and the world swoons. I suppose you love the thing."

That last was directed at Rose.

"I know what it's worth to you," she said. "It's pretty much the only thing you've got left. They've taken everything else. Lose that as well, and you're a debtor. It doesn't sound all that clever to me."

Grom's face seemed to set. So that was what Grom looked like when he was angry. Perhaps she should have a greater sense of self-preservation but she didn't have much to lose. He could kill her any time if he chose to.

"So what's your plan now?" she asked. "Why do you need me? You've got the painting. This isn't about Fairchild again, is it? You may be disappointed there. I sent him away, you see. He's probably long gone by now. So whatever you do to me would achieve nothing except satisfy your own sadistic urges. Again."

Grom was still looking at the painting. His hand hovered over it and traced the direction of the brush strokes. Maybe he was more appreciative of this masterpiece than he was letting on. He gave Rose a dismissive glance.

"You may have some value to someone. We'll find out, I expect."

They'd skirted Marseille and were still going east, towards Nice, but on the coast road now. There was no point sitting there in silence. She may as well find out what she could.

"You'll be wanting to get out of the country now, I guess."

"That's your interrogation technique, is it?"

Lightly said, but heavy on the irony. She tried another tack.

"Okay, how about this for a question? Why did you betray your country? What had Britain ever done to hurt you? Where did that even come from?"

He looked up, less dismissively now. "You have a lot of faith, don't you, in good old Blighty. How far back do you remember? Oh, you probably weren't even born. You don't know about standards of living in the fifties, the sixties, the seventies. It wasn't great, let me tell you. America had it all but good old GB was neither one thing nor the other. Didn't want socialism but didn't much like capitalism either. There was a lot of propaganda about the USSR. Sure there was censorship, but let's be honest, how important is freedom of speech? Most ordinary people have nothing of interest to say anyway. In the Eastern Bloc, if you kept out of trouble you could enjoy a good education, a good healthcare service, a guaranteed job. Was that so bad? You could travel as well, to anywhere on that side, which was a lot of countries back then. Countries people in the West were embarrassingly ignorant of. Still are. All dog food and gulags, that was the image everyone had. Our home country, Rose, has always had a blind faith in its own rightness, perpetuated by a narrow gene pool of public schoolboys who had no idea what life was really like in an inner city high rise, in slum housing or some grim town with no economy. It was all self-preservation really."

They were gradually ascending a switchback road, each turn revealing stunning views of the coastline, towns perched on green hillsides, beaches nestled within sweeping bays.

"Baloney," said Rose. "You're not interested in the ordinary man. You have no principles whatsoever. This was personal. Something pissed you off. You just don't want to say what it was. Maybe you don't even know. Or maybe it was nothing. You wanted to feel important, have an influence, sing to the world, only you had no tune. Maybe that was all there was to it. Then after you started, you perpetuated it by continuing with some grudge in an attempt to give your life meaning. Fairchild's parents – why go after them ten years later? And why target their son? He had nothing to do with any of it. You were looking for a fight. What's that line from Macbeth? 'Full of sound and fury, signifying nothing.'"

"Got a lot to say, haven't you?"

"What's that, an old-fashioned view of women? We should shut up, should we? I was rather thinking you'd gone a bit quiet yourself. Maybe there are some things you don't want to talk about."

She was playing with fire, baiting the guy. But he might give something of himself away. A pause, then:

"John Fairchild. You like to hold him at arm's length but you owe him a lot, actually. You'd have lost your job if it weren't for him. What would you be now? A bank clerk? An insurance saleswoman? But no, he saved you from all that and became your way back in. Then your peripheral involvement in all of this gets you some big promotion. One you don't deserve, that's pretty obvious. Yes, you've done well out of John Fairchild. But you won't be honest about it. That's the modern woman, isn't it? Just as dependent on men as you ever were, but you won't admit it any more. You sent him away? Nonsense. The idea that someone like you could send someone like him away! As if he's on a leash."

He laughed quietly and his gaze returned to the canvas on his knee.

Two interesting things about that, thought Rose, intellectualising her way out of the rising mist of anger. One – he knew a lot more about her than she was comfortable with, even her role within MI6 after he'd left Russia and the resources of the FSB behind him. Two – he actually admired John Fairchild. It made sense in a way. They had certain things in common.

With the most gentle of touches, Grom repositioned the paper over the surface of the painting and rolled it up again on his knee. He levered the roll into a backpack that was by his feet, fastened it tightly and put it by his side on the seat, keeping his hand on it as though it were a favourite pet.

They drove on in silence, winding ever upward.

Chapter 52

Once the sails were set and the course steady, they sat on deck, Zoe at the helm, Fairchild barefoot stretched out on the starboard side. Silence for half an hour, then Fairchild asked:

"So what's the plan?"

"Corsica. Plenty of places there to load up."

"And then what?"

A small shrug. Out here some of Zoe's bravado had melted.

"Corsica is quite an obvious destination from Monaco. Someone on your tail will look there for sure."

"Then we just have to be quick. Stop overnight, set sail at dawn."

"That's not quick enough." She already knew that, he could tell. "You can't outrun them. They can always get there faster."

"Then what?"

"Outsmart them. Like you have already. But if you want an easier life, be invisible."

"Invisible how?"

"Change identity. Don't be Zoe any more. You and the boat."

"A fake ID? You know people who can get those?"

"Sure."

"On Corsica?"

"Maybe."

She thought. "You're not invisible, are you?"

"No. I'm John Fairchild and I live that way even though plenty of people don't like me very much. But I can disappear if I want. Get through borders, go off grid."

"I need to be Zoe Tapoko. At least some of the time."

"Why?"

"I got holdings in my name. I need to sign to get to it. Show my ID."

"You can be different things to different people. As long as they stay separate. What kind of holdings?"

She looked pleased with herself. "Big ones. Offshore ones."

"And where did it all come from?"

"I stole it." No trace of shame. "I stole from people who steal from other people. Or worse. Nothing they can't afford."

"Well, they won't see it that way."

"I know a lot about them," she said. "Wouldn't be worth them causing a public stink."

"Public, no, but what about private? Do you know how to use a gun?"

She looked up at the unexpected question. He carried on.

"Can you disarm someone who has a gun? What if someone boarded this boat at night? Would you wake up in time?"

She looked queasy. He knew what was going through her head. Was this her life now?

"You'll get used to it," he said. "But that threat will always be there."

She looked up at the mainsail, tears in her eyes.

"I'm not ready. I'm not ready for that. This is all too quick."

"You can get ready. You just need to get through the next few days. You stole from Yunayev. He isn't going to forgive that. He'll track you down and so will the Russians. It wasn't difficult for me to find you, Zoe. They'll do the same."

A long inward breath. Anguish in her eyes. What had she done? He knew that feeling well enough. It was a part of his journey just as much as hers.

"You just need to know they're coming," he said. "Plan for it. What do the tacticians say? Don't start a fight you can't win."

She swallowed and looked straight at him, brave.

"So let's be tactical, then," she said.

Chapter 53

They drove on, ever upwards. Grom stared out of the window. The driver was intent on the road. The other guy was on a mobile phone. Every time they came to a sharp bend they slowed right down. The car doors were locked. Could she unlock them from the inside? There was only one way to find out.

Approaching a curve, the land fell away on Rose's side, disappearing behind a low stone wall. A sizeable four-wheel drive was approaching the bend the other way. The driver stepped on the brake. The slowest part would be the middle of the turn. Rose tensed. All eyes were elsewhere.

The car turned into the bend. With one movement, she pulled the handle and rammed herself against the door. It opened. She rolled to the ground, scrambled to her feet and ran.

A screech of brakes. Shouting broke out. She vaulted the wall and landed badly on the scrubby slope. Her ankle gave way. Heavy footsteps were right behind her. She half-slipped, half-ran, gritting her teeth every time her foot jarred the rock. She let gravity help, unsure if she could stop if she wanted to. She could see nothing below except the slope and, a long way down, waves gently breaking on rocks making swirls of white.

The footsteps were still right behind, two sets. She tripped and lurched head first, managing to turn so that she fell on her side. She was rolling down and couldn't stop. Panic set in. She was gaining speed, had to slow down. She grabbed plants and rocks, but nothing held. She reached a hand and found solid rock. Her wrist took the strain as she held on against the downward momentum. She got a grip with her other hand, feeling the force in both elbows. Her legs now below her, she lay on her front gripping the rock, gasping for breath, her mouth full of dust. She looked up. Two pairs of feet stood on either side of her.

They weren't gentle, pulling her back up to the road, one on either side. Grom was standing leaning on the car with his arms folded.

"An admirable attempt, though futile," he said. "If you behave like that all the time, you're your own worst enemy. Search her." The latter was to his men. "Be thorough."

They were, and that was the end of her mobile phone. She was surprised they hadn't taken it off her earlier. All their phones had location trackers. When her team started to search for her, they'd be able to place her here, but no further. The men pushed her back into the car.

They set off. Grom settled himself just as before and looked at her dourly. Rose was covered in dust. Her foot and wrist throbbed and her skin was grazed in a dozen places.

"Like I said before," she said. "I don't know why you need me anyway. You've got what you want."

Grom's hand settled again on the backpack. "I've got one thing back that was stolen from me," he said. "But there's still the other. I suppose you think I don't know about that."

His gaze was pointed, but Rose had no idea what he was talking about. She kept her face neutral.

"You're not denying it, then?" he asked. "That it was you lot? It has your smell all over it. Typical of some bureaucrat's petty envy. Any symbol of success, any hint that someone's managed to rise above their own small-mindedness, how snippy and vindictive they get. So what happened to the proceeds, then? Gone to charity? Or into someone's back pocket? Quite a decent sum you got for it, though a lot less than a craft like that is worth."

His yacht. He was talking about his yacht.

"Oh, I know some of it went on some fancy sloop or other," he continued. "Someone's hobby, unless it's going to be used for MI6 training days or some such excuse. I don't know if that was supposed to be a secret, but I'll find that little side-interest, don't worry. Wherever it's gone I'll track it down and whichever bent officer did this. People don't play with me without getting burned."

Rose focused on looking calm, but a deep sense of dread was building up in her gut.

Zoe. This had to be Zoe. What had the woman done?

Chapter 54

They had to carry Pippin out, thick hands gripping him under each armpit. He couldn't keep his head up. It lolled from side to side as they manhandled him into a large sunlit room filled with period furniture. A reception room. Pippin was being received. That was after he'd been punched and kicked and slapped and left for hours, and then had it all done again.

In the kitchen they had hung him up by the wrists like a piece of meat, pulverised and tenderised. It was just the two Russians, Clem's friends, not Clem.

"You talk?" they would say in French, offering respite from the onslaught. Pippin wanted to talk. But he had nothing to tell them. They spoke to each other in Russian.

"You think he knows anything?" one of them said to the other before he rammed his fist into Pippin's stomach. Pippin spewed what was left from his gut, vile-smelling acid dripping off his chin. His feet slid around on the slimy floor. His wrists chafed. Every muscle in his arms burned.

"Maybe he does," said the other. "Or maybe Khovansky's lot are worse than us."

They looked at him thoughtfully. Pippin could only see through one eye. The Russian landed a punch on the other one.

When he was carried out to be received, his shoes dragged over a polished parquet floor. He dripped on it. They threw him onto a sofa. Not a sofa: a chaise longue, elegantly tapering at one end. It was bright pink. Fuchsia. No – incarnadine. Pippin curled up, expecting them to stop him, but they didn't. He was getting blood on it. It bothered him more than it should, that he was bleeding onto the chaise longue. He lay, eyes closed, not moving, while his body shrieked at him from head to foot.

Something moved; he heard it but didn't see it. He opened his eyes a crack. A large form was seated in the high-backed armchair opposite. It was Clem, of course, watching him. Clem watched Pippin and Pippin watched Clem. Pippin wasn't capable of anything else.

"You ever been beaten up like this before?" asked Clem.

Pippin shook his head.

"Never been in prison?"

He shook his head again.

"I've been on both sides. I've given and taken. I didn't enjoy either, but you do what you have to do."

He leaned forward in his chair.

"They came to me, these people. You must understand that. French, Italian, Corsican, those are my contacts. That's my world. But worlds collide. One of them heard something, thought there might be some pieces in the Freeport worth having. Then the Russians got word of it. They approached me. These people aren't nice. I say that as a warning. Don't try and resist, Pippin. Give them what they want. To survive. I did. And now you must."

The words kept blurring. Clem was kind, wasn't he? He didn't try and shoot him, anyway. Clem was in the same situation as Pippin.

"Can I have a glass of water?" asked Pippin.

After a pause, Clem carried on as if Pippin had said nothing.

"Why did you take it to Arles?"

There was no point in denying anything. Pippin took a breath and answered in a low voice.

"To hide it."

"Why not lock it up somewhere?"

"What kind of lock would keep something like that safe? Locks just tell people there's something to steal. Hiding it…" He felt dizzy. "Hiding it – somewhere no one would think…"

"Why Arles?"

"I told you before. I was taking it home. Back to where it came from."

"Why didn't you tell your contact about it?"

A pause. "I wanted to keep it for myself." It was weak, but he couldn't give Clem the real reason.

"It's not where you said it was. Someone took it. Who?"

"I don't know. I didn't expect anyone to take it. I thought it would stay hidden."

It could have been there for years, lying where no one would think of looking. And if it were found, it would be discovered by someone who knew what it was, what to do with it. But already it was gone. Despite everything, despite the situation it left him in, somewhere deep down that gave Pippin a tiny spark of hope.

Clem shifted. Pippin opened his eyes and tried to focus. Clem was standing up now, looking down at him curled up on the chaise longue.

"Time to sit up now, Pippin," he said.

Pippin didn't move. Clem grabbed his arm, sending shards of pain into his body. He pulled Pippin upright so his feet were on the floor. He reached out for a small stool and lifted Pippin's left foot onto the stool.

"You expect people to believe a story like that?" He leaned in close, head to head. "People like those Russians in there? People like me?"

Pippin felt faint. He had nothing more in him. He couldn't lie any more. He was finished with that.

"It's the truth," he said.

Clem stayed still for a few moments, as if absorbing this.

"Okay," he said. "Okay. If that's what you say, that's what you say."

He straightened. Pippin took a breath. Was it over? Did Clem believe him? Surely Clem would believe him.

Clem looked up, out over Pippin's head, as if admiring the view from the window. Then he lifted his foot high and stamped down hard on Pippin's raised knee.

Something snapped. Pippin screamed.

Chapter 55

They turned up a track leading to tall wrought-iron gates which swung open on their approach.

"This is your luxury villa, I suppose," said Rose.

"Don't be stupid," said Grom. "I know full well my villa is already crawling with Kremlin acolytes. I do have spies, you know."

They wound up a long drive and approached a complex of pinky-brown buildings with tiled roofs, like a reconstructed Provençal village.

"This is a rather exclusive hotel," said Grom. "From where we will exit. As you said, I've got what I want."

The blue of a swimming pool started to emerge amidst the pseudo rural cluster, and beside that the *H* of a helipad, on which a helicopter was sitting. In the front of the car the guy in the passenger seat was on the phone again. He pointed the driver straight to the helipad.

They stopped on the tarmac next to the pad. The heavies in the front came round to Rose's door and gripped an arm each as she got out. Grom, the backpack casually over his shoulder, strolled over to the chopper without looking behind. Rose tried a few moves on her guards but they were good, very good, rock hard responses to everything. She gave up and let them walk her over. It was early evening by this time, and the sun was setting over a spectacular view of the coast. The exclusive hotel was in a very nice spot. Of course it was.

They all got in. The pilot's seat was empty.

"Tell him to hurry up, for God's sake," said Grom. One of the men jumped out. Grom's gaze fell on Rose.

"I've decided not to take you with me," he said. "You're too annoying. Too mouthy. But none of it interesting. Just blah blah blah."

Rose kept quiet. It was a compliment, coming from him.

"But I'm not letting you go, either," he said. "I just want rid, to be honest. In the easiest way possible. Probably I'll throw you out once we've cleared land."

Rose glanced out at the expanse of sea.

"Oh, I know what you're thinking," said the old man. "We won't be all that high, the sea's warm, the coast isn't far for a strong swimmer, pretty good chance of survival. I'm afraid not, though, because I'm going to shoot you first."

Rose let her gaze wander over the man's form. It was news to her he was carrying a gun. Maybe he hadn't felt the need to show it before, or maybe he was bluffing. But it didn't sound like a bluff.

The pilot door opened.

"About time," said Grom.

The pilot strapped himself in and flicked a few switches. They powered up. Grom was passed headphones and a mic; clearly the other passengers would have no audio except for the roar of the engine. They took off, Grom and the pilot in dialogue. The craft turned as it lifted and headed seawards.

Movement on the ground caught Rose's eye. Cars, big black saloons, were speeding up to the helipad. People jumped out. People with guns, semi-automatics. They took aim. Grom gestured at the pilot, his shouts almost audible. A loud drumming as bullets hit the undercarriage. They rose. As the nose dipped, a bullet caught the glass. Cracks rippled upward directly in front of the pilot. This he didn't like. He was shaking his head, gesturing to Grom, who shouted back. They hovered, the ascent paused.

The gunfire stopped. Grom carried on shouting at the pilot, but whatever he was saying had less and less impact. An intractable look settled on the man's face. They descended towards the pad. Grom was screaming now, but the pilot was unmoved.

Once the bird was safely down, the pilot put his hands in the air. A clear message to the shooters who now surrounded the pad: this isn't my fight. Take your man and leave me alone. Rose was hoping the same might apply to her.

The door opened and a barrage of angry Russian voices replaced the dying engine roar. They knew exactly who they were after. Two of them stepped up and forced Grom out. One of the bodyguards struck out. Fists and bodies collided. A muffled gunshot. The loyal bodyguard yelped and collapsed. The Russians dragged him and his more passive colleague out. While this was going on, Rose silently reached for Grom's backpack and put it on.

If she were hoping to slip away unnoticed, it wasn't going to happen. The helipad was as crowded as a Moscow metro station at rush hour. Arms grabbed her and forced her into the back of a saloon. Large bodies clutching weapons piled in on either side of her. They joined the convoy out towards the coast road.

Clearly Grom wasn't the only person who had spies.

Chapter 56

The fuel station at the port of Ajaccio, Corsica, was busy into the evening. It was pretty late when the sailboat *Ocean Joy*, bearing a Monaco flag, arrived and came aside to fill up, before berthing at a floating pontoon. Lovely looking boat, traditional wood finish, very nice. The skipper wasn't bad either, according to the dock attendant, who liked to chat. The rules were that the skipper had to stay on board during fuelling while everyone else disembarked. It was immaterial to this one, though, because she was single-handed. Pretty unusual, and on top of that she was a young black woman. She'd just come from Monaco and was keen to get away the next day. On destination, she was a little vague, probably Italy but nothing definite.

Anyway, this skipper had a lot to do. She went off and came back in a taxi, laden down with groceries, frozen food, ice cubes, a few bottles. She spent some time on deck checking the rigging then called in at the chandlery shop, which was open late. She spent a lot of money in there, the dock attendant was told. Paid cash, too, which was interesting. Flares, lifejackets, spare halyards, motor parts, cleats, pins and screws: she knew what she was asking for all right. She browsed as well, asking a lot of questions about auto pilot kits, self-steering and winches. Single-handed was an interest, she said, but for the next stretch a crew would be good, if anyone could be found at short notice? The dock attendant's friend at the chandlery shop knew exactly which bars she could still find the yachties in, even this late. And that was where she went later on, asking around herself to see who might be up for a two or three day trip. It was pretty last-minute, but others had done it before and she was easy-going. With a smile like that she'd probably have a choice. She didn't seem short of money either. Probably a story behind that. There usually was.

Word spread quickly in a port like this. By the time the quayside restaurants were closing their doors and the lights were going out in the boats moored across the bay, plenty of folk in Ajaccio had heard about the *Ocean Joy* and its interesting young skipper.

Chapter 57

A reinforced metal gate with video intercom greeted the Russian motorcade. The gates swung open to let them all through. Inside, two armed guards stood on either side of the gate. Rose spotted others in the grounds, though it was dark by that time. They'd been travelling for no more than an hour. At the top of a driveway, steps led up to an imposing door ranked with classical-style white columns, reminding her of the extravagant Moscow dachas owned by Russia's super-rich, but this seemed more genuine somehow, and not fake like the hotel they'd just come from. Either it was a Kremlin safe house or this was Grom's luxury villa recently appropriated by the Russian state.

Four cars, four prisoners. Grom was in the first car, Rose in the last. They marched Grom inside. He looked slight between his two captors, with his white hair and shorter frame. Grom's two men were also led inside, the injured one half-carried, and taken down steps into a cellar. Rose too. She didn't resist. There were too many men with guns for that.

The door clanged shut behind them all. Was it some kind of bunker or panic room? The door was certainly fortified. It was pitch black. The two bodyguards were muttering to each other in Russian, trying to find a light switch but failing. Their captives would have no reason to think that Rose wasn't part of Grom's entourage. The men gave up on the light and sat or lay on the floor. Rose was about to do the same when she heard movement from further within the room. They weren't alone.

"Who's there?" she called, in Russian.

No answer, but, straining to hear, she could make out laboured breathing. Then, a thin voice, but a voice she knew straight away, though the answer was short and also in Russian.

"I am."

Alastair! Her old university friend and MI6 fellow officer. She could have called out his name with the joy of recognition and relief, but didn't know what Grom's posse would make of it. She felt with her hands.

"Where are you?" she whispered in English.

"Here. I'm here."

God, he was weak. What had they done to him? On hands and knees she moved towards the faint voice, feeling along the cold concrete floor. She touched part of a body, then a hand came towards hers and held it. They stayed motionless in the dark for several seconds, just gripping hands.

"Pippin?" said Rose, using what she now knew was Alastair's cover name.

"More or less."

Alastair answered in French. Consistent with his cover, and also the least likely Grom's Russian goons would understand, though there was no guarantee of that.

"What are you doing here?" he asked.

"Special project. How long have you been down here?"

"Hours. They – think I know where the painting is. You know about that?"

"Oh yes, I know about that."

"I told them where I put it, but they're saying it's not there."

"It's not."

Alastair stiffened. "You found it?"

"We realised Pippin was you. I got to thinking about where you might hide it. And Vincent's letters were in your room. We go back a long way, Alastair." She squeezed his hand. "I'm sorry. Sounds like I got you into a lot of hot water."

"You weren't to know. Where is it now?"

She hesitated. "Not far from here." Her backpack suddenly felt heavy. No one had searched her: too focused on Grom himself, maybe. If it had to be, it could be their way out of here.

"You're here working for the French, right?" she asked. That much she'd learned via Walter.

"Yes. It was all about Gustave. One of the thieves. They thought he was dangerous because of some group he was mixed up with in Paris. But he was just – I tried to tell them…"

His voice faded.

"Take it easy," said Rose. "Are you badly injured?"

"That bastard broke my leg! Christ."

"Who?"

"Clem. The other robber, the driver. He's working with the Russians. He's the one they should have been worried about."

Rose was piecing it all together in her head.

"Why didn't you just walk away after you stashed the painting? Tell them where to go?"

A pause, then:

"My handler. I spotted her meeting secretly with someone. She was compromised. I thought with Russia but didn't have any proof."

"That's why you didn't tell her where you hid the painting?"

"Yes, and that's why I came back. I needed evidence."

"And?"

He guided her hand to a pocket on the front of his shirt.

"I hope it's still there. It's sewn into a fold. But they shoved me about pretty hard."

Rose felt around, rubbing the material through her fingers. It was damp and clammy, with sweat or with blood she couldn't tell. Her fingers found something that felt like a spare button.

"That's it?"

Amazing how tiny a listening device could be. Alastair was always up to speed with the latest gadgets.

"That's it."

"It's a recording?"

"If it worked okay. It should have picked up a conversation I had with Clem, earlier today. Take it." His grip on her hand tightened.

"Why? Where are you going?"

"Nowhere. You take it. You're in much better shape than I am."

"Pippin, we're both going to walk out of here," she said with what she hoped was calm determination.

"Rose, I'm not walking anywhere. You should see what he did to my leg. And that's not all. Take the thing. Don't let this be for nothing."

His voice almost broke; he was close to tears. Now Rose understood. Alastair, vulnerable under cover, couldn't trust his handler but went back in despite the danger, to gather proof that she was selling secrets. Then he couldn't get away because she, Rose, had taken the painting. He'd paid a huge price and Rose was partly to blame.

Rose had to use both hands and tear the material to get the device off his shirt. God knows what Grom's men thought was going on over here. She pocketed it.

"Okay, maybe not walk," she said. "But we're getting out of here. I have some collateral, you see. Something to bargain with."

"You know where the portrait is."

"Yes, and I'll tell them if it means we walk free. Besides, better that it's going to the Russians than Grom."

"Grom? You mean Khovansky?"

Alastair would only know what had been said publicly about him.

"Yes. I've been tracking him for the past six months. Long story. Anyway, the good news is that he's now upstairs, captive of the Russians."

"And the bad news?"

"He has a pretty good idea where the painting is as well."

"But he won't tell them, will he?"

That was an interesting one. If Grom figured out that Rose picked up the backpack, would he prefer Rose to have the painting than see it fall into the hands of the Kremlin?

"I really don't know," she said.

Chapter 58

It was impossible to keep track of time in that pitch black cellar. It could have been hours, it could have been shorter. Grom's two men were silent. Alastair drifted in and out of sleep. He was in a bad way. But he was still thinking like Alastair. At one point he whispered her nearer.

"When they had me strung up in the kitchen," he said, "I was looking around to try and distract myself. You know they have smoke alarms in every room up there."

"Really?" That wasn't unusual, but it was the thought behind it that interested Rose.

"You know, not all of Gustave's ideas were crazy," he said.

Rose knew what he meant. A distraction, like a fire, might provide a means of escape, activating those smoke alarms.

"What can you remember about the layout up there?" she asked.

Alastair gave her a pretty detailed schema of how the rooms on the ground floor interconnected. The training they both did was paying off. Then he sank into silence again. Rose got to thinking about how this could be achieved. She had nothing flammable on her and neither did Alastair, but Grom's people might. They were both smokers, she'd already noticed.

She shifted over to them.

"Hey! Do either of you have a light?" She spoke to them in Russian.

Silence.

"I mean, matches or a cigarette lighter," she said brightly.

"What do you want that for?" one of them asked.

"To get the hell out of here."

"How?"

"Never mind how. Do you have something?"

A long pause, then: "Too late for him. He's dead."

"Who?"

"This guy. The one lying here. They shot him in the helicopter. Now he's gone."

Rose couldn't see a thing but imagined the guy talking, sitting there in the dark with a dead body slumped next to him.

"I'm sorry," she said.

She waited. Eventually he spoke again, his voice flat.

"Why should I help you?"

"You want to get out too, right? We all do. So give me the lighter and maybe it'll work out. What do you have to lose?"

Another pause, then a rustle and a clatter as he sent a cheap plastic lighter across the floor to her. She put it in her pocket.

"Stay ready."

"What for?"

Rose didn't reply, and went back to sit over with Alastair, who now seemed to be sleeping or unconscious. If they spent much more time stuck down here, he'd go the same way as Grom's guy. How could she get the attention of their captors?

As if answering her prayers, the cellar door clanged as someone turned a key in the lock. The door swung open. Beside her, Alastair jerked into consciousness. Light flooded down the steps behind the man who stood in the doorway, turning him into a huge silhouette. Rose heard Alastair take a sharp breath. The man was enormous with a shaved head and some serious muscle. He shone a torch round, resting its beam on each of them in turn as they sat blinking in the sudden light.

"You." He pointed to Rose. "You come with me." He was speaking French.

The language and Alastair's reaction told her that this must be Clem. She got up.

"Why me? What's this about? You know I'm not one of Khovansky's lackeys. I just got caught up in this."

"Never mind. You're coming with me."

While Rose was talking, she managed to get the backpack on without drawing attention to it. She wanted it with her. It could be their passport out of there.

Clem led the way. Odd that he came for her on his own when the place was crawling with Russians. But it gave her the chance she needed. With Alastair's description fully in her mind, as soon as they got up the steps she darted back, off into another room. Clem turned and sprinted after her instantly. She was already through another door before he got there. She hung around behind the next door as he went straight ahead. She double-backed. What she wanted was half a minute in the kitchen, which Alastair remembered with extraordinary detail, without Clem knowing she'd even been in there.

Why didn't Clem shout out for help? Alastair was sure he was with the Russians but he didn't seem to want their assistance. Never mind: it was better for her.

In the kitchen she turned one of the huge ovens right up to the highest setting and put the cigarette lighter inside. She stuffed the oven with whatever she could find that would burn: towels, pages from a recipe book. On the hob she turned on the gas without lighting it. Then she ran through to the front of the house, discarding the backpack and throwing it into a corner.

It worked. Clem grabbed her as she made towards the front door.

"Do that again and I'll break your jaw."

He gripped her wrists behind her back and shoved her forward into a large room full of parlour furniture. On a variety of elegant soft furnishings sat Grom and some unamused Russians. It took her a moment to realise that Grom's hands were tied behind his back and his ankles bound to the legs of his chair. Other than that he looked relaxed and in control.

A particularly annoyed-looking Russian addressed Clem in French.

"Why you bring her? We wanted to talk to others."

"That was my idea, I have to admit," said Grom smoothly in Russian. "I actually think that Rose here might have the best insight into the whereabouts of the painting." He turned to Clem.

"What was the scuffle? Did she try to escape?"

That was in French.

"It's fine," was Clem's short response.

Grom looked directly at Rose. "I'm right, aren't I?" Now he was speaking English. "You were the last person off the helicopter. You know where the painting is. The question is, what price do you want for it?"

Rose then understood why Grom was sitting there as if he were holding court. He was a fluent speaker of English, French and Russian, like herself. Clem spoke only French. The Russians' grasp of English and French was limited. Clem may be working with the Russians, but Grom was doing all he could to turn them against each other. From the body language in the room it seemed to be working.

Now Grom addressed the Russians.

"She knows where the painting is. She was the last person to see it."

They didn't look impressed.

"You don't have to believe me," he said. "Work it out for yourselves. It wasn't on the helicopter, was it? So someone must have carried it off. She was the last one off, apart from you."

"She's one of yours," said a Russian. "Just make her tell you."

"Oh, she's not one of mine," said Grom. "Far from it. She's a British spy. Sent here to try and get the painting off me. She's unlikely to want you to have it either."

He made a sudden switch into French, which he spoke too quickly and quietly for the Russians to follow.

"Did you see a backpack anywhere? It must be in the house. She brought it here. She's hidden it somewhere."

Clem's face didn't change.

"I'm giving you a chance to get it first," Grom said, more urgently. "Go look for it! Now!"

"Enough! Enough!" One of the Russians interrupted this flow. "You stop talking to him. You talk to us. You're our prisoner. Our property. You tell her to tell us where it is."

Something could happen in the kitchen any second. The longer this confrontation went on, the more chance it had to build up into something big. Grom looked at the Russians with no sign of fear or defiance.

"You'd better tell her yourself. She isn't going to listen to me."

The Russians turned to each other. If her kitchen stunt didn't work, she was headed for an interrogation session like Alastair's. But just then, what she'd been waiting for finally happened.

The explosion was loud enough to make everyone jump. The Russians were on their feet. Tinkling glass, then a deep roaring. Two of them ran out. Grom was looking at her, a curious smile on his face.

"What have you done, Rose?"

Rose looked blank.

The smoke alarms went off, a deafening clanging. The remaining Russians ran out, leaving her, Grom and Clem together. Rose looked up to the ceiling.

"Do they have sprinklers in this place?" she asked innocently, in English.

Grom's face changed. Clem was still standing there.

"Go! The backpack! Find the thing before it gets ruined!" Grom shouted in French.

Still Clem didn't move.

"What are you doing! Go and get it! It's in the house, I'm telling you! It'll end up burned, or soaked! I said I'll give you a cut, just get the thing before it's destroyed!"

Clem remained. He didn't trust either of them enough to leave them on their own. Or else he didn't take kindly to being shouted out. Impossible to tell which. His face had no expression.

"I'll tell you where it is if you get me and Pippin out of here," said Rose, in French.

"Who the hell is Pippin?" said Grom.

"One of the thieves. He's in the cellar. He's injured. Clem here broke his leg."

Clem didn't seem repentant.

"What's so special about him?" asked Grom.

"What do you care? I'll tell you where it is. Once Pippin and I are clear of the house and grounds I'll tell you. I don't care about the painting. I just want out."

"So go and get the guy!" Grom was shouting at Clem again, straining at his ties. The air was filling with smoke. Shouts were coming from the kitchen. The roaring got louder. Rose turned and ran.

"Untie me! Untie me for Christ's sake!" Grom's scream stopped Clem coming after her as he turned to free Grom instead. Rose ran to where she'd stashed the backpack. The alarms were everywhere; the piercing sound vibrated through her head. Was this smoke getting down to the cellar? No time to find out now. She ran out of the front door into the driveway.

Grom and Clem were only seconds behind her, but that was all she needed. She hurled the backpack as far as she could into the darkness of the garden.

"Go get it!" she shouted. "You're welcome to the thing!"

Grom and Clem both made off after the backpack. Rose ran inside, hitting a hallway full of smoke. She could hear sirens now, fire engines approaching. She made straight for the cellar. No one tried to stop her; the Russians were trying to tackle the blaze but it was pushing them out. Smoke was snaking down the cellar steps and pooling at the bottom. She couldn't breathe without coughing. Her eyes were gritty.

The key was in the lock of the cellar door. She turned it. The door flew open, almost knocking her over. Grom's surviving bodyguard sprinted up the steps past her, holding his shirt over his face.

The cellar was full of smoke.

"Pippin!"

No answer. She got to her hands and knees and crawled inside.

"Alastair!" she shouted.

She heard nothing, but upstairs was pandemonium. The sirens were very close now. The Russians were shouting at each other. When her hands found Alastair he was warm but he didn't respond. She turned him on his back and dragged him by the armpits to the door. She looked up the smoke-filled stairs. She couldn't see the top. She lifted Alastair under his shoulders and pulled him, going backwards one step at a time. After the second step she had to stop. This was taking too long. She forced herself to move more quickly despite her aching muscles. Nearly half way up she looked round.

Grom was standing at the top.

"Where is it?" he said. "Where's the painting, Rose?"

He was too quick for her. Or else he'd realised the backpack was a bluff.

"Help me and I'll tell you."

"If you don't tell me, I'll kick you both down the stairs."

"Go to hell, Sutherland." She was pulling Alastair up another step.

Sirens squealed to a halt outside the front of the house. Running feet, shouts into radios. The authorities were here.

"You won't get him out of there unless you tell me," said Grom. He took a step down. From where he stood he could send them both tumbling with a kick of his boot.

"Okay, I'll tell you then," said Rose. "It was in the kitchen. I put it in the oven. It's gone already. Ashes. Cinders. Burned."

She looked straight at him, her face serious, letting it sink in.

"No!" His face showed genuine shock.

"And the French authorities are here. Fire service, police, I'm sure. You want them to find you? How are you going to explain all of this to your creditors? The painting's destroyed. You're finished, Grom. Get the hell out of here. Run away and hide. While you still can."

She turned back to Alastair. He was her priority right now. Grom was her target, but he was finished anyway. She had to get Alastair out, and if letting Grom escape was the only way to do it, she'd do it.

She struggled up two more steps. When she looked up again, Grom had disappeared.

Firefighters were coming into the house now. They would find them both in a matter of seconds. But Rose didn't want to be found. Some things were too difficult to explain. She'd done all she could for Alastair now.

She left him, his head on the top step, and made for a window at the back of the house. Glancing behind before she climbed out, something on the wall of the room caught her eye. Even through the smoke and the sirens and the people shouting, it made her stare for a few moments. But there was no time. She jumped out of the window and ran for cover into the grounds. Filthy and suppressing a cough that wouldn't stop, she lay in the undergrowth and waited until she could slip past the flashing lights and uniforms, into the darkness of the hillside.

Chapter 59

Rose worked her way down onto the coastal road and found a small restaurant still open. Her car caught fire, she said. Mobile not working. Can I phone for help? She made a call using pre-agreed emergency codes, resulting in an arrangement to rendezvous in a hotel room near Cannes in three hours. She wanted it quicker but the protocols didn't allow for much negotiation. She cleaned herself up as best she could, accepted a diner's offer of a ride to Cannes, and killed time trying not to think of either Alastair lying on those steps, or Grom's expression when he talked about his stolen yacht.

Three hours later she wasn't all that surprised when the hotel room door was opened by none other than Walter himself.

"I thought you might show up," she said as she walked in. "As soon as we found out Grom was in the area."

"I've clearly become very predictable."

Rose sat on a satin-upholstered chair. The room was grand but shabby. The window looked out over the ocean, large and black. With a spy's caution, Walter pulled the curtains closed. He sat, quiet and alert. It was the next day by now, the early hours.

"What do you know already?" Rose asked.

"When you went missing, your team tracked your phone to somewhere out on the coast road before it stopped transmitting. Then, reports of a fire at Sutherland's villa. Police in attendance. It's being described as a confrontation between two rival Russian mafia gangs."

"Casualties?"

"One death. One injury. Taken to hospital."

"Alastair?"

"Yes, though he's still going by his French identity."

"Will he be all right?"

"He's stable, apparently."

That was good news at least. Rose retrieved the listening device from her pocket and passed it to Walter.

"Promise me you'll do the right thing with this. Alastair's handler was working with the Russians. He risked everything, went back in knowing he might be blown, just to get the proof. It's on there."

Walter examined the tiny item on his palm.

"Well, that certainly explains a thing or two. Why he didn't remove himself from the situation much sooner, for one. Some people ought to be very grateful for this."

Rose felt a surge of anger. "What was he doing under cover here anyway? Don't the French have their own people they can use?"

"Someone owed someone else a favour, apparently. His art expertise gave him the right credentials. They furnished him with a stock of stolen pieces to use as bait. Pieces that had secretly been recovered but were part of ongoing investigations. And he was enthusiastic about doing it. Felt he had something to prove."

"Prove? Prove what? To whom?"

"You can ask him yourself in due course."

She would certainly be doing that. "There was only one body? One of Grom's Russian bodyguards died in the cellar from a gunshot wound. That's all?"

"Yes, my dear."

"So Grom got away. That was my doing, I'm afraid." She recounted what happened on the cellar steps. "It was more important to get Alastair out. Grom would have stopped us.

You know how vindictive he is. Besides, he'd lost the painting by then."

"And the painting is where, exactly?"

"Destroyed, I'm afraid. Burned."

"Destroyed?"

"Yes." She told him how she started the fire. Walter frowned.

"You burned it deliberately?"

"There was too high a risk Grom would get his hands on it. I'd already given it to him once that day."

She told Walter what happened in Arles. "And not much better if it ended up with the Russians. Or Clem."

"Clem?"

"The fourth member of the heist team. Some local gangster. He was working with the Russians, but Grom was trying to turn him against them."

"And you're sure about the Van Gogh? It's definitely – gone?"

"Yes, like I said. I threw it in the oven. It'll be ashes now. I wonder if Alastair will ever forgive me."

There'd been a moment when she stood in the kitchen with the roll, so carefully packaged, in her hands. Could she bring herself to throw such a unique and precious object into what would become a fireball? A Van Gogh! Five hundred million dollars, irreplaceable. But what did these sums of money really mean? It was oil on canvas at the end of the day, and lives were at stake.

Walter was still struggling with it, though.

"Could anyone have got into the kitchen after you stuffed the oven and before the explosion?"

"No, Walter. It was only a couple of minutes and nobody knew I'd been in there. It's gone. A painting nobody even knew about until a few months ago doesn't exist any more. What's the big deal?"

There was something guarded about Walter's expression when he looked at her. Then he seemed to shake himself out of it and move on.

"Your team didn't seem to know why you were in Arles."

"When I realised Pippin was Alastair I thought again about where he might have hidden the painting. There was a copy of Van Gogh's letters in his room."

"A clue?"

"I don't know about that. I'm not at all sure he wanted it discovered, to be honest. Maybe he was trying to bury it by putting it somewhere obscure, but also where it ought to be safe. If that was his plan, I scuppered it."

"You certainly did, my dear."

That look again. But he returned to his main point.

"Keeping your team in the loop would be helpful next time, Rose. Some of this might have been avoided."

"What difference would it have made? We were already too short-handed to cover what we were trying to do. And besides, the objective was to rid Grom of his resources, and we did, didn't we?"

It was undeniable, though Walter seemed to have a problem with exactly how she'd done it. But never mind that now. Something else was more important.

"Walter, Grom will go after the yacht. It sounds like our rogue informant stole it from him." She told Walter what Grom had said. "Now the painting's gone he's got nothing. He'll go after Zoe, even though the Russians had already commandeered his yacht. He's blaming us for the theft. He's not going to spare her when he catches up with her, and she'll have no defences. We've got to find her first."

Walter shifted in his seat.

"You want to track down a sailing boat that probably left port yesterday and could have gone anywhere? And then do what?"

"Bring her in, Walter. Make her safe."

"Didn't you try that before? She didn't show up, as I recall."

"She's got no idea what she's up against. We have a duty to her."

"Well, I think I know what Salisbury would say about that, my dear. If our agents reject our help then it's really very difficult to protect them."

"It's not as simple as that. We're the ones who put them in that situation."

"Really? This woman? We made her steal a yacht, did we? It sounds like her own actions have put her in that position, as well as jeopardising the entire operation."

"She wouldn't be out there if it weren't for us. I can't just let her go knowing who's after her and what he's like. You understand that, don't you? The things this man has done! And the way he's done them. He's messed up, Walter, and he messes other people up."

Walter was gazing at the curtains as if imagining the sea on the other side of them.

"Do you know where she's gone? The identity of the boat, even?"

"We'll find out. Where's my team?"

"Standing by."

"We don't have long. Grom has people in the area. They'll have been working on this already. Can you get me connected? Can I work from here?"

Walter looked sad, baggy around the eyes.

"I can't say I fancy your chances, I'm afraid. Where's Fairchild?"

"Oh, no idea." He frowned at her breezy tone. "I sent him away. As I expected, Walter, he was just acting in his own interests all along. He tracked down the heist gang in Marseille but all he did was recover his own property and then leave. He could have incapacitated them or freed Alastair. He could have prevented Alastair from going through all of that."

"Well, to be fair, Rose, he couldn't have known who Alastair was."

"It's the kind of thing he does know, though, isn't it?"

"Not always. Alastair decided to stay under cover to gather evidence against his handler. So he may not have gone anyway. And your team weren't available when all this was happening, were they?"

"We were trying to locate Zoe. Fairchild was also aware that Zoe was getting too involved, and he didn't tell me."

"Really? How did Fairchild even know about our informant?"

"He shouldn't have done. But they became acquainted somehow. This is what he's like."

Walter was still frowning. Rose didn't want to think about how useful an extra pair of hands would be right now, particularly Fairchild's. But she didn't regret her decision. You can't work with people you don't trust.

"Let me do this, Walter. I have to try."

He raised his hands. "I can see you want to, my dear. Very well, then. But I fear it may already be too late. You can't blame yourself."

Rose didn't want to waste any more time philosophising. "Right. I need a mobile phone. And wheels."

She was already working through what she needed to do. Walter may be right. But she couldn't give up on Zoe, not yet.

Chapter 60

The two representatives of the Ajaccio harbour police were moored along the sea wall keeping an eye on a classic sailing yacht anchored out at a distance in the bay. They'd been tipped off that there might be some trouble there. Hard to believe on such a calm peaceful night, everything quiet and the boats bobbing in the mildest of breezes, particularly as they'd been waiting there for some time already. But this source was generally accurate, and nothing else was going on, so they held their ground. And then, just as the sky was starting to show a slight hint of dawn, they heard the sound of a motorboat.

A beam of light crossed the waves as the craft rounded the headland. The boat slowed, chugging quietly, nosing its way between the anchored boats, torchlight playing out onto their hulls. They were looking for one boat in particular. But they knew where to look, that was the interesting thing. And sure enough, when the light picked out the elegant tapered woodwork of the *Ocean Joy*, the launch turned in the water to go alongside.

Through the binoculars they watched two figures climb up, one of them big, the other smaller. Older, but agile enough. A third guy, a beefcake with a shaved head, stayed in the launch. The sailboat was dark and quiet. They only had the torchlight and the beam of the launch to go by, but it was enough to see that one of the men at least was carrying a gun.

On to the radio, then. The two of them weren't equipped for firearms, but backup was only minutes away. Quick enough for whoever was in the boat? They'd have to hope so.

The call made, they waited. The boat remained dark. No shouts or movement. One figure appeared on the deck. Then the other. They were talking, gesturing. Not going very well, by the look of it.

Then, the sound of another approaching boat. This one was loud and fast. They all heard it, the guys on the deck looked round too. This wasn't the backup. It was something else.

Another launch came round the headland. Bigger, and fast, too fast, making a huge wake that set all the boats rocking. A more powerful searchlight, which also found the *Ocean Joy*. Seemed a lot of people were interested in this boat.

It slowed and circled a distance away. A figure stood up, holding something long and large. Then, unbelievable what happened next.

A massive bang and a flash, and the scene exploded with light. They'd launched some great missile at the boat! It was on fire, properly burning, with a huge hole in the side, listing already. Whatever did that was proper military grade. No markings on the boat that they could see. Well, there wouldn't be, would there? It wasted no time, anyway. A sharp circle in the water and it tore off the way it came.

The police were on the radio, screaming all this but still no backup. It was in a bad way, the sailboat. Lights were going on everywhere now, on all the anchored craft and those in the harbour behind them. Who was on that boat? Their source hadn't told them that. They were in trouble, whoever they were.

Through the binoculars they saw a guy on the deck, the older one, holding on as the boat tipped even more. It was sinking, no doubt about it. But now what? The first launch was already speeding off. The beefcake was making a getaway, not even waiting for the two on the yacht.

Now, finally, backup was arriving. Vehicles driving into the port, and more speedboats. Now they could go in. They pushed away from the jetty and set off. But when they looked ahead again, the guy on the deck was gone. Did he jump? Did he fall? They'd missed it.

Another explosion and flames leaped into the sky. That would be the fuel tanks. Now the police were speeding over there, watched from decks all around by horrified boaters. The worst nightmares all at once, fire and sinking. Yes, *Ocean Joy* was doomed. She would soon be no more. Their job was to see if she'd taken anybody with her.

Amazing, their source had known all this was going to happen. Who was it again?

Chapter 61

The scene was still being processed when Zoe and Fairchild quietly motored in early the next day. They'd spent the night on the other side of the bay nestled in a small mooring. Fairchild wanted to be further away but Zoe insisted they stayed nearby. Let's get off the water, Fairchild said. Get rooms on shore. We'll have more options. But Zoe insisted on staying on the boat, once everything had been carried over from *Ocean Joy*. She didn't tell Fairchild why. Didn't quite trust him enough, yet.

They were close enough to see the explosion, like a distant fireworks display. Fairchild got the details on the phone afterwards from his friends at the police. Zoe's hands were shaking as she watched that distant column of flame. This was who she was up against now. On the deck of the tiny motor cruiser that Fairchild had picked up for cash the previous evening, she watched her beautiful sailboat break and sink, and felt herself crying. Fairchild saw, but he didn't say anything. She was realising now what she'd done, what her life would be like.

Fairchild didn't even want to go back to Ajaccio at all.

"We don't have to see it. There's no benefit. We know what happened. The plan worked. They both got word that you were here. Yunayev came first with his crew, and while they were on board the Russians showed up and sank the thing with some missile. We'll find out in time who survived and who didn't. Going there won't help. Either of those lot could still have people watching. Once they realise you weren't there they'll be all over this place. We need to be long gone by then."

"And we will be," said Zoe. "But I want to see what they did to my boat. I just want to see. It won't take long."

So they motored in and kept a good distance. Police everywhere. Some of *Ocean Joy* was still floating, blackened and ruined. Zoe cried again looking at those charred pieces. Then divers brought up a body. The emergency services had screened off an area of the sea wall, so they only got a glimpse as it was pulled close in. But it was a body, no doubt.

"With a bit of luck," said Fairchild, "they'll think that's you. For a short while at least. We need to be well out of here by the time they discover it isn't. How does it feel to be dead?"

"Weird," she said. Actually she felt sick. It so easily could have been her.

She turned the binoculars to the sea wall where a small crowd had gathered.

"Oh," she said. Fairchild heard, but she said nothing more. She'd seen a familiar face. Anna was there, standing very still, arms folded, looking out at the remains of the yacht. She'd have seen the body. Zoe focused on her. Anna had promised to keep Zoe safe. Now Anna thought Zoe was dead. How did that make someone feel? The woman's face said it all.

"Can I look?"

She handed the binoculars to Fairchild. He took in the scene over the water, the divers, the wreck, then panned over to the spectators on the sea wall, and stopped. He stared for quite a while. Then he put the binnies down and said, voice changed:

"Let's get out of here."

They were out of the gulf before they spoke again, headed for Italy as planned. Whatever was buried deep behind

Fairchild's eyes, he pushed it down so that when he next spoke he sounded almost normal.

"Why didn't you want to leave the boat last night? There's something you're not telling me, isn't there?"

She stared out over the sea. She hardly knew this guy. He could walk off with everything she had, if he wanted to.

"Do I have to tell you every last thing? Can't I keep some things to myself?"

"It's a secret?"

"It's private."

A long pause with just the droning sound of the engine. Motoring was so boring.

"You know what would have happened if I weren't here," Fairchild said. "I'm not bragging. This is my trade. It isn't yours, or hasn't been so far. You've got a way to go before you can do this on your own. I'll help you, but you've got to tell me everything. What's on this boat that you don't want out of your sight? Is it in those boxes we hauled over? Because if you don't think it matters now, it will."

She looked over at him. Truth was, if he'd wanted to steal from her or take her for a ride, he could have done it by now. He knew how much cash she had. He didn't say it in those words, but if he weren't here, she'd be dead. He was offering to set her up in this life, this post-Zoe life, this life after death, and that was a generous offer. She'd been confident with M. Bernard that she could safeguard the bearer shares, but after the sound-and-light show last night she wasn't so sure. She was going to have to chance it with this guy.

Fairchild was steering. Zoe got up from the windward deck and came to sit next to him. She told him everything.

Chapter 62

Things changed after Corsica. In Naples Zoe gained a new identity as an Italian national, thanks to a contact of Fairchild's. Useful that she spoke the language fluently. She picked up a new sailboat, like *Ocean Joy* but better, slightly bigger, more customised. They registered it under a Cypriot flag. From Cyprus they went to Greece, Malta, Sardinia. As the shock of Corsica wore off, Fairchild could see Zoe focusing more on what she'd gained, not what she'd lost.

Private Life, she named her new boat. "You know, like the song. Grace Jones." Clearly it meant something to her.

That trick with the bearer shares was genius. As the days turned into weeks, Fairchild thought a lot about how that could best be dealt with. He phoned Zack.

"Have you traced your elusive drug baron yet?"

"What do you think? Quesada may as well have flown to the moon. Thanks for all your help, by the way."

"That's what I was calling about. I know someone who may be some use to you."

"I'm listening."

"Someone with a detailed and unusual perspective on offshore money laundering. She may be able to help in – let's say – informal ways."

"How disreputable are we talking?"

"Not very, in the grand scheme of things. She has a requirement for secure storage. Maybe you could help each other out."

"You're saying she. Hey, Fairchild, you finally got yourself a girlfriend? Wonders will never cease."

"It's not like that. Did you hear what I said?"

"Secure storage? Not the usual request but we can work something out. Want to introduce us?"

"Sure. Can you get to the Caribbean?"

As Fairchild expected, Zack was very open to the idea of a business trip to the Caribbean. Zoe had already mentioned her ambition to cross the Atlantic. More distance from this part of the world would do her no harm. He liked the idea even more once he started thinking about going with her.

They settled into a kind of lifestyle out at sea, moving around each other in the boat with more ease, planning routes, testing the sailability of the craft, eating, and as they relaxed and travelled further, drinking too. Zoe was at home on the water. She could live here, she said, only going in to port for supplies and repairs, constantly roving. He'd been sceptical at first but she might be safer like this. Fairchild taught her what he could of the skills he'd gone out to acquire himself, when he realised he was on his own in the world. In some ways Zoe was doing what he did, determined to make her own path, refusing to fall in line with anyone, unable to return to normality.

She sucked up whatever he taught her like a sponge. His contact in Naples supplied them with weaponry, and she learned how to use it. They kitted out the boat for any eventuality. They covered Tradecraft, ways of slipping in and out of existence. And then self-defence moves. She was athletic and liked to use her body. He wasn't naturally at ease around women, choosing to ignore sexual attraction far more often than act upon it. But as the days went by on the water it became more natural to be physically close. At anchor, on deck, their combat sessions by necessity involved contact, but over time their hands lingered on each other's bodies longer than was necessary.

There was laughter, in these sessions, and optimism, and the feeling that he was finally getting something right by doing this. Their routine filled the days and sometimes even stopped him thinking about Rose. The inner paralysis that set in whenever he remembered that he'd never see her again seemed to loosen around Zoe, who was so different in every way. Zoe was warmth, sunlight, wind and tide, sensation for its own sake but behind all of that a wealth of intelligence and capability he didn't think the world had seen yet. With Zoe he could be someone else, not the bitter self-serving mercenary Rose had shown him, but a friend, in some ways a mentor, in other ways a student, happily learning a more carefree and physical approach to the world. They were companions more than anything else, alone out here, and he hadn't had too many of those in his life. In Zoe's company his interactions with Rose came to his memory as complicated and cold, though painful still. He tried not to think at all of that last sight of Rose, guilty and horrified, standing on the sea wall at Ajaccio.

One quiet morning at anchor, he showed Zoe a defensive move and she used it on him with greater success than he imagined, throwing him hard on his back onto the wooden deck.

"Sorry," she said. "Sorry, sorry!"

Laughing, she leant over him and brushed his mouth with her lips. And it was only then that he realised how much he wanted her.

Chapter 63

She could have done it herself eventually, Zoe knew. She'd have figured it out somehow, but without John Fairchild she might never have got past Corsica, never had the chance. Why did he come with her? Right from the start it felt like something he needed for himself, and saw an opportunity with her flight to flee as well, but wrap it up as charity. She didn't mind. It was an arrangement that suited both of them and he was good company.

Her thoughts about her future were only just starting to take shape as they sailed. She'd thought of the boat as a way to get out of Monaco in a hurry. But why not keep doing this? People did. She had what she needed here on board and in port. She wouldn't be lonely, though her heart ached every time she thought of Noah. But she'd always known she'd have to live with that.

Fairchild was a mine of information and know-how. Yes, it was about guns and self-defence, but also shedding shadows in public places and becoming a shadow yourself. This they practised on some of their stops; it reminded her of Anna. Fairchild knew people everywhere, knew how to get what was needed and seemed happy to share some of that with her. And it was a whole new mindset to learn. She needed to change how she thought, see the world from a different angle. Scary, but exciting too.

Monaco drifted further away as this new life took shape, fraught with risk and danger. But she sensed she could manage and thrive here, see opportunities and play the game everyone else was playing. The feeling she had at the penthouse that Fairchild was patronising her, had gone, and the longer he stayed the more she felt that she was in some ways supporting him and not the other way round. This feeling came to a head one morning when they were fooling about with defence moves on deck, and on a whim she leant over and kissed him. This unleashed something in him, but in her as well. His depth of need surprised her, but so did her own. It was easy to say she wouldn't be lonely, but from now on there would be parts of her life that she wouldn't be able to share with anybody. Just then, at that time, John Fairchild knew her, and the person she was becoming, more deeply and more closely than anyone.

They sailed, they ate, they drank, they touched every time they came close to each other. They made love, they enjoyed a warmth and ease that was truly private, miles away from everything and everyone they knew. The sun, the wind, the waves became the beat of their lives. Zoe made plans to cross the Atlantic, visit some of those places that before had only been names on office paperwork. She shared it all with Fairchild. He got it, and not everyone would. He got why she'd done this and not just followed orders, why she'd willingly made an outcast of herself.

Then one night as they lay in bed he said something about coming with her.

"Are you surprised?" he asked, following her silence.

"A bit. I thought you had other things going on. Your work, your business."

Something else as well, Zoe knew, some darkness inside that he buried, but was there on his face at Ajaccio when he turned away from the sea wall.

"That's all over," he said. "That life. I messed up. I need to start again somewhere else. The Caribbean would do for a while. If you can put up with me."

She warmed to the idea. Oh, it was a plug, a stopgap for him, she knew that, but she was getting kind of used to having him around.

At Gran Canaria they set a date to start the crossing. Ten days of preparation: a thorough rigging check, motor servicing, spare parts, careful provisioning filling every space below decks. They got as far as day six when the message came.

Fairchild was on the bow checking his phone. When he turned to Zoe, his face was pale.

"What is it?"

A death, she thought. Something terrible to cause a shock like that. But it wasn't. He never said exactly. Only that someone had asked for him and he had to go. He stayed for another day, helping with cleaning and washing, but part of him had already gone.

When he got his things ready to leave, he said:

"Zack will meet you in Panama. Be tough with him. Don't do anything you're not happy to do. But he's a good guy. He'll bend the rules. He hasn't forgotten who the rules are for."

Then he left, with few further words and certainly without thanks. There was no need. She didn't know where he was going and was focused anyway on the trip ahead, the gear that still needed fixing, the crew she'd want.

It hurt more than she thought, after he'd gone. But she knew he had to go, and that he didn't really want to. Unfinished business. It was etched into his face.

And she knew someday she'd see him again.

Chapter 64

The land felt solid and unyielding compared to the constant motion of the waves. Fairchild didn't want to go. He ached to stay with Zoe, to cross the Atlantic with her, to carry on in that sun-filled windswept rhythm. But the message was from Rose. Rose wanted to see him. Rose asked him to come back to France. And when he saw those words on his phone he realised that it didn't matter what had gone before. If Rose wanted him, he'd be there. She was his core, the person who made everything mean something. She always would be, whether he liked it or not.

So here he was in the town of Aix-en-Provence. They met at an outdoor cafe in a cobbled square with a fountain. The town's refined elegance, the chink of spoons on coffee cups, the hum of polite conversation, seemed cold and colourless. Even the sun had gone; the sky was an empty grey.

Rose was there already. She looked contained, withdrawn. He sat. She was drinking tea. He ordered an espresso. How long this would take he had no idea.

"You've been having a nice time?" she asked.

Weeks on deck had turned Fairchild's skin brown.

"Well, it was you who sent me away."

He tried to sound light, but it didn't work.

"I over-reacted," said Rose. "I shouldn't have done that." Her voice was low. It took a lot for her to admit it. "We could have done with your help in the end."

"I heard about the incident at the villa."

He saw the story when they were out at sea, and it gnawed at him then. He should have been there too, not floating off somewhere. Even though she'd told him to go.

"The media reported it as a fight between rival Russian mafia gangs," she said. "During which the famous portrait was destroyed. Not great PR for the Kremlin. Nobody believes their claim that they weren't involved. Sutherland got away, though."

"I know. He showed up in Corsica."

She stiffened. "You were in Corsica?"

"With Zoe. She's all right. She's going to be okay."

Some heaviness lifted from her face, he thought, maybe.

"Where is she?"

"At sea. That's where she'll stay."

"But the boat?"

"She's got another one. Another boat, another identity. She's not Zoe any more. At least not all the time."

Rose frowned. "How did she manage all that?"

"She's rich. She has resources. Contacts. She's off the grid but she'll be fine."

Was there some recognition in her face of his role in that? It was hard to say.

"Thanks for letting me know."

A genuine thanks, or a chiding for not telling her before now?

"No further news of Sutherland?" he asked.

"Nothing so far. He's penniless, though. No real influence or network."

"Not considered to be a present danger, then."

A flash of annoyance crossed her face. She must be off the job. Her team would have been disbanded, the mission over, declared a success, no doubt. Why was she here, then, in France? She hated being purposeless, he knew that about her. He let his gaze flick around the square. She didn't like that, either.

"Pippin was MI6," she said. "Working undercover for the French."

This was news to him, but it explained a lot. There was always something reserved, something unrevealed, about Pippin.

"You didn't know, I take it," he said.

"Different teams working at cross purposes. The bane of large organisations. Especially those that have a policy of not sharing. I'd started to guess, though. After we'd been to his room. But I wasn't sure enough to say anything."

She already knew Fairchild could have had no idea. But he had to make the point anyway.

"Of course, if I'd known that in Marseille, I would have done more—"

"Yes, yes."

Her cut-off was further admission she'd been wrong to blame Fairchild for his inaction. Her eyes travelled to the fountain again.

"He put himself in danger to incriminate his handler," she said. "She was working with the Russians. It worked. She's out, now. But he's still in hospital here in Aix. He was pretty damaged by what they did to him. Not just the physical injuries. He's been changed by all of this."

A pause that spoke volumes. Rose Clarke spending weeks off the job to be with a friend in hospital? They were more than just friends, then. Of course, someone in the business, someone who went back years, traumatic experiences shared, that was right for Rose. It needed to be a colleague, a collaborator in the spy world of some kind, for it to work for her. Something squeezed his heart, though after all that had happened he had no expectations of her at all.

"What about you?" he asked.

"I resigned."

She was matter-of-fact but there was a catch in her voice. He couldn't help staring. MI6 was her life, the only thing that mattered to her.

"Another informant lost. A colleague beaten to within an inch of his life. It's too high a price," she said, looking at the fountain again. "It's too much to take. Grom's in the wind. That was my fault. I let him get away. Whatever I said to Zoe, I gave her ideas but she didn't trust me enough when I could have helped. And I should have realised sooner about Pippin. Alastair."

Alastair. So that was the man's name. It fell somewhere, like a rock sinking to the bottom of a pond. He could tell her it wasn't her fault. But they were all judgment calls that she made. It was the nature of the business that lives were weighed up against each other. That she'd become repelled by it made him love her more, though it hurt him too knowing what walking away would cost her.

"They both got through it," he said. "And Grom has slipped away from all kinds of things. He's a spent force now. Bankrupted. His people have deserted him. Even in Corsica, even on the boat, they didn't stay by him."

She looked directly at him now.

"You saw what happened?"

"We were watching."

"You and Zoe?" He saw her adding it up. "You've been with her ever since?"

He didn't try to deny it, though his face felt warm.

"I've been preparing her for what's coming. The life she's chosen. The skills she'll need to survive."

"Right."

It sounded tawdry even to his own ears, even without Rose's one-word verdict. But then came a prick of anger; he had saved Zoe's life after all.

"What was it you wanted?" he asked.

For a moment he thought she was going to get up and walk off. But she took a breath and started talking.

"When I was in Grom's villa, I saw a print on the wall. It was a Japanese print. Very similar to the one in his penthouse."

The prints. He'd almost forgotten about them. Her reminder was like being slapped.

"How similar?"

"Well, I had about a second to look at it, and the place was on fire. But from that one glance, the similarity was striking. That's why it caught my eye."

She waited for a response but he couldn't muster one.

"So there are three of these prints. At least. One that was in the Freeport, one in Grom's apartment, and another in his villa. You have two of them, right?"

He nodded vaguely. He'd passed the prints to a colleague at his letting agency with instructions to store them safely somewhere.

"I don't know if that third one has survived," she said. "The villa suffered extensive fire damage in the end." Another expectant pause. "Are you at all interested in this, Fairchild?"

He wasn't sure. He wanted to be back at sea, slowly forgetting it all.

"Why are you telling me?" he asked.

She stared at her cup, gathering thoughts.

"When I told Walter that there was a second print, he was pretty dismissive. Described it as a coincidence. All these prints are alike, and so on."

"Not this alike. They date from the same time. Same artist, same printer."

"And now there's a third one. Maybe."

"I suppose Walter isn't your boss any more."

He'd not heard Rose doubt him before like this. Maybe there was more to her resignation than she'd said.

"You always claimed he knows more than he lets on," she said. "I got the impression he didn't want any focus on the prints. That it wasn't something he wanted anyone to think about."

That didn't surprise Fairchild at all, but Rose being this overt was astonishing.

"Why does it matter to you?" he asked. "You've resigned."

She smiled, with a little sadness. "I resigned. But then I took back my resignation. Life outside the Service just seems meaningless. Pretty pathetic, isn't it?"

Something caught in his throat. She felt trapped in this life, just like he did. He'd have done anything then to have been able to hold her.

"There's something else," she said. "Our team was being watched. Right from the start. Did you ever see anything?"

He shook his head. "Are you sure?"

"I wasn't. But now I am. It was Grom and his people. They were playing games, deliberately letting themselves get seen, then disappearing. Making us doubt ourselves. Doing enough to spook us, but not enough for us to act on it. Game-playing, like he does."

Fairchild was trying to work through the implications.

"When you say right from the start…"

"I mean, from the day we set up in Nice. Grom may only have arrived after the robbery, but his team was here from day one. Our day one. They didn't latch onto us in Monaco, Fairchild. They knew we were coming."

A silence, filled with water running at the fountain and footsteps on cobbles.

"Someone within MI6 tipped him off?" he asked.

"How else could he have known?"

"You think it was Walter?" He may as well be blunt.

Rose sighed. "No, not really. It was Walter who was so keen to set up the team in the first place. But he's holding something back. He has something on Marcus Salisbury as well."

"The Chief?"

"Salisbury almost canned this op but Walter pushed it through. How was he able to do that? And why did Salisbury not want it to happen?"

"Could just be a difference of opinion. Limited resources and so on."

"Well, that's what they say, but I'm starting to think there's more to it."

"A secret intelligence service is going to have plenty of secrets." He was playing devil's advocate. Defending MI6 wasn't his natural position.

"True. But this affected me and my team, work we're doing now. It's not some Cold War grudge that doesn't matter any more. If someone's passing things on…" her eyes went back to the fountain.

"Did you mention any of this to Walter?"

"No."

One word could say a lot. Rose wanted to trust Walter, but somehow she didn't, quite. She was telling Fairchild all of this for a reason.

"What do you want me to do?" he asked.

"Follow up on those prints. Find out what they mean. Find out whatever Walter doesn't want you to know. These things all relate somehow, I'm sure. Sutherland, your parents, Walter, Salisbury, you. There's more to dig up. It's got to be someone outside the Service doing the digging. You have the means to do it."

"You want me to investigate MI6?"

"Nothing as formal as that. I'm just – I'd like to see you continue to look into your own affairs. As you would do anyway, probably. Because I think they might shed light on what happened here, and whether Grom has too many friends where he shouldn't have any at all. I appreciate I can't ask you for anything. I've hardly been fair to you." She couldn't bring herself to look at him while she was saying this. "But this is real. I haven't taken this to anyone else. Only you."

Now she looked at him. No guardedness for a moment. In her eyes he saw hurt, fear, anger: symptoms of the betrayed. Rose had put her life on the line for the Service, and the lives of others. The idea that someone there wasn't playing straight would make her foundations crumble, bring her world tumbling down.

A yacht at full sail, the swell of the Atlantic, green islands far away, a warm touch on his skin. That was all gone now. He would do it, of course he would. Zoe and Zack would have to fend for themselves. He had another mission now.

Chapter 65

Rose watched him walk away across the square. She wasn't sure if he'd come. He'd be forgiven if he hadn't, after the way she'd treated him.

She knew the body off the yacht in Corsica wasn't Zoe; it turned out to be male, a Russian national. But she'd just assumed then that Zoe's body was lying elsewhere, yet to be discovered. Fairchild's reassurance eased something inside her, though she didn't want it to show. He'd clearly given Zoe a lot of help and probably saved her life. But he also got something out of it if they ended up sleeping together. Wasn't that a little bit exploitative of him? Something about it left a bad taste.

She ordered another tea. She didn't have to be anywhere. Her team was disbanded, Ollie back in London, Yvonne in Paris. Though she wouldn't be surprised if the two of them met again. They had a rapport which reminded her of herself and Alastair during their training days. But they were a little reserved towards her, she felt. Maybe it was the painting. Like Walter, they couldn't quite believe Rose had chucked a masterpiece into an inferno with such ease. All that about the value not meaning anything, it was still sacrilege to destroy a Van Gogh. Disturbed though Rose was by these responses, she'd run through the whole train of events and was sure she did the right thing. She'd do it again, too. People were more important than paintings. Especially Alastair.

She sat thinking about Alastair. It had been an intense few weeks. Always, back at university, she'd wondered if something might happen between them, but they'd only ever been friends. In the cellar he'd held it together, but this experience had scraped layers off him, left him raw, exposed, contemplating his own death and the meaning of his life. He was needy and clingy, and Rose was happy – more than she'd imagined – to be the person he could cling to. They became inseparable, Rose spending nights at the hospital, ready to comfort him when he woke disturbed and confused. She'd never been this close to someone for so long.

By day, when awake and not in pain, Alastair related the story of Pippin's life, how he came to be and what happened to him. At night, he cried out in his sleep about tones of gold green and dark lilac-grey, whirling autumn leaves, wind-bent corn under whirling skies. Always an obsessive – or maybe they all were in this business – Alastair had gone to work in his creation of the character of Pippin, and the quiet little thief had become entwined with the vivid imagination of Vincent Van Gogh himself, the artist's anxieties and sensitivities becoming those of Pippin as well. Pippin saw what Vincent saw. At night Rose sat by Alastair's bed and listened to it all unravelling, Vincent and Pippin and Gustave, because Gustave was there too, his overbearing self-belief, his crushing artistic passion dominating those around him, just as Gauguin had dominated Vincent. How did we all get so complicated? Rose mused on this during those long nights, wondering how much of the old Alastair would emerge from this maelstrom of fevered minds.

She challenged him too. Walter said Alastair went undercover to try and prove something. What was he trying to prove, and to whom? Was it self-centred to think it might be her? There was a certain rivalry between them during training, and since then Rose had been involved in more risky operational stuff than him. He never said it was her, but then he wouldn't have laid it on her like that, even in the state he was in. Rose had enough to deal with knowing that Alastair was tortured because she'd taken the painting. When she finally found the nerve to tell him what she did with the portrait, he laughed. Was that the real Alastair or was he still in some mixed-up state? She'd find out.

They became close, holding hands without even thinking about it, needing each other, needing to share what neither of them could share with anyone else. In the meantime the treatment continued, procedure after procedure, all painful, none entirely successful. She couldn't leave him, not like this.

But things were changing again. The nightmares were receding. Alastair had moments of stillness, not holding back, just not having anything to say. Like he was before – a quiet, kind listener. He needed time to think and get to grips with who he was now. Time alone, not with Rose distracting him with her own angst. They were becoming companions now; intimacy was too strong a word. What was next? Maybe Alastair would go back to Hong Kong, manage to take up his old life somehow. Or maybe the world of secrecy wasn't for him any more. They hadn't had that conversation yet.

It left her feeling empty. Even more so with Yvonne and Ollie, Fairchild and Zoe. Was there something wrong with her that she couldn't be close to anyone? Always before, she'd blamed her job and the difficulties of having to keep so much a secret. But she had no such excuse with Alastair, and still she knew, even now, already, that they weren't going to become a couple. They were friends. Good friends, lifelong friends, but that was all. This episode was born out of danger and fire and trauma, and those would all fade, although they would both be changed, particularly Alastair, whose leg would give him pain for the rest of his life. Now the emotional weight was lifting, she felt a sense of loss which stabbed her particularly as she watched John Fairchild walking away.

And now she couldn't trust the Service any more. There really was nothing in her life except MI6; the moment she'd sent the resignation email she'd been overwhelmed with a terrible emptiness. But now she had to reconsider all that, look over her shoulder all the time, wonder if Grom or his acolytes would show up for her next assignment. He should be history, but not if he was getting help. She was alone with this; even Ollie and Yvonne didn't know that she'd recognised the moped rider in Arles, that she knew for sure Grom had been tracking them.

She didn't like being in Fairchild's debt. She made it clear she was trusting him, and him alone, with this. And she told him about the print. If she hadn't, he'd never have known. He ought to feel he owed her for that. His disaffection with the UK establishment was something she'd never liked about him, but now it was useful. His motivations may be selfish but she understood them. He was the only person she could think of who could really get to the bottom of this. What that meant, of course, was that they were tied to each other until this thing was resolved. She thought she wanted nothing more than an end to John Fairchild in her life, but she'd called him back in, and this could go on for some time.

She called the waiter and asked for the bill. Walter would shortly assign her elsewhere. A fresh start with no Grom on the horizon. At least in theory. There were still threats, there was still work to do protecting British interests. She still believed in all that. She just didn't know any more if everyone else did. She needed to commit once again, send other people into the battlefield and maybe go in herself as well, no longer sure that everyone was fighting the same war.

She paid the bill and got up to leave. She'd done what she could.

Whatever was coming next, she'd have to be ready.

The Clarke and Fairchild series

Thank you for reading *The Colours*! If you want to stay in touch and hear about new releases in the series before anyone else, please join my mailing list. Members of the Clarke and Fairchild Readers' Club receive exclusive offers and updates. Claim a free copy of *Trade Winds*, a short story featuring John Fairchild and set in Manila. It takes place before the series starts, and before Fairchild and Clarke meet. Another short story, *Crusaders*, is set in Croatia and features Rose Clarke's fall from grace from the British intelligence service. These stories are not available on Amazon but are free for members to download. You can unsubscribe from the list at any time. Visit the website, www.tmparris.com, to sign up.

Reviews are very important to independent authors, and I'd really appreciate it if you could leave a review of this book on Amazon. It doesn't have to be very long – just a sentence or two would be fine – but if you could, it would provide valuable feedback to me to and to potential readers.

Previous books in the series are *Reborn* (Book 1, set in China and Tibet) and *Moscow Honey* (Book 2, set in Russia and Georgia). After *The Colours* comes *The Secret Meaning of Blossom* (Book 4, set in Japan), and subsequent novels will be wherever there are interesting political stories to tell. Both characters grow and develop over the series; Fairchild will eventually discover everything about his past and Grom's motivations. My inspiration for Rose is the Judi Dench interpretation of M in the later Bond films, and an imagining of what this M would have been like earlier in life when she was in the field.

I hope you stay with us for the journey.

Author note

While I did a good amount of research for this novel (see my Facebook page for more), I didn't hesitate to take liberties and stretch, or even completely transgress, the boundaries of what would be possible in real life.

The idea of a Van Gogh worth half a billion dollars is inspired by the true story, as told by Ben Lewis in *The Last Leonardo*, of the *Salvator Mundi*, a recently discovered masterpiece attributed to Da Vinci which was eventually sold at auction for US$450m. Given the question marks over whether any of it was really painted by Da Vinci, the idea that a clearly authenticated Van Gogh could sell for $50m more doesn't seem unfeasible. The lawsuit described by Laurence on his lunch date with Zoe is based on one that's detailed in this book and in numerous other places.

The *Portrait of Theo* is of course fictional, though Vincent's close relationship with his brother and differences with Paul Gauguin are documented in Van Gogh's letters. Many of Pippin's observations, particularly about colour, are drawn from these letters.

Browsing in a bookshop (yes, people still do that!), I was delighted to discover *The Secret Lives of Colour* by Kassia St Clair. It's a beautifully-presented book (this one wouldn't work as an e-book, you need the physical copy) detailing the history of dozens of tones and shades of colour, where they came from, how difficult they were to produce, and how expensive and in fact poisonous some of them were. I made extravagant and perhaps sometimes self-indulgent use of the evocative names of some of these colours throughout the novel.

We are all indebted to the International Consortium of Investigative Journalists (www.icij.org) for opening the lid on the huge and secretive world of offshore finance, following the leaking of the Panama Papers and others. *The Laundromat*, by Jake Bernstein, illustrates some of the stories that the Panama leak exposed, and was also made into a Netflix film starring Meryl Streep. Some details, including for example the use of blank pre-signed forms when setting up offshore accounts, are drawn directly from that source. My inspiration for Zoe comes from a reference to the fact that the company directors of thousands of offshore companies are often "low-paid employees" of the firms which set them up.

Without doubt, things have tightened up since those leaks, with truly confidential banking becoming increasingly rare. Bearer shares, in particular, have been outlawed now in numerous domains. I will freely admit I do not know if Zoe's stunt could be pulled off in the real world. It really is a "*what-if?*"

Various other things: I spent a lot of time looking at online brochures of super-yachts for sale. Much of what's said about Freeports originates from an article in the Economist written in 2013. Finally, Pippin's supposed thefts are loosely based on real cases, including the replacement of a painting with a photograph, which happened in Bel-Air and is described by the LA Art Theft Detail on their website.

Acknowledgements

I haven't included an acknowledgments section before, because my list is always so very short compared with other authors, for whom writing a book seems to involve a cast of thousands. That sounds great and I wish my writing were more social.

That said, there are some people who I rely on to help get these books together, and have had an influence not just on the Clarke and Fairchild story but my writing as a whole.

First, my beta readers, the people who read each draft at the earliest possible stage and comment on it. Thank you for always being so lovely and tactful! But also thank you for being honest and letting me know what's not so good, doesn't work at all or is downright inexplicable. I never ignore you, though I don't always follow your suggestions. Special thanks to Julia Blewett, Matt McAvoy and Snyman Rijkloff who have read all of them and have shaped the whole series.

Thanks to Ryan O'Hara at Rhinobytes for his excellent covers. It's only when I get the first draft of a new cover from Ryan that I start to believe I'm actually going to publish a book. He puts a lot of thought into the imagery and I love them all.

A mention for Jericho Writers, in particular my developmental editors Sharon Zink, Eve Seymour and Russel McLean. Harry Bingham's evangelism on the theme of self-publishing, on his video course and also at the

Festival of Writing, is probably the single thing which has most encouraged me to self-publish.

There's so much out there for trainee writers, but I want to make special mention of Emma Darwin's excellent blog, This Itch of Writing. Emma is wonderfully articulate, and this blog is an incredibly rich – and free – resource of detailed, original and well informed material which debunks quite a few myths and explains many of the "rules" that are so often thrown at those who dare to pick up a pen. It has changed my writing for sure.

Facebook is a great place to connect with other self-published authors, who are generally a mutually supportive bunch. I'd like to make special mention of the administrators of the awesome 20BooksTo50K Facebook page which has almost 50,000 members and a Top Posts document which again takes several days of reading. It's influenced the role of writing in my life, how I do it, when I do it, and far more.

Also a special mention for David Gaughran, whose hairy face is a familiar sight to many of us self-published authors. His enthusiasm and openness as well as his expertise, particularly in all things to do with marketing and getting along with Amazon, are invaluable, and once again much of it is freely given.

I would also like to thank everyone who's reviewed any of my books. Even if you didn't like it very much, it means a lot that someone's gone to the trouble of feeding back. Some have reviewed more than one, and I thank you in particular.

Now whaddayaknow – I've run out of space!

About the author

After graduating from Oxford with a history degree, T.M. Parris taught English as a foreign language, first in Budapest then in Tokyo. Her first career was in market research, during which she travelled extensively to numerous countries and had a longer stay in Hong Kong which involved visiting many of the surrounding countries. She has also taken sabbaticals for a long road trip in the USA and to travel by train from the UK through Russia and Mongolia to Beijing and around China to Tibet and Nepal.

More recently she has played a role in politics, serving as a city councillor in Brighton and Hove on the south coast of the UK.

She currently lives in Belper, a lively market town near the Peak District National Park in the centre of England.

She started writing seriously in 2011. She published her first novel, *Reborn*, in 2020, the first in a series of international spy thrillers. She is drawn to international settings and the world's most critical political issues, as well as the intrigue, deception, betrayal and secrecy of clandestine intelligence services.

Crime and action thrillers are her favourite book, film and TV choices. She occasionally plays the trumpet or the Irish flute. She enjoys walking, running, cycling and generally being outdoors in beautiful countryside, as well as cooking and baking and, of course, travelling.

Email: hello@tmparris.com
Facebook: @tmparrisauthor
Twitter: @parris_tm

Printed in Great Britain
by Amazon